"I'm her[...] **take care of Evan and your house. By the end of four weeks you'll see you couldn't do better."**

"But *you* could do better." That's what had Hugh so confused. "Better than a man eight years your senior with a four-year-old boy who might never get over the way he's been treated."

Annie's eyebrows arched as if surprised by his statement.

He hurried on. "You're young. You're beautiful."

She blinked rapidly and gave an almost imperceptible shake of her head. Did she not believe him on the latter observation?

"I'd like to know why you are so set on such an arrangement." He meant the marriage she so stubbornly sought. And why was he resisting her offer so vehemently? Because of the very things he'd told her. She deserved better than an older man with a troubled child.

All he wanted was to be enough for his son and for that he needed a helpmate. One who wouldn't regret her choice and perhaps run off with someone younger and more suitable as soon she discovered she could do better and he had no doubt Annie would soon discover that.

Linda Ford lives on a ranch in Alberta, Canada, near enough to the Rocky Mountains that she can enjoy them on a daily basis. She and her husband raised fourteen children—four homemade, ten adopted. She currently shares her home and life with her husband, a grown son, a live-in paraplegic client and a continual (and welcome) stream of kids, kids-in-law, grandkids, and assorted friends and relatives.

Books by Linda Ford

Love Inspired Historical

Big Sky Country

Montana Cowboy Daddy
Montana Cowboy Family
Montana Cowboy's Baby
Montana Bride by Christmas

Montana Cowboys

The Cowboy's Ready-Made Family
The Cowboy's Baby Bond
The Cowboy's City Girl

Christmas in Eden Valley

A Daddy for Christmas
A Baby for Christmas
A Home for Christmas

Lone Star Cowboy League: Multiple Blessings

The Rancher's Surprise Triplets

Journey West

Wagon Train Reunion

Visit the Author Profile page at Harlequin.com for more titles.

LINDA FORD

Montana Bride by Christmas

HARLEQUIN LOVE INSPIRED® HISTORICAL

Recycling programs
for this product may
not exist in your area.

LOVE INSPIRED BOOKS

ISBN-13: 978-0-373-42542-6

Montana Bride by Christmas

www.Harlequin.com

Printed in U.S.A.

We love him, because he first loved us.
—1 John 4:19

Dedicated to the reason for the season:

For unto us a child is born, unto us a son is given:
and the government shall be upon his shoulder: and
his name shall be called Wonderful, Counsellor,
The mighty God, The everlasting Father,
The Prince of Peace.
—*Isaiah* 9:6

Chapter One

Bella Creek, Montana, winter 1890

Annie Marshall shook the sheet of paper. "Mr. Arness— I'm sorry, Preacher Arness—I'm here to apply for this position."

Hugh Arness did his best to deliver God's word every Sunday, and on numerous occasions between Sundays he faithfully helped those in need. At the moment he was the one in need of help but Annie Marshall was not the person to fill that need. "How old are you, Miss Marshall?"

"I'm nineteen but I've been looking after my brothers, my father, my grandfather and until recently, my niece since I was fourteen. I think I can manage to look after one four-year-old boy."

That might be so and he would have agreed in any other case but this four-year-old was his son Evan, and Annie Marshall simply did not suit. She was too young. Too idealistic. Too fond of fun.

She flipped the paper back and forth, her eyes narrowed as if she meant to call him to task. He'd seen her reaction to things before. A little fireball was not what Evan needed. He'd also witnessed her riding about with her friend Carly Morrison. They were a wild pair who seemed to think they could do as they pleased.

"Are you going back on your word?" she insisted, edging closer.

Hugh was grateful for the wide desk between them. He glanced out the window. Her grandfather, Allan Marshall, whom most people called Grandfather Marshall, sat in the wagon waiting for Annie to complete her business. Poor man must be cold out there but he was too crippled to get down by himself and seek shelter indoors.

Hugh turned back to the girl opposite him. "I've not given my word to anything." He meant to point out leaving her grandfather outside in the winter wind did little to prove she was as capable as she wanted him to believe but before he could, she read aloud the words he'd so carefully penned.

"'Widower with four-year-old son seeking a marriage of convenience. Prefer someone older with no expectations of romance.

I'm kind and trustworthy.

My son needs lots of patience and affection.

Interested parties please see Preacher Arness at the church.'"

"I'm applying," Annie said with conviction and challenge.

"You're too young and…" He couldn't think how to voice his objections without sounding unkind, and having just stated the opposite in his little ad, he chose to say nothing.

Her eyes—blue eyes like her three brothers—narrowed. She had blond hair like her brothers too. And she was tall like them, but completely feminine. He pushed aside that foolish thought. He didn't need or want anyone that made him aware of such things. No sir. At twenty-seven, he was admittedly jaded but he wanted nothing to do with romance and love. His wife leaving him had taught him the foolishness of expecting such stuff.

"Are you saying I'm unsuitable?" She spoke with all the authority one might expect from a Marshall... but not from a woman trying to convince him to let her take care of his son.

He met her challenging look with calm indifference. Unless she meant to call on her three brothers and her father and grandfather to support her cause, he had nothing to fear from her. To answer her question, yes. Had he not seen her and her friend racing through the streets, seemingly unmindful of those in the way? Hadn't he heard her father complain that she left them to fend for themselves on many a Sunday? No. He needed someone less likely to chase after excitement and adventure. She'd certainly find none here as the preacher's wife.

"I would never say such a thing but like the ad says, Evan needs a mature woman." And he'd settle for a plain one, and especially a docile one.

"From what I hear, he needs someone who understands his fears." She leaned back as if that settled it.

He wondered what she'd heard and from whom, but living in a small town and being the preacher made it impossible to keep anything hidden. "It sounds like you think you would be that person." He kept his tone moderate even though the girl was starting to get on his already tense nerves. "What would you know about being abandoned?"

"My mother died when I was younger. I'd venture to say I might know how little Evan feels."

"There's a whole lot more to it than that." Hugh had come to Bella Creek in the spring to find his son. It had taken him several months to locate him. He couldn't begin to guess what had happened to the boy since Hugh's wife had disappeared with him eighteen months ago. He'd learned she had died months ago and he had frantically searched for his son until he located him a few days ago.

"I found him in a home where he was treated like an animal." His throat tightened and he couldn't go on.

Annie's eyes clouded. "Poor little boy."

"In many ways he acts like an animal."

"Can't hardly blame him, can you?"

No, he couldn't but after meeting Evan, the only other women who had come in response to his ad had hurried away, no longer interested in marrying the preacher. There weren't many eligible women in the area so he'd sent notices to papers in several cities. But it would take time for a reply to come from any interested parties. And would their interest wane once they met Evan?

In order to conduct this futile interview with Annie, he'd left Evan with the elderly woman who normally came in several times a week to cook and clean for him. Evan had been sitting in the corner with a bowl of mashed potatoes in the circle formed by his folded legs. From the far room came the sound of crockery breaking and Mrs. Ross shrieking a protest.

"You'll have to excuse me." Hugh leaped to his feet and hurried through the open door, across the sitting room and into the kitchen.

Evan stood facing Mrs. Ross, his eyes wide, his mouth a grimace far too like a snarl for Hugh's peace of mind. A shattered dish lay between them.

Mrs. Ross flung about at Hugh's approach. "He slapped the bowl out of my hands." She backed away from Evan. "Hugh, I'll clean your house. I'll make your meals. But I'm sorry, I can't handle this child of yours." She looked about ready to weep.

Hugh patted her back. "I understand."

The distraught woman grabbed her thick woolen shawl and hurried out the back door.

"Hmm. Looks like you need someone immediately." Uninvited, Annie had followed him.

He would not look at her…would not let her see how desperation sent spasms through his jaw muscles. How was he to care for his son? Would the boy ever recover from his state?

Somehow Grandfather Marshall had managed to get down from the wagon despite his crippled state and hobbled into the kitchen, his canes thudding against the floor.

"Annie, you listen to me," he said with some authority.

Hugh hid a grin. The elder Marshall ruled his family and half the territory.

Annie jammed her fists on her hips and glowered at her grandfather. "How'd you get down?"

"Called to the blacksmith to help me. I had to talk sense to you. Marriage is not a business deal. Whatever reason causes a man and woman to get hitched, it's forever. Forget this foolish advertisement for a marriage of convenience and let's get home before winter sets into my bones and I freeze into a solid block." He turned back toward the outer door.

Annie didn't move. Didn't give any indication she'd even heard his remarks. Instead she lowered her arms, tucked them into her skirt and looked at Evan.

Hugh's eyebrows rose a fraction of an inch. The girl must be the only one within the whole of Montana who dared ignore the old man. A young lady who wouldn't heed the directions of someone in authority. It further reinforced his opinion that she was unsuitable.

Evan huddled in the corner, his eyes wide as he watched the adults. No doubt he wondered what they would do that involved him.

"Well," Annie said after a few seconds of silent study between the two. "Looks like someone should sweep up the mess." She spied the broom behind the stove, swept up the broken dish and looked about for a place to dispose of it.

Hugh sprang forward, holding the ash bucket and she dumped the debris into it.

The look she gave him was part pity, part curiosity and all challenging. Before he could think how to divert her from her goal, she shifted her attention to Evan.

She squatted down to the boy's eye level, keeping far enough away not to frighten him. "It's okay, Evan. It was an accident. No one is cross with you."

She waited a moment then slowly straightened and brought that determined blue gaze back to Hugh.

"You need someone. It might as well be me."

Her grandfather banged one of his canes on the floor. "I forbid it."

"No need, sir," Hugh said. "I've already told her no."

Annie shook her head. "What about Evan? Who is going to look after him while you do whatever it is preachers do?"

He resisted an urge to list all the things preachers do but she was right. He couldn't prepare a sermon, visit the shut-ins and the ill, listen to people's worries in his office or even read his Bible if he had to constantly wonder about Evan and keep an eye on him. *God, I beg You. Send me someone to help with Evan.* Knowing God understood his heart, he didn't bother to add, someone older, less attractive, less likely to want a life of adventure…or at the very least…less likely to want courting and all that went with that.

He leaned to one side to watch the door to his office, fully expecting it would open and the perfect solution to his problem would step inside.

"I have the perfect solution," Annie said.

Hugh did not share her opinion.

Her grandfather thumped his cane again. "Forget this nonsense and take me home."

She shook her head. "Grandfather, I'm pretty sure that Conner and Kate would prefer to have the house to themselves."

Her words caught Hugh's interest. He'd married her brother Conner and his wife Kate a few months ago. They'd adopted the baby that had been left on Conner's doorstep, spent a few months in a cabin and then had moved into the big ranch house. It seemed Annie was feeling like an extra spoke in a crowded wheel.

She went on facing Hugh with what appeared to be patience and a whole lot of determination. "Here's what I propose. Give me four weeks to prove I can handle the job. If you aren't satisfied I'll leave. If I prove I can handle the task, then I expect you to honor your offer."

Why was she so desperate for a marriage that he'd clearly indicated would not be a love arrangement? What sort of whim or desire to prove something drove her to seek this position? How long before she changed her mind and chased after another fancy?

"Annie," her grandfather bellowed. "I will not allow it. You can't live in the house with a man you aren't married to."

She smiled sweetly at him. "I expect you to live here too."

The old man blinked, opened his mouth and closed it, then sank to the nearest chair and leaned over his canes. "You are determined to do this, aren't you?"

She nodded.

"Then I might as well stop arguing. But it still depends on Hugh's agreement. What do you say?"

Annie waited for Preacher Hugh's reaction. He was a big man, with strong features. At the moment, his expression was troubled but she knew he had deep dimples when he smiled and his smile was beautiful. His dark brown hair was rumpled, his dark brown eyes troubled as if worried how he would cope with his young son. As she'd said, her suggestion was the perfect solution. After four weeks he'd be used to her

and have learned to appreciate all she could do. Then
they'd marry. A marriage of convenience would give
her a home without any risk to her heart. One thing
she'd learned in her—according to Hugh's opinion—
few short years, was that it hurt to care. People, pets,
everything either died or left, and when they did, a
part of her heart fractured off and lay dying. Her
mother's death had ripped a huge hole in her heart.
Her brothers had married and she rejoiced for them
but it made her feel lonely. Her pa had left to see more
of the West. Said he'd always wanted to see the Pa-
cific Ocean. She hoped he enjoyed his travels but for
her, it was another goodbye.

And don't get her started about how easily beaus
left. Rudy Ryman had taught her that lesson very
well. She'd been foolish enough to unreservedly give
him her heart. Not even her family realized how thoroughly she'd loved that scoundrel...or imagined she
had. It still hurt to recall how easily he'd left when he
decided he would sooner live a life of adventure than
share his life with her.

Besides, no matter what Kate and Conner said, she
and Grandfather were in the way.

She'd admired Hugh from afar from the day he
arrived in Bella Creek, drawn to his unwavering determination to find his son and to his kind but challenging words on Sunday morning. He was a man she
could trust to keep his word. A marriage based on
mutual needs was perfect for her. She had no intention of ever again giving her heart to a man.

She swung her gaze toward Evan. Poor little boy.
She could feel the fear coming from him. It rivaled
the sour smell of him. He needed clean clothes and a

good bath. She tucked a smile away as she imagined Mrs. Ross trying to bathe him. The little guy had a feral look to him. Had Hugh tried to get Evan near water and clean clothes?

Hugh still hadn't given his answer and she shifted her attention to him, amused at the desperate look in his eyes that she guessed he tried vainly to hide.

"Four weeks?" he asked, his voice full of doubt and regret.

She nodded.

"Or until I find someone more…"

She knew he meant to say *more suitable* but he quickly changed his mind at the way she silently challenged him. How dare he consider her less than ideal! Why she could out-bake, out-clean, out-take-care-of anyone in the entire West.

"More mature," he substituted with a little cough.

She raised her eyebrows. "I hope they don't break down the door in their urgency."

A flicker in his eyes informed her that he understood her little sarcasm. After all, how many unmarried young women were there in the wild West of Montana? A worrisome thought raised its head. She could think of two spinsters in Bella Creek area. Had they seen the ad? How far abroad had he sent the ad for a wife? Well, she was here and not anyone else and in the weeks they agreed to she would prove herself so invaluable he would never want her to leave.

Hugh shifted his attention to Grandfather. "And you're willing to stay here?"

Grandfather nodded. "Wouldn't want her reputation ruined." The men studied each other, some sort of agreement forming.

Annie resisted rolling her eyes. What was it about men that they thought they could hide their feelings from her…from any woman for that matter? As plain as the nose on either of the male faces she knew they both thought she would get this out of her system and they could all get back to their ordinary lives.

She could have informed them it wouldn't be that simple. She had no intention of staying at the ranch and becoming the spinster sister that everyone endured and pitied. She could almost hear the whispers of her brothers and their wives. *Can't you take her for a few months? She's been with us long enough.*

Hugh turned to his son. "You think you can deal with him?"

Annie smiled at Evan. "What do you think, Evan? Can you and I get along?"

For an answer, he sank to the floor and pulled into the corner as far as he could. He wasn't ready to trust her nor should he. For all he knew, she meant him harm and not good. It was up to her to prove otherwise.

"We'll get along just fine." She spoke as much to Evan as to Hugh.

Hugh rubbed at his chin and sighed. "I'm desperate enough to accept your offer."

"Try not to fall all over yourself in gratitude."

He had the grace to look embarrassed. "I'm grateful and desperate."

She had the grace to overlook his predicament. "Grandfather, we need to return to the ranch and get our things." She studied the weary old man. "Actually why don't you stay here and get to know Evan while I get our things?"

Grandfather gave her a grateful smile. "Don't mind saying that's the best offer I've had in a long time. That cold is bitter."

"I'll be back." She looked around her at the unwashed dishes Mrs. Ross had left in her hurry to escape the frightened boy in the corner. "I'll take care of things when I return." She hurried outside. Winter afternoons were short and she had to pack up enough to last her and Grandfather a few weeks and get back to town before the cold deepened as darkness settled in. She could arrange for her other things to be delivered after she and Hugh were married.

Her jaw muscles twitched. She liked the preacher just fine. A marriage to him would suit her. A home and a family of her own without the risk of opening her heart.

She ignored the blaring warning that it might prove more difficult to guard her heart than she imagined, especially with a little boy who needed a wagonload of patience and understanding.

Heavenly Father, give me wisdom and patience to deal with little Evan.

She had gone into the parsonage wearing a stylish red winter cape but now pulled on a heavy winter coat that her brother Logan had outgrown, wrapped a buffalo robe around her legs and turned the wagon toward home. Wanting to spare the horses, she kept them to a slow trot. By the time she'd covered the four miles to the ranch, her hands were numb and her face ached from the cold.

Her brothers Conner and Dawson both ran out as she drove up as if they'd been waiting and watching for her return. Her brothers did their best to take care of her even though she didn't need it. Besides they now had wives. Dawson, the eldest at twenty-six, had married beautiful Isabelle Redfield and they made a home with his daughter, six-year-old Mattie, in a house to one side of the main house.

Conner, twenty-four, had married the doctor's daughter Kate. They had recently left a cold cabin and moved into the main house with little Ellie.

The youngest brother, Logan, at twenty-two and three years older than Annie, had married Sadie the schoolteacher and they lived in town with the three children they had rescued and adopted.

Everything had changed. Like Pa had said when Ma died, *You can't hang on to things. They don't last. But life goes on.* Her brothers had moved on as they should. It was time for her to move on as well.

Dawson lifted her from the wagon and hollered at one of the cowboys to take the outfit to the barn.

"Don't unhitch," Annie said. "I'm going back to town."

Conner and Dawson rushed her indoors, pulled the heavy coat off her and faced her like two defending soldiers.

"Where's Grandfather? Is he sick?"

"What's this about going back to town?"

Kate came to the doorway. "You look half frozen. You two let her come in and have a hot drink before you cross-examine her."

Her brothers stepped aside and allowed her to follow Kate to the kitchen. Little Ellie smiled at her from the high chair where she ate bits of bread.

"Hey, pumpkin," she said to the baby before she sat at the table and took the tea Kate offered.

"Grandfather and I are going to live in town." She explained about Hugh and little Evan. "They need someone."

Both brothers spoke at once, making their opinions clear. They didn't like the idea. They didn't think she should settle for such an arrangement. She had no reason to pack up and leave.

On and on they went. Annie ignored them, grateful Logan wasn't there to add to the ruckus.

She finished her tea and pushed to her feet. "I'd like to get back before dark. Anyone going to help pack things for Grandfather and me?" She didn't wait for their answer but left the kitchen, crossed the big dining room and smaller sitting room to Grandfather's bedroom and then pulled out a satchel and begin filling it.

Conner followed. "I don't like this."

"I think he'd like some of his books. There's a crate in the closet off the sitting room," she said.

Still protesting, Conner went to get the box and fill it with books.

If Annie thought that was the end of it, Dawson soon cleared up that notion. "You belong here with the rest of us."

She didn't point out that the *rest of us* had spouses and homes. "I'd like to take Grandfather's armchair. Do you think you and Conner could load it in the wagon?"

Making a sound of exasperation, Dawson went to do her bidding.

Annie climbed the stairs to her own room. She paused to look around, an ache the size of a vast desert sucking her heart dry. This had been her room as long as she could remember. She'd spent happy hours here dreaming. No more dreams for her. She'd cried her share of tears on the bed. There'd be no more tears either. She'd stared out the window searching for something to fill her heart. A smile smoothed her tension. She'd found what she needed and pulled the sampler from the wall.

For where your treasure is, there will your heart be also. Matthew 6:21.

The sampler included a stitched house and the date she'd finished making the hanging. March 15, 1887.

She'd been fifteen and struggling to cope with the pain of loss from Ma's death and the heavy load of responsibilities in trying to take her place. Working the words of the verse had helped her deal with it all. Her treasure was in heaven. In her faith. In God's love.

She touched the red roses she'd embroidered in front of the needlework house. How many hours she'd spent on this project. She'd started the project right after Christmas and finished as the trees burst into leaf that spring.

Christmas! It was only four weeks away. If she proved herself, she would have made a loveless match by then but with her own home. She would do everything in her power to make the season special for her very own family. Her heart swelled with anticipation and she smiled as she put the sampler in the bottom of the satchel she'd brought from the hall closet and then opened the wardrobe to choose what to pack.

"You're sure this is what you want to do?" Kate stood in the doorway, Ellie perched on her hip.

"I've made up my mind."

"Is this because Conner and I moved into the house?"

Annie folded a warm woolen skirt and added it to the contents of the satchel, considering her answer. "You need your own space but it's more than that." Not that she was sure she could put it into words. "It's time for me to move on."

Kate continued to look troubled. "But you're prepared to enter into a loveless marriage if Hugh agrees?"

"Seems to me love is only asking to be hurt. Besides, it's not that he's ugly or a criminal or anything."

Kate chuckled low in her throat. "It sounds like you better be careful if you're hoping to avoid love."

Oh, she'd be careful. She had no intention of falling in love. "We both understand the terms of our agreement." She kept her attention on her task. "Which at this point does not include marriage. I have yet to convince him it's the perfect solution." Satisfied she had enough clothing, she glanced around the room, picked up her brush and hand mirror, her Bible and the picture of Mama and Pa on their wedding day. She tucked those into her bag. "I'll get the rest of my things later."

"We'll miss you," Kate said as they descended the stairs.

Annie encountered her brothers as she made her way to the outer door.

"You're sure this is what you want to do?" Conner asked. Dawson hung over his shoulder, silently echoing the question. "There's only one reason to get married," Dawson said.

Conner nodded. "If you love the person so much you can't imagine life without him or her."

The two of them silently challenged her.

"This is my chance to pursue the life I want."

They backed down in the face of her determination.

"I'll take you to town," Conner said.

Dawson elbowed him aside. "I'm taking her. I'm the oldest plus you have a wife and baby." He chucked Ellie under the chin, winning him a giggle.

"You have a wife and a daughter as well," Conner pointed out.

"Yes, but Mattie is old enough to be of help to Isabelle."

Annie pushed past them. "You two can stand here arguing all day but I want to get back before dark." She hurried to the loaded wagon. By the time she climbed aboard, Dawson joined her and took up the reins. "Guess it helps to be the oldest."

"It's got its perks. I wish I could change your mind."

"Grandfather will worry if I'm not back soon."

"Fine." They made the trip to Bella Creek with little conversation. Dawson seemed to have accepted Annie's decision.

In town they went directly to the parsonage. Dawson lifted Annie down and hurried her inside to the warm kitchen, where Grandfather and Hugh sat at the table and little Evan remained huddled in the corner.

Annie had explained about Evan but Dawson still looked a little shocked to see the boy in such a state.

"You need a hand with things?" Hugh asked, and at Dawson's affirmative reply, went out to help carry in Grandfather's chair and the other things Annie had hastily packed.

The bags were taken to two of the rooms down the hall. The previous preacher had six daughters and two sons so there were plenty of bedrooms to choose from. Annie chose one close to the kitchen with Grandfather next door. Hugh indicated the second hall where he and Evan slept.

Annie said goodbye to Dawson then turned to consider the kitchen. Mentally she began to plan the evening meal and how to take care of Evan.

Hugh returned from waving goodbye to Dawson. "Annie, could I please speak to you in my office?"

At the hard, flat tone of his voice, Annie's heart sank. Had he changed his mind?

Chapter Two

Hugh waved Annie to a chair across the desk from his own. He waited for her to sit. Instead she crossed her arms and gave him a look full of challenge. He sighed. Seemed this discussion was to take place while standing and with her all set to argue. If this was the way it would be to have her here he already regretted agreeing to her "perfect solution."

He perched on the corner of the desk. His position allowed him to see through the adjoining rooms to where Grandfather sat watching them. So far Evan hadn't objected to the older man, perhaps interested in his canes or knowing the man posed no threat if only because he couldn't move around too quickly. Evan had not had the same reaction to Hugh. It had taken Hugh two hours to persuade Evan to let Hugh take him home and then he'd had to bodily move him and hold him firmly the entire way to prevent the child from throwing himself to the ground.

Or perhaps Evan respected the air of authority from the older man. Hugh almost smiled as he thought of how Grandfather Marshall ruled with just a firm word and a look that stalled men in their boots. His smile faded to a worrisome thought. Seemed Annie had inherited some of her grandfather's stubbornness and forcefulness.

"You wanted to say something?" she said, her sweet words laced with annoyance.

"Yes, I did. I think we would do well to establish some ground rules."

"Rules?" Somehow she managed to convey a snort even though she kept her tone neutral.

"Maybe not rules. What I mean is I would like to understand a few things."

She jammed her hands to her hips, seemed to realize how belligerent it made her appear and dropped them to her sides. Did she realize her fists curled? "What's to understand? I'm here in response to your ad. I'll take care of Evan and your house. By the end of four weeks you'll see you couldn't do better."

"But *you* could do better." That's what had him so confused. "Better than a man eight years your senior with a four-year-old boy who might never get over the way he's been treated."

Her eyebrows arched as if surprised by his statement.

He hurried on. "You're young. You're beautiful."

She blinked rapidly and gave an almost imperceptible shake of her head. Did she not believe him on the latter observation?

"I'd like to know why you are so set on such an arrangement." He meant the marriage she so stubbornly sought. And why was he resisting her offer so vehemently? Because of the very things he'd told her. She deserved better than an older man, with a troubled child.

The words that haunted him blared through his mind. *Not good enough.* Not good enough to please his mother even though he'd tried so hard. Not good enough to please his wife, Bernice, even though he'd again tried hard. Now all he wanted was to be enough for his son and for that he needed a helpmate. One who wouldn't regret her choice and perhaps run off with someone younger and more suitable as soon she discovered she could do better and he had no doubt Annie would soon discover that.

She looked at the window. Night had turned the glass into a mirror that reflected back the room.

He waited. In his experience those with a secret usually responded best to patience. There was not a doubt in his mind that she had a secret that drove her to seek this position. He needed to know what it was and if it constituted a threat to him or his child. Moreover, he knew Evan needed security. Not housekeepers who came and went, but a woman committed to staying.

She brought her gaze back to him, her blue eyes full of midnight shadows. "Let's just say that I have a concern for a little boy who doesn't know where he belongs."

Was she telling Hugh that was how she felt? How could that be? She came from a large, supportive family.

"I'm guessing he's had lots of losses. If you allow it, I'll show him that he can believe in permanency."

They studied each other like wary opponents. He considered her words, trying to find the hidden mean-

ing in them. He appreciated that her concern was for
Evan. He respected her for that. But the why of her
choice refused to be dismissed.

He reviewed what he knew of her. Her mother had
passed away several years ago. Annie couldn't have
been much more than a child but she'd taken over the
care of her family. Recently her three brothers had
married. Did that explain her rash decision?

"Are you feeling your family has moved on and
left you behind?"

Her eyes narrowed. "Nothing stays the same. Life
goes on."

He measured her words, seeking the hidden truth
in them. "So you've decided to move on too. But why
to this?"

Her eyes were innocent yet he got the feeling she
hid a world of meaning.

"I don't care for secrets," he said. If patience didn't
work then the direct approach was the best.

"I suppose we both have our share of them."

"Perhaps." He was beginning to think getting information out of her was like trying to pull an un-
willing mule out of a bog. *God, please make hidden
things plain, dark things light.*

She spoke firmly. "I suggest we agree to honor
each other's right to have our secrets."

It sounded reasonable enough. "On one condition—"

Her eyebrows arched letting him know she'd be
reluctant to give a promise. A parallel truth blared
through his mind. Maybe she was also reluctant to
believe a promise. Had some young fellow hurt her
with a broken promise? He hadn't heard about a failed

romance and now couldn't ask without seeming to be too interested. However, it would explain why she was willing to settle for the sort of arrangement he offered. Trouble was, she would get over that hurt as soon as someone more appealing came along. He couldn't put Evan through that. No, he needed someone who accepted a businesslike union as her best choice.

She tapped a toe, reminding him he hadn't finished his statement.

"The condition I would like your agreement on is that no secret can be allowed that hurts Evan."

Her countenance underwent a transformation. A smile wreathed sparkling eyes. "I can promise you I would not do anything by omission or commission to hurt that little boy." She held up a hand before he could reply. "That is not to say I won't make mistakes. I ask if you see me making one that you speak to me about it." She chuckled low in her throat. "I might not thank you at first but once I'm past my annoyance I will." She ducked her head. "I might not tell you though."

Something about her rapid shift of moods, her honest admission of pride—if that's what he chose to call it—made him want to share a laugh with her. Made him wonder what it would be like to witness both the pride and the humor in action. Seemed he'd get that chance in the next few weeks unless some other woman showed up on his doorstep in answer to his ad because, at this point, he really had no other option.

He shepherded his thoughts back to the moment. He could have wished for more information from her but understood he had to settle for this compromise. He pushed off the corner of the desk.

"Very well. As long as we're both in agreement about doing what's best for Evan."

She tipped her head in acknowledgment. "You can trust me to do what I think is best for him. Speaking of which—" She indicated the open door. "Perhaps I could get to work."

"Of course." He followed her from the office.

In the kitchen he paused, uncertain what his role was. "Do you want me to show you around?"

She turned full circle. "I know my way around a kitchen. But could you show me where the vegetables are?"

He opened the small door by the pantry. "My cold room. You'll find frozen meat in the cupboard in the woodshed. Milk is delivered every morning. I have an account at your uncle's store for anything else you need. Feel free to purchase whatever is required."

Both their gazes circled back to Evan, crouched in the corner, watching them warily.

"I don't know what to do about him." Hugh spoke softly but he couldn't keep the despair he felt from his voice.

Annie smiled and it somehow lifted a portion of his worry. "Give him time. We're all strangers and he has to know he can trust us."

"I don't know what's happened to him," Grandfather Marshall said. "But it's obvious he'll need lots of patient handling."

Annie smiled at her grandfather. "We have time and patience, don't we?"

The old man nodded. They turned to Hugh.

He would do everything in his power to give his son whatever he needed. "I have the rest of my life."

His answer earned him a smile of approval from both of them.

"Feel free to do whatever you need to do." Annie's words were kind yet Hugh felt dismissed. As if he was in the way. The words often spoken echoed in his head. *You'll never be enough.* He pushed them away. That was his mother speaking and he no longer had to listen to her. Hadn't needed to since he was twelve when she died of what the preacher said was a broken heart.

Hugh knew it was because his brother, whom his mother loved so completely, had died some months before at age seventeen. Hugh had tried to fill his brother's shoes but every time he did something he thought would help, Ma had uttered those oft-repeated words. *You'll never be good enough to take his place.* He had no pa to voice an opinion contrary to hers.

Annie continued speaking, unaware of the thoughts tangling through Hugh's mind.

"I'll prepare supper and make friends with Evan."

Evan stared at her, his gaze revealing absolutely nothing. As if the boy had shut off all connection with the world.

Anger, pain and sorrow intermingled in Hugh's heart. Bile burned the back of his throat at how his wee son had been treated. He had to escape before he erupted.

"I'll be in the office if you need anything." He fled to the far room leaving the door half-open so he could hear if Evan or Annie required rescuing.

He pulled his sermon notes from the drawer and set them on the desk in front of him but didn't read a word he had penned.

How could a nineteen-year-old girl from a protective family begin to understand what Evan had been through? He couldn't help thinking this agreement with Annie was a mistake. The depths of his desperation drove him to prayers that came from the darkest corner of his heart.

Annie had no idea how to get through to Evan, how to prove to the child she could be trusted. She might have asked Grandfather but he had settled into his armchair by the stove and snored softly.

However, she knew what it felt like to be lost, alone, afraid. She'd felt that way after her mother had died even though she was surrounded by a loving family. When Rudy had left her, she'd known the same feelings, intensified this time because he chose to leave and she'd willingly opened her heart to him despite knowing the pain of loss. She hadn't felt she could voice her feelings to her family. Even so, she'd received strength and comfort simply by their presence.

What would she have done if she'd been alone? Without family? Or worse, treated poorly? *Heavenly Father, heal the hurts of this little boy. Help him learn to trust us. Give me wisdom in comforting him.*

She'd have wanted someone to reach out to her, to show they cared, and that she mattered. She could offer that to Evan but she must proceed slowly, letting him set the pace. So she did the only thing she could do at the moment. She talked to him.

"It's time for me to make supper. What would you like, Evan?"

Not so much as a twitch of interest to indicate he heard.

"Do you like stew?"

Not a flicker.

"Potatoes and gravy?"

Still nothing.

She listed item after item, all the while her hands busy, washing dishes Mrs. Ross had left from lunch and then peeling potatoes. "Bread and gravy?"

The slightest movement of his eye. "Good. Then you shall have it. I'll make pork chops, mashed potatoes, green beans and lots and lots of gravy." She'd found a generously stocked pantry with jars of canned vegetables and several items of baked goods. Two loaves of bread that appeared to be freshly made. Mrs. Ross had done a good job caring for the preacher. Annie was confident she could do just as well.

She brought out one of the loaves and set it on a cutting board. "How thick do you like your bread?" She placed the knife to indicate a very thin slice. When Evan gave no response, she moved it slightly. Still no response. She widened it so the cut would result in a slice two inches thick.

Evan's gaze came to hers.

She smiled. Despite whatever had happened to the boy, he wasn't beyond interest in the things around him. "Too big?" She brought the knife closer to the end of the loaf and paused at a generously thick slice but nothing out of the ordinary. The knife hovered.

Evan watched and she knew it was where he wanted the bread cut. She did so.

"One slice or two?"

Evan's gaze returned to the loaf and she understood he wanted two.

She chuckled at the way they'd been able to communicate. "You and I will do just fine, won't we?"

His gaze held hers a second then he ducked his head. He had his father's dark eyes and dark hair and would no doubt grow into a man as handsome as Hugh. Right now it was hard to see past the shaggy hair, the guarded eyes and the need for a good wash.

Annie turned her attention back to supper preparations, more than a little pleased with the way things had gone so far. Given time she had every expectation that Evan would become a happy, normal little boy. Four weeks would be plenty enough time to make Hugh see that he and Evan needed her. She'd gain her own home and family.

She hummed as she finished meal preparations and set the table but paused as she chose the plates.

Four places? Or did Hugh allow Evan to take his meals sitting in the corner? It wasn't right. There was no need to continue treating him like an animal and she carried four plates to the table.

"Supper is almost ready." She put down one plate. "For Grandfather." She put down the second one. "For me." Then the third plate. "For your papa." She set the fourth plate down on the side closest to where Evan huddled but before she could say it was for him, he made a noise half grunt, half growl and kicked out one leg, catching Annie behind her knee. Her leg buckled. She caught at the back of the chair but it slipped from her grasp and banged to the floor.

Evan continued to swing his legs at her, making feral noises.

She fought for balance, trying to get out of his reach.

Hugh strode into the room, scooped his son into his arms and held him tight, restraining the flailing limbs. "Evan, you're okay. No one is going to hurt you. I won't let them." He sent Annie a look of accusation.

She lifted her chin. She would not defend herself, would not say she had done nothing to Evan. The attack had been entirely unprovoked though she realized her expectation that he sit at the table had been a little hasty.

Evan continued to struggle in Hugh's arms but Hugh held him firmly. "I won't let you go until you stop kicking and hitting."

The boy bared his teeth.

Hugh held Evan's head immobile. "You can't bite. You aren't an animal."

Again Hugh's gaze hit Annie's with the force of accusation. Did he think she would judge the child? She shook her head. "It's my fault. I set a fourth plate on the table and he knew I meant for him to sit at the table. It's too soon."

She tore her gaze from Hugh's and looked at the boy in his arms. "Evan?" She waited, hoping he would acknowledge her but he continued to struggle. "I understand you aren't ready to join us at the table. That's okay. When you are, you can sit with us like a little boy who belongs in a family."

He began to calm.

She continued. There were so many things she wanted him to understand. "This is your home, your papa."

Hugh sucked in air like he had forgotten to breathe

the last few minutes. "I will never let you go again." His voice broke on the words.

Annie knew from what the preacher had said in the months since he came to Bella Creek that his wife had disappeared along with their son. Knew he'd discovered his wife had died and his son was missing. She wondered about the details. Did he let her go? Why? Or had she left because of something he did?

So many questions. So few answers. Would knowing the facts help her deal with Evan? Or did she want to know because she wondered why Hugh was so set on a businesslike marriage? One would think with him being a preacher he would insist on love being present in such a relationship. But despite the questions flooding her mind she couldn't imagine asking him about his wife.

Was this one of those secrets they had agreed could exist?

"Supper is ready." She turned back to the stove, put the food in serving bowls and set them on the table.

Meanwhile, Hugh lowered Evan to the floor where the boy crowded into the corner.

Tears stung Annie's eyes at the fear on Evan's face and she vowed she would prove to him that he was safe and life could be fun.

She found a tin bowl and put the two slices of bread in it, drowning them in gravy. She cut the bread into small pieces, put a spoon in the bowl and set it on the floor close enough Evan could reach it but not so close he would feel threatened and lash out again.

Hugh watched her every move. Prepared, she supposed, to intervene.

Grandfather had wakened at the ruckus and observed the whole time.

Annie knew he would not hesitate to give his opinion and wondered what it would be. She stood by the table waiting for Hugh to take the lead. He waited, perhaps for the same reason.

"Shall we eat?" she said.

"By all means. Where would you like me to sit?"

She stood behind the chair closest to the stove and indicated the one across the table for Hugh. Grandfather sat at the spot closest to his armchair and across from where Evan sat on the floor.

Hugh stared at his plate, the picture of despair.

Annie wished she could offer some encouragement to him but she wasn't sure a touch would be welcome and there seemed no adequate words.

"I'll ask the blessing," he said and Annie bowed her head, silently praying her own words. Gratitude for the food, and for the chance to earn her own home, but more than that, a request for God's healing love to fill their hearts.

Grandfather waited until the food had been passed around and everyone had a good start on eating before he voiced his opinion. "We have our job cut out for us with that one." He tipped his head toward Evan who had pulled the bowl close and turned his back to them.

There was no clang of the metal spoon against the metal dish and Annie knew the boy ate with his fingers. At the moment it seemed the least of their worries. But Grandfather's words encouraged her. He had made it clear he meant to ally himself with her and Hugh in winning this boy's trust and cooperation.

Hugh put his fork down as if he'd lost interest in the meal. "Any suggestions?"

Grandfather also lowered his fork to the table and considered his words. "I once knew an old Indian so weathered and wrinkled you could get lost in the crevasses of his face. He and I worked for the same outfit back before I got married." He paused and grew somber as he always did when he thought about his long-dead wife. "I knew him several weeks before I heard him utter a word. When I asked him about it he said he never had anything to say until then." Grandfather's gaze went to Evan. "I expect it's the same with him. Same with leaving his corner. He'll do it when life beyond that spot is more interesting, more enticing than the walls he's pressing into."

Hugh turned his gaze toward his son.

Annie watched him, her heart slowly melting as sorrow intermingled with hope in his face.

She was needed here and she could think of no better reason for seeking an arrangement with Hugh than to offer one little boy a safe home.

Hugh's concern for Evan would guarantee Annie a safe home as well.

Unless a more suitable woman appeared on his doorstep in the next four weeks. She had to assume he had sent advertisement for a wife beyond the possibilities of Bella Creek.

Outside the wind battered the walls of the parsonage. A cold draft swept by her feet and she knew the temperature had dropped. If it snowed, travel would be difficult. Perhaps too difficult for any interested woman to be willing to venture to Bella Creek in answer to a request for a mail-order bride.

Being a ranch-raised young woman she couldn't bring herself to pray for a storm to break all records but perhaps God would see fit to send enough snow to keep visitors away.

Surely that wasn't too selfish a request.

Hugh tried to relax. Grandfather Marshall's words of support and encouragement meant a great deal to him. As did Annie's insight into why Evan had struck out. He noticed she rubbed her leg when she rose to make the tea.

"Did he kick you?" he asked, softly, not wanting to upset Evan.

"It's nothing." She glanced at Evan. "He didn't do it out of spite."

Again, she had an understanding of the child that rather surprised him. The few times he'd seen her before led him to believe she cared only about having fun though if he'd stopped to think he might see that she carried a huge load of responsibility and some lighthearted activity on occasion might be in order.

The thought only darkened his mind. There would be little enough time or opportunity for fun while caring for Evan. Hugh had consulted Dr. Baker who would offer no assurances that Evan would ever be okay.

"Some children," the doctor said, "are permanently damaged by being treated so poorly. Others, however, respond to patience and love. Just look at little Ellie." He referred to the baby his daughter and Conner Marshall had adopted. The difference being that she was so young compared to Evan.

As Hugh drank his tea, he tried not to dread the

upcoming bedtime. Three nights Evan had been with him and three nights had been an experience he wouldn't wish on anyone. It would surely test Annie's commitment. But if she left, what was he to do?

He again prayed for a suitable woman. Again no one came to the door except for the wind and he shifted his attention to Evan. He'd soon learned that to look directly at him caused the boy to shrink into the corner and turn his back to Hugh so he pretended to look out the window.

"Sounds like the wind is getting worse. We might get a storm." He watched Evan out of the corner of his eye. The boy looked at the window, then, from under lowered eyelids, watched Hugh. What was he thinking? What did he see when he looked at the adults? Was he able to assess their reliability?

Annie quietly cleaned the table and did the dishes while the dread in Hugh's thoughts continued to grow.

She finished and stood watching Evan. He wished he could read her mind. She brought her gaze to him, her eyes holding the darkness of the night. "What do you do about getting him to bed?"

He pushed to his feet. "Can we talk in my office?" He turned to the older man. "Would you mind staying with him?"

Grandfather waved them away. "Sort things out. You'll need to be in agreement if you're to reach him."

Hugh followed Annie to his office, careful to leave the door open so her grandfather could see them. He could tell by the set of her shoulders and the tip of her head that she expected he was going to take her to task about something. Nothing was further from the truth.

"About bedtime," he began and was relieved to notice her shoulders relaxed. "It's been difficult so I thought it best to warn you."

"Tell me about it." She sat in the chair he'd indicted earlier and he sank to his own across the desk.

"As you can see, he doesn't like to be touched and doesn't like anyone to get too close. I think the woman who kept him let him sleep on a mat in the corner. He relieved himself in the slop bucket." His throat tightened with the memory of how he'd found the boy and the words poured out as he described the situation.

"I've searched for him for months. At times I thought I would fail to find him. It wasn't until I offered a reward of twenty dollars that the woman came forward. Twenty dollars! That's all my son was worth. She told me when Bernice was dying—"

"Bernice?"

"She was my wife."

"I see."

She couldn't begin to see what it had been like. Bernice's dishonesty, her sneaking about with other men and then her disappearance.

"I'm sorry. Please continue."

He sucked in air. "Bernice told her to hang onto Evan until I came and I'd pay for him. The woman should have been charged with abuse or something. She barely kept him alive and now I don't know if he'll ever be right." He couldn't go on.

She had her head down, as if studying her hands folded in her lap.

What was she thinking? Had she been moved at all by Evan's plight?

He was about to go on, describing bedtime when she lifted her head and he saw a sheen of tears.

"How can anyone treat a child that way?" Her voice was a hoarse whisper. "It's criminal."

"It *is* criminal, in my opinion, but Sheriff Jesse assures me there isn't anything he can do about it."

"I hope that changes someday soon." She spat out each word as if she couldn't wait to get the bitter taste of them off her tongue.

His estimation of her rose several degrees. At least she wasn't one of those men or women who thought children were of little value unless they could work. "Me too. But it won't undo what has happened to Evan."

"I'm sorry and angry at the same time." She almost choked. "So sorry for Evan." A beat. "And you." Her voice strengthened. "But so angry at that woman. Please don't ever tell me who she is or where she lives. I might hunt her down and exact justice."

He imagined her in buckskins carrying a long gun and the fire of vengeance upon her face. It so tickled him that he chuckled. "I think for everyone's sake that will be one of my secrets."

Their gazes locked and he got the sensation that she saw far more than he wanted her to but he couldn't pull away.

"Hugh—may I call you that?"

He nodded. Hardly seemed they could stand on formality if they were going to be living under the same roof.

"Hugh, what happened to your wife?"

Her question slammed through him, leaving him

floundering for footing. Having a son who exploded at his slightest touch made him feel helpless and frustrated but being reminded of Bernice brought a flood of failure. "I don't want to talk about it."

"Another of those secrets?"

He couldn't tell if she found the idea annoying or if she didn't care.

She studied her hands again, examining one fingernail after the other.

Just when he thought she had accepted he didn't mean to tell her more, she began to speak. "In this case, I think it affects Evan. If Bernice left after a squabble, he might have heard you and…well, it might make him frightened of you."

"We didn't squabble." There were times they hardly talked. Bernice preferred to talk to other men. "She found me sadly lacking."

Annie stared at him. "Lacking? In what way?" She seemed to find it hard to believe.

He told himself her surprise didn't please him. After all, what did she know about him? Yet it did his ego good to think she might not think it possible. He shrugged. "I wasn't exciting enough. Didn't offer enough adventures. I found it difficult to please her." Just as he had with his mother.

Annie made a derisive noise. "That sounds to me like she had a problem, not you."

Hugh knew there was more to it than that. Just as he knew he was far too old to be flattered by Annie's defense of him. Knowing all that didn't change the fact that he felt like grinning like a silly kid. Instead, he coughed a little. "About Evan's bedtime…"

Annie tipped her head and grinned. "That is why we're here, isn't it?"

He grinned back then sobered. What was wrong with him that he responded to a young girl's attention so readily? He had to concentrate. "I can't let him stay in the kitchen on his own any more than I can let him sleep on a mat like an animal." He held up his hands in exasperation. "I know. You wonder how letting him sit there all day is any different but somehow it is. At least I know he's safe during the day."

She nodded.

"So I carry him to my room. As you can imagine, he kicks and screams the entire time." He couldn't help the little tremble in his voice. The whole procedure left him dazed and defeated. "I have a mattress on the floor for him. As soon as I put him there, he scrambles off and pushes it away. It's like he's resisting me, not the bed."

"Hugh, he's afraid if he trusts you he's going to be disappointed or worse, hurt."

She spoke with such certainty that he realized more lay behind her observation than she wanted him to know. Her little secret. And it did affect Evan. It made her more understanding. He was about to ask for her to explain but she spoke again.

"Does he eventually use the mattress? Does he sleep?"

"The first night he curled up in a ball in the corner. I covered him after he'd fallen asleep. Yesterday he waited until he thought I had dozed off before he crawled to the mattress and pulled the quilt over him."

"That's great progress." She grinned widely.

For the first time since he'd found Evan, he almost

felt encouraged. "I was so afraid of what he'd do the first night, I pulled my bed against the door to make sure he wouldn't run off."

"Somehow I don't see him running. Now if he was still with that woman I would wonder why he didn't but I guess it means he's smart enough to know he couldn't survive on his own."

Hugh couldn't help but smile. "I guess that shows that the boy has a good mind despite the way he acts."

"Oh, he's bright enough." She told him how she'd been able to tell what he liked to eat by his reaction. "I regret that I thought we had made more progress than we had. It was my fault he acted the way he did."

"I don't suppose it's anyone's fault. We just have to learn to understand him."

"I've been praying that God would give me wisdom and patience."

To hear how she'd been able to communicate with Evan and to know she'd prayed for him renewed his courage. "Thank you. Do you mind if we pray together before we head back to him?" Normally he had no hesitation about offering to pray for others but this was his need not someone else's.

"I'd like that." She leaned forward, her hands clasped together on top of his desk and her head bowed.

He stifled an urge to cradle her hands between his. Instead, he bowed his head and prayed for wisdom, understanding and healing for his son. Silently, he additionally prayed for a more mature woman to come to his door because, despite his resolve to keep things completely businesslike, he found Annie's concern and care very appealing and it frightened him. He must, above all else, guard his heart against the risk of caring for a woman, especially one who would soon realize that she could do far better than spend her life with a man who could offer nothing but a home with him and his hurting young son.

Chapter Three

Annie kept her head bowed several seconds after Hugh said *Amen*, waiting for God to direct her thoughts. When an idea came to her mind, she took it as from Him and lifted her head.

The look in Hugh's eyes almost made her forget what she'd been about to say. He watched her, looking both weary and hopeful at the same time. That was good, she told herself. He was beginning to see how helpful she would be. But the way his gaze clung to hers as if looking for something more left her breathless. She couldn't say if he found what he sought or if she could even offer it. There were far too many unknowns between them.

There was no need for her to know more about him. And she certainly didn't want to know about his marriage nor why his wife found him lacking. In what way? She tried and failed to imagine what he meant.

She slid her gaze past his to the night-blackened window. They had a common goal—taking care of Evan. She recalled something she'd heard somewhere. *Begin as you mean to go on.* She meant to become

Evan's mother and Hugh's wife. Therefore, she must begin to act like it.

"I think a bedtime routine is essential. So could we establish one starting tonight?" She couldn't keep looking past him and gauge his reaction so she brought her attention back to him. The quirk of one eyebrow informed her that her request had caught him off guard.

"It seems we have a routine," he said with a large dose of irony. "I pick him up. He fights me. I take him to the room and keep him there." His laugh lacked mirth.

It certainly wasn't how she wanted to go on. She smiled. "Maybe we could work at improving that routine."

"What do you suggest?"

Did she detect a note of hope? She wanted to believe so. "My mother always read to me at bedtime and said prayers with me. When my papa was home, he came in to hear my prayers." Her voice deepened. "When I look back, I wonder how I could have taken such ordinary things for granted."

"I'm sorry about your mother."

She tried to break from his compassionate look but found herself unable to do so. Her insides clenched. Tears stung the backs of her eyes. Mama had been dead more than four years. Annie knew she should be over her grief but it often welled up inside her like a bubbling pot of hot jam, about to overflow. She swallowed hard, striving to control the sudden rush of sorrow. "Thank you." She hadn't been able to keep the emotion out of her voice and wondered how he would react. "I shouldn't be upset by the memory."

His smile was soft and gentle. "Some sorrows never go away. A person simply learns how to be at peace with them."

She met his gaze, practically drinking in the comfort he offered. "I can see why you're the preacher." She managed a little smile. "You know the right words to say."

"Thank you." Did she detect a bit of a catch in his voice? That seemed strange. But a trickle of hope entered her heart. If he needed to hear words of encouragement, she could give them. But not right now. "I'd like to start a bedtime routine such as I knew but I don't think he'll be in a frame of mind for stories and prayers after a struggle to get him into bed. Instead, why don't we let him stay in his safe corner while I read a story? And then you could say his bedtime prayers." She didn't want to exclude Hugh from the opportunity. "I think we need to establish normal behavior for Evan as quickly as he'll let us."

Hugh nodded slowly. "I like the idea. Just so long as you don't expect too much of him."

"I hope I've learned my lesson about pushing him too hard."

Hugh got to his feet and waited for Annie to go ahead of him.

"I brought a storybook."

He remained in the sitting room as she hurried to find the book from among her belongings and then rejoined him. Together they entered the kitchen.

Grandfather nodded in his chair. He must have been exhausted. It had been a long day. She would suggest he go to bed but knew he wouldn't go while both she and Hugh were still up.

"I'll make tea." She set the kettle to boil and brought out a selection of cookies from the pantry. As she waited for the water to boil, she talked, knowing Evan listened even when he gave no indication of it.

"I think it's nice to have tea together before bed," she said, looking to Hugh to see if he understood her need to explain for Evan's sake.

Hugh's slight nod and barely-there smile encouraged her to go on.

And brought a sudden stutter to her voice. She forced herself to speak firmly and steadily as she continued. "When I was about Evan's age, I remember my mother making milk tea for me. And I always got two cookies. Of course, I always chose the two biggest ones." She contemplated how best to connect with Evan. "My mother died a few years ago. So no one reads me bedtime stories anymore but that's okay because now I can read them to Evan."

From the slight tilt of his head she knew he listened.

She poured the tea and gave a cupful to Hugh and Grandfather. She made milk tea and set the cup and a small plate holding two cookies before Evan then sat across from Hugh.

He gave her a smile that seemed to say he approved of her efforts. Good. It meant they were headed in the right direction. He'd soon learn she had much to offer him and his son.

She sipped her tea slowly and enjoyed the two cookies she had chosen and then opened the storybook. It was the same one her mother had read from when Annie was Evan's age and as the memories of those days assailed her, tears filled her eyes and clogged her throat. Not wanting Hugh to see how fragile her emotions were, she kept her head lowered.

"Are you okay?" he asked after a moment.

She nodded, unable to speak.

Grandfather squeezed her hand. "It's okay to miss your mama."

"Of course it is," Hugh assured her.

A strangled squeak drew the attention of all three adults to Evan. His shoulders twitched. As if he cried? It was impossible to tell as he kept his back to them.

Annie looked to Hugh. Raised her eyebrows to silently ask if they should go to him.

He lifted his shoulders ever so slightly. He didn't know any more than she did and his mouth worked.

Her heart tore at the sign of his uncertainty. She couldn't imagine how difficult it would be to watch his son struggle with so many problems and not know if any offer of comfort would send him into a fury... one born of fear, she was certain. It made her doubly grateful to have had a tender mother and a supportive family and she promised herself she would give Evan the same if he would let her.

It seemed no one quite knew what to do and she could only think of one thing so she cleared her throat and began to read. The book was a collection of Bible stories and moral tales and her favorite had always been about the old farm dog who rescued some orphaned kittens and raised them. The dog fought off a coyote that tried to get the kittens and chased away a hawk. At one point she was sorely injured but kept on tending the three kittens.

"The moral of the story," Annie read, "is that God loves us even better than that dog loved her kittens.

He claims us because He loves us. He takes care of us—1 John 3 verse 1 says 'Behold, what manner of love the Father hath bestowed upon us, that we should be called the sons of God.'" She needed to say more for Evan's sake. "Some children are in families they weren't born into and they are loved. My brother Logan and his wife adopted three children." It struck her that the children's circumstances were somewhat like Evan's. They'd been neglected and abused by a man claiming to be their stepfather. Perhaps now was not the time to talk about that. "And my brother Conner and his wife have adopted a little girl and love her dearly. My oldest brother Dawson has a little girl but his wife died so Mattie had no mama." She sensed Evan straining toward her. "Dawson married a very fine lady by the name of Isabelle and Isabelle is Mattie's new mama. They love each other very much. God loves each of us even more."

She and Hugh considered one another across the table. The tension seemed to have left his face. If the things she'd said had accomplished that then thanks be to God for guiding her words.

"My mama or papa always said prayers with me before bed."

Hugh nodded. "I'm the papa so I will do it."

Annie knew he wasn't excluding her but simply helping Evan understand his role in the family.

"Let's pray," Hugh said and the adults bowed their heads.

Annie stole a look at Evan. He had turned his head slightly to watch his father. She knew the boy would have showed her his thin back if he realized she watched him and would have disguised the longing in his eyes. Seeing it gave Annie hope. Evan knew what he wanted but was afraid to trust it could be his.

It was up to Annie and Hugh and even Grandfather to prove to Evan that he could trust their love and concern.

Hugh prayed for a good night's sleep for them all. He asked for people to be safe in the cold winter wind and he especially thanked God for allowing him to find Evan and bring him home.

Annie continued to watch the boy from under the curtain of her lashes and saw wonder and doubt intermingled in his face.

"Amen." Hugh met Annie's eyes across the table. His eyes were troubled.

She understood he didn't look forward to getting Evan into bed. She rose. "My mama always said it was time for me to go to sleep after the prayers were said."

Evan crowded into the corner as if he wanted to become part of the walls.

Annie tipped her head toward Hugh. It had to be done. She went to Hugh's side. "We're in this together," she murmured.

"Thanks." With a deep sigh, he got to his feet and faced his son. "Evan, it's bedtime and I'm going to take you to bed."

The boy stiffened and then his legs windmilled.

"Evan," Annie said. "We all have our own beds and we all sleep in them. That's what people in a family do. Grandfather sleeps in his bed. I sleep in mine. You sleep in yours with your papa in his."

Hugh sucked in air like his lungs had no bottom and then gathered the boy in his arms. As expected,

Evan tried to kick, tried to squirm from Hugh's grasp, but Hugh was prepared and held his son firmly.

Seeing the look of distress on both of their faces, Annie started after Hugh.

"I'll be right here," Grandfather said.

"I have to help with Evan," Annie said, following Hugh down the hallway to the room he and Evan shared.

She had taken care of three brothers, a father and grandfather so stepping into a room where a male slept was nothing new to her and yet this was different and her cheeks burned as she glanced about. There was a mattress against the far wall and a tangle of blankets. There was also a narrow bed with the covers pulled tight. Odd, the men in her family never made their beds. She had assumed men simply didn't know how or didn't care. She took in the rest of the room. A wardrobe with the door closed. A coat hanging from a hook on the wall. A table next to the bed which held a lamp, a Bible and three books stacked neatly. From under the bed peeked a valise.

Hugh was a neat, orderly man.

She liked that. However she couldn't dwell on her reaction as Hugh struggled with Evan.

He reached the mattress and set Evan down. "Time to go to sleep, son."

The tenderness in Hugh's voice caused Annie's throat to constrict.

A keening sound came from Evan's throat and he scrambled off the mattress and into the corner, watching his father with wide eyes.

Grooves appeared in Hugh's cheeks at the way Evan shrank from him.

Annie wanted so badly to comfort both of them she acted without thinking. She went to Hugh's side and squeezed his arm as she spoke to Evan.

"Evan, honey, your papa loves you and wants to help you. So do I. We are both going to be here to take care of you, to protect you, to help you learn to trust us."

Hugh's hand came over hers. "That's right, son. We are here for you. Always and forever."

Evan grabbed the quilt off his mattress and clutched it to him.

"Good night, Evan," Annie said. She longed to kiss him but knew she couldn't. She slipped from Hugh's side and left the room. In the hall, she paused. Had Hugh really said they were in this together for always?

He stepped from the room and pulled the door closed behind him. "Thank you for all your help with Evan. I truly appreciate it."

"Did you mean what you said?"

"I hope so. What specifically do you mean?"

She shouldn't have brought it up. She didn't want easily made and as easily forgotten promises. Yet if he'd already made up his mind about her staying she wouldn't have to worry about it.

"I will do whatever it takes to help Evan, if that's what you mean."

It wasn't and yet it answered her question. He would accept her if he thought it was in Evan's best interests. "I feel the same."

He shifted so he looked into her face. "Then we are agreed on the most important thing."

She nodded. Caring for Evan ensured she would have a home and family of her own.

She wanted no more than that.

* * *

Hugh lay on his bed in the darkness, listening to Evan's quiet breathing. The boy had slipped to the mattress and pulled the quilt over himself a short time after Hugh had turned out the lamp. Probably when he thought Hugh had fallen asleep.

Sleep did not come easily for Hugh as he reviewed the events of the day.

He'd advertised for a woman to become his wife and a mother to Evan and the only one to show up, eager for the task, was Annie…an unsuitable, unlikely match. And yet he had agreed. Out of desperation only.

His eyes widened in the darkness as he recalled the words he'd spoken as she helped put Evan to bed… though *help* and *put to bed* were but idealistic terms. Evan had allowed neither. *We are here for you. Always and forever.* He groaned and regretted it immediately when he heard Evan scuffle to the far edge of his mattress.

Annie could easily take his statement as a promise that he would marry her and make this agreement permanent. He couldn't imagine doing so.

Apart from her young age, she was a Marshall and he had quickly learned that the family had high expectations of themselves and others. Grandfather Marshall had founded the town of Bella Creek to provide a better place for people to live than the wild town of Wolf Hollow closer to the gold mines. When most of a block had burned down last winter, the Marshalls had spearheaded the rebuilding and finding a new teacher and doctor. It was Grandfather Marshall and two other men—one also a Marshall—who had interviewed Hugh for the preaching position. Annie was the younger sister and cherished daughter and grand-daughter. If Hugh failed in any way to treat her as he should, he would face the combined wrath of the large Marshall family. It wasn't something he would enjoy. How could he hope to live up to their high standards?

How could he make this right? Make her under-stand he had spoken carelessly? He eventually fell asleep without finding an answer and woke up know-ing he must clear up the matter.

The room was still dark and Hugh stiffened lis-tening for Evan's breathing. He didn't relax until the boy snuffled. The rattle of pots and pans informed him the young woman troubling his mind had risen.

He slipped into his clothes before he lit the lamp.

Evan woke up and lay in a bemused state for about two seconds then jerked upright, his eyes blinking rapidly. He retreated to the corner then rushed from the room to the kitchen.

Hugh followed on his heels.

Evan skidded to a halt as he saw Annie at the stove and Grandfather in his chair nursing a cup of coffee then he sidled past them and sank into the corner he had claimed as his own.

"Good morning, Evan. Good morning, Hugh," Annie said, cheerful as the morning sun that had not made its bleary way over the horizon.

"Morning." Hugh wasn't yet ready to be as cheer-ful as she.

Grandfather also greeted them.

Annie poured a cup of coffee and offered it to Hugh. "I don't know what you take in it. Cream, sugar?"

"This is good." He sat at the table. "I hope you had

a good sleep." He had a hundred things on his mind, things he wanted to clear up, but that was all he could come up with?

"Fine, thank you."

She hummed as she prepared breakfast. Grandfather swirled the bottom inch of his coffee. Evan hunched in the corner. Hugh wrapped his hands about his cup. Seems the male members of the household did not wake as bright-eyed as Annie. The thought brought Hugh's attention to her. She had a spring in her step that had her almost dancing in front of the stove. She reached for the salt with a quickness that made Hugh smile. She flung about and her gaze collided with Hugh's.

He couldn't say what he saw in her face or perhaps, more correctly, didn't want to admit he might see an eagerness. His fingers tightened around his cup. Was she recalling the careless words he'd spoken last night? *Always and forever.* Wasn't that what he wanted for both himself and Evan? Why not with her?

He couldn't answer the question except with his previous doubts that she would soon enough decide she could do better.

She shifted her attention to Evan. "Hey, little man. What would you like for breakfast?"

Evan, as expected, gave no sign of hearing.

Annie wasn't deterred and she began to list possibilities.

Remembering how she'd said Evan gave subtle clues, Hugh watched the boy. When she asked if he liked eggs, Annie nodded. "Good. One or two?"

He wasn't sure how she knew his answer but again she nodded. "Two it is."

She flicked him a triumphant glance. He wanted to believe she really saw a response but caution warned him she might only be saying she did in an attempt to impress him.

Smiling, she turned back to the stove and soon had a bountiful breakfast prepared. She filled a bowl and placed it in front of Evan then served those at the table.

Hugh glanced at those he was about to share the meal with. Grandfather, Annie and Evan. Somehow, despite his reservations about this arrangement, it felt right. He allowed himself to hope the future might provide better things. All he had to do was trust God and not expect too much. Which, he warned himself, did not have any bearing on what expectation the others would have of him.

He asked Grandfather to offer the grace and the old man bent forward to bow his head and prayed a simple prayer of gratitude.

As they ate, both Hugh and Grandfather came to life.

Grandfather looked about. "Is there anything I can help you with, Hugh?"

Hugh's fork stalled halfway to his mouth. The last thing he expected was such an offer from the old man. He shifted a glance to Annie. Her eyes were quiet and watchful. Did she have an expectation of something from him? If so, he couldn't begin to guess what it might be and turned back to her grandfather. He could understand the man wanting to feel he was useful but what could Hugh give him to do? Thinking of a task he had put off a long time, he chuckled.

"I don't suppose you would visit Mr. Barret for

me? I promised I'd drop by this week and here it is already Friday."

Grandfather grunted. "He'll understand when he learns how you've been occupied." His gaze slanted toward Evan.

Hugh couldn't say so but he'd gladly accepted the excuse. Mr. Barret—cranky, complaining and bitter—was no joy to visit. "He expects me to keep my word."

"He expects a whole lot more than that from what I've seen." Grandfather shook his head. "Seems to me he thinks the world owes him far more than it's given him."

That was the truth. "I try to tell him that God has a purpose for his life but he won't believe it."

"Son, you deliver the Word. It's up to him to receive it."

"Thank you." Hugh had seen so little of his own father that he barely remembered him. The old man's words fell into his heart like a sweet, warm drink on a cold day. "You make me think of a kindly man, Stewart Caldwell by name. He and his wife took me in when I was twelve. He was a preacher. Because of him, I became one."

"You honor me to say so."

Hugh felt Annie studying him and met her gaze. "Were your parents both dead?" she asked.

He nodded.

"I'm sorry. There's so much I don't know about you."

"And I about you." The moment grew longer with each heartbeat.

Grandfather chuckled. "You want to know anything about Annie, just ask me. I can give you all the details."

Hugh could ask Grandfather but would sooner have Annie tell him. Her cheeks looked like she was too close to the stove and she shifted her attention to Evan as did Hugh.

The boy had cleaned his bowl and watched the adults until they looked at him and then he shifted away from them.

Hugh's coffee cup was empty but he took it and squeezed it between his hands as if doing so could relieve the heaviness sucking at his body. Would his son ever learn how to properly relate to people?

Annie rose and reached for the coffeepot. "Can I give you a refill?"

He held up a hand. "No thanks. I must go to the office and study for my sermon. Will you be okay?" He inclined his head to indicate his concern over Evan.

Annie gave Hugh a steady, promising look. "We'll be fine."

"You're going to ignore Mr. Barret?" Grandfather's voice carried a mix of humor and accusation.

"I'll visit him this afternoon." Not until he reached his office did he realize he had not addressed the careless words he'd spoken last night. Of course, he could hardly say anything in front of her grandfather. The old man would surely see it as wrong to withdraw words that could be taken as a promise.

He'd deal with the matter later, though he couldn't keep putting off unpleasant duties.

Before he started he sat quietly in prayer. *God, show me how to help Evan. Give me insight into Your Word that I might deliver hope and encouragement to*

Your people. He readily admitted he needed to hear from God as much, if not more, than those who would gather on Sunday.

He pulled out his notes, opened his Bible and dipped his pen in ink. Dishes rattled from the kitchen. Grandfather grunted as he made his way to his easy chair. The poor man must be feeling pain today. Annie murmured something.

Hugh leaned closer to catch her words.

"Evan, did you enjoy breakfast? I'm glad to see you ate it all. I hope you got enough." She chattered away as if Evan understood and responded to everything she said.

Grandfather's deeper voice chimed in. "Hurts my bones to watch you sit on the floor, young man. Sure do enjoy my soft chair."

Hugh bent his head, determined to concentrate. He could close the door but he didn't. How else was he to know what was going on in the other room? And if he wished, even a tiny bit, that he could be there observing, it was only because he cared about Evan. He refused to admit he wished he could see the expression on Annie's face as she talked to the unresponsive boy.

He forced his attention to sermon preparation and read over the Bible passage he meant to preach from.

A knock rattled the back door. Hugh set aside his pen and pushed to his feet. By the time he reached the office door, a blast of cold air indicated Annie had let in the caller.

"Hi, Logan. What brings you here? Did you want to see Hugh? I'll get him."

"I'm here to see you." Logan's voice rang with authority.

"Well, here I am. Can you see me?"

Hugh hung back. Someone would call him if he was needed.

"Dawson told me you moved in here." Logan's voice rang with disapproval.

"Would you like a cup of coffee and some cookies?" Annie sounded unperturbed by her brother's attitude.

"Fine but don't think you can keep me from speaking my mind." The coffeepot scraped across the stove and china clattered on the table as Annie served her brother.

Should he join them? Hugh thought.

After a moment or two, Logan spoke again. "Tell me what you think you're doing."

Annie chuckled. "I know Dawson told you everything and nothing has changed since yesterday."

"You can't seriously plan to marry in response to an advertisement."

"Have you never heard of mail-order brides? Isn't that what they do?"

Hugh marveled at the calm way she answered.

"You aren't an old spinster. You have a family that gladly wants you to stay with them. Why are you doing this?"

"Why do you object?"

"Because you deserve better than a loveless marriage."

"I'm not married yet." She drawled out the final word as if to inform Logan it was only a matter of time.

Hugh had to put a stop to this. He hadn't promised her a marriage…only a four-week trial period.

Was that long enough for someone to answer his ad? Someone more suitable. As he headed for the door, Grandfather spoke.

"Annie thinks she can protect herself from pain by settling for less than love."

"Why," Logan demanded in an aggrieved tone, "would she want to do that?"

Hugh slowed, wanting to hear her response.

"Because of that young fella who courted her— what was it?—a year or two ago."

Logan made an explosive sound. "Rudy Ryman! That milksop? Good riddance to him, I say. If he hadn't left, us boys were about to suggest he should."

Silence greeted his remark. Hugh wished he could see Annie's expression. Was this the real reason for her eagerness to marry him?

Annie's soft response came. "Nothing stays the same but life goes on and I intend to go on in the way I choose." No mistaking the conviction in her words.

"Dawson told me you wouldn't listen to reason," Logan continued. "But you and I have always been closer than that. I hoped you'd listen to me."

Annie continued to speak in gentle tones. "I'd like you to accept that this is what I want."

There came no response. Was she changing her mind under pressure from her brother? Hugh had to know what was going on and crossed the sitting room. As he reached the kitchen doorway, Logan's look blasted him. Hugh, having dealt with harshness all his life, kept his own expression bland. "Hello, Logan. What brings you here so early in the morning?"

"My sister. No offense, Preacher, but I'm trying to talk her out of this arrangement."

Hugh's gaze skimmed those at the table and settled on Evan who huddled in the corner, his shoulders hunched forward, hearing every word and wondering what these adults would decide and how it would affect him.

Hugh met Annie's look. Saw desperation and determination. She inclined her head slightly toward Evan signaling that she was concerned about how the boy would react to this conversation.

Her look, her concern about his son and Logan's comments about a beau of Annie's made up his mind. "Annie and I are agreed that she should stay here for now. Evan and I need her. Your grandfather provides chaperoning."

Annie's smile rewarded him.

Had she heard the limitation of his offer? *For now.* Until someone more suitable, more likely to find this situation to their satisfaction answered his ad. Why was he having to remind himself of that so often?

Annie poured Hugh a cup of coffee as he sat to visit with Logan. What Logan said was true. They had always had a closer relationship than she'd had with her other brothers but nothing he could say would change her mind about her decision. In less than twenty-four hours, she had already proven to Hugh how much she was needed here. And she meant to prove she was invaluable.

As the men discussed the weather, she mentally planned the next few meals and observed Evan out of the corner of her eye. The boy gave the appearance of indifference but she was certain he listened with interest to every word. He glanced at the window as they mentioned the possibility of a storm. His hands twisted as Logan wondered if the cows would find enough shelter.

Logan pushed aside his cup. "I better get home and tell Sadie how our discussion went. She will be disappointed I wasn't able to change your mind."

"Assure her I am fine. We are all fine."

"That's a fact," Grandfather added. "I rather like the notion of spending the winter in town. That drive in the cold gets less and less appealing."

Logan chuckled. "Are you admitting you're getting old?"

"Nope. Just cold. And don't try and convince me you enjoy riding out to the ranch every day." Grandfather knew as well as Annie that Logan didn't go out every day since the fall work ended.

Logan managed to look slightly embarrassed. "I've got things to do in town. Come spring I'll be out more often. In fact, Sadie and I are talking about building a house on the ranch property. We like the idea of the kids being around family more."

Annie slid an overt look at Evan, noting the way he watched them from the curtain of his eyelashes. It was the word *family* that drew his attention and she vowed to use the word as often as possible.

With goodbye to all in the room, including Evan, Logan made his departure. Hugh returned to the office and Annie turned her attention toward cooking, though her thoughts were not on the familiar tasks. No. Instead, she prayed for guidance. A thought came and she began to speak.

"Evan, that was my brother. I have three brothers and they are all married and all of them have children. We are a big family. The reason my brothers come to see me is because they care. They would do anything for me. That's what families do."

She prepared a pot of soup for the noon meal and described everything she did from peeling carrots to chopping onions.

"Onions make me cry." She wiped her eyes on the corner of a towel. She looked directly at the boy and caught a look of concern in his face before he jerked away. "Not because I'm sad but because they give off a juice that stings my eyes." The fact that he showed emotion over her tears so encouraged her she wanted to run to the office and tell Hugh.

The office door remained ajar. How much could he hear? She half considered raising her voice so he wouldn't miss a word. Somehow she would make an opportunity to tell him of Evan's reaction.

While the soup simmered on the stove, Annie swept the floor and then got down on her hands and knees to wash it. Not because it was dirty. Mrs. Ross had seen to that. But in order to have an excuse to get to Evan's level. As she worked, she continued to talk.

She told him how Grandfather had started the Marshall Five Ranch, and Grandfather told of his early days. She spoke of the first horse she could remember riding.

Soon enough it was time for dinner and she went to the office. Hugh sat with a fan of papers before him. He held what looked like a photograph in his hands. She observed for a moment, then rapped on the door.

"Dinner is ready."

He looked at the picture a moment longer before he let out a long breath and laid the picture faceup on the desktop.

Curious, she tried to see it.

He noticed her interest and tipped the picture toward her. "Evan's mother."

She studied the likeness of a very pretty young woman. "Bernice?" Why was he showing her now when he'd refused to talk about her last night?

"Do you remember me mentioning Stewart Caldwell?"

"Wasn't that the preacher who took you in when your parents died?"

"Yes, after my mother died. My father had disappeared before that."

"I'm sorry. You've had a lot of loss."

He drew his finger along the edge of the frame holding the photo. "Stewart warned me not to marry Bernice but I thought I knew better."

"Why did he warn you against her?"

"I suppose he saw things I refused to see." Hugh's gaze slammed into Annie so that she gripped the door to keep from falling back. "She had a reputation for wildness. I put it down to her youth. I discovered it was more than that. She couldn't seem to get enough of..." He hesitated, as if searching for the right word. "Life, I suppose. She lived in a permanent state of excitement and when I could no longer offer that, she sought it elsewhere."

"She left you for more excitement?" It was so much like Dawson's first wife, Violet, that she could barely keep the shock and anger from her voice. She'd watched Dawson and Mattie suffer when Violet sought what she wanted elsewhere. At least Dawson had his family to help him.

Hugh stared at the picture. "She left and she took Evan." The agony in his voice echoed inside Annie. The little boy had paid a heavy price for his mother's foolishness.

She took the three steps to Hugh's side and rested a hand on his shoulder, feeling the tension beneath her palm. "It's an answer to prayer that you found him. My whole family prayed daily that you would and now you have. Evan has you and me and Grandfather and my whole family to teach him what life should be like." She stood there, quietly waiting and silently praying for healing for both father and son.

The tension eased from Hugh's shoulder and she removed her hand lest he think her too forward.

He slipped the picture into the right-hand top drawer and closed the drawer firmly. "I have to trust God that Evan can be helped."

"I'm positive he can be. He sees everything. I believe Evan understands what is being said around him and even more important, he is aware of other people's feelings." She told him how she had seen concern in Evan's eyes when she cried while chopping onions. "It's a very good sign."

He pushed to his feet and stood facing her, barely eighteen inches between them. She was overwhelmed by his nearness, felt his strength and his powerful personality just as she had from the first time she saw him.

"I hope you are right and I admit I'm willing to believe anything that offers me hope about my son."

She smiled what she hoped was an encouraging

smile though inside, she trembled just a little at all the longings rushing through her. She did not want to care about this man any more deeply than as a partner sharing concern about Evan. "How can he fail to get better with so many people on his side?" Her words were meant to make her remember she was here only to do a job of caring for Evan and his father.

He caught the door and pulled it wider, waiting for her to go ahead of him. They walked side by side to the kitchen. And Annie told herself it meant nothing but common courtesy. Perhaps also mutual concern over a little boy. But nothing beyond that. It was something they were both agreed on.

After they ate soup and thick slices of bread, followed by the remains of a cake discovered in the pantry, Hugh announced he was going to visit Mr. Barret.

Grandfather, who had spent the morning reading or snoozing in his chair, said, "Would you like me to go with you?"

Hugh looked about to say yes, then shook his head. "It's bitter cold out there. You're better off staying inside and keeping warm. Thanks for offering."

Grandfather looked so relieved that Annie's estimation of Hugh rose several notches. She followed him to the door as he donned a heavy woolen coat. "Thank you for realizing it's best for Grandfather to stay home." *Home* stuck momentarily on her tongue. She gave a decisive nod of her head. She would soon get used to this house being home rather than the ranch house.

Hugh seemed surprised at her words. "I'm not about to take advantage of an old man." He studied her a moment. "Or of a young woman."

Before she could challenge his assumption that he was taking advantage of her, he stepped outside and closed the door, a cold blast sweeping across the floor. She reached for the knob, about to call out a protest but pulled her hand back and turned away.

She'd given up on love and meant to keep her heart safe from emotional involvement but she had not given up on this arrangement. She had four weeks to prove to him that it should be made permanent. Surely four weeks would be long enough.

Chapter Four

Hugh walked four blocks down Silver Street and turned right. He passed three houses and reached the home Mr. Barret shared with his elderly sister, neither of whom seemed to have a cheerful bone between them. He paused outside the door to pray for strength, wisdom and a large dose of Christian kindness. The elderly pair had followed Mr. Barret's married son to Montana to look for gold but his son had been killed in an accident several years back and his wife, the younger Mrs. Barret, had returned east to her kinfolk. Neither of the elderly Barrets could see any reason to leave their home in Bella Creek although they had no family here. According to Mr. Barret, they had no relatives anywhere. Surely that was enough to make the pair morose.

As he stood before the weathered door, he thought of the morning's events. Annie had promised her whole family would work together for Evan's benefit. A most generous offer and one that made him more hopeful than he had been all week. Don't count on too much, he warned himself. Annie was young and beautiful and would soon find greener pastures.

The cold knotted the muscles in his chest. Strange that frigid air had never had that effect on him before. He would not admit it had anything to do with the thought of Annie leaving and the need for him to start the process over again...with a more suitable woman.

Gathering his thoughts together, he rapped his gloved knuckles on the door. Knowing from past experience that it would take a few minutes for Miss Barret to come, he waited. After several minutes when she hadn't answered, he removed his glove and banged harder then bent his ear to the door to listen, concerned that she might be unable to cross from the kitchen. Perhaps she'd fallen.

He thought he detected a shuffling sound and waited, ready to barge in if he thought it necessary.

He was about to do so when the doorknob rattled and the frail, white-haired woman opened the door. "Come in, pastor," she said in her reedy voice.

He hurried in so she could close out the cold.

"Clarence was just saying that you had forgotten your promise to visit. He'd have had to scold you if you did."

Hugh knew Clarence Barret's scoldings took on the form of fire and condemnation but perhaps Hugh needed to be reminded occasionally that he was a man with many flaws.

"I've been otherwise occupied this week but I promised and here I am."

She led him through the unheated parlor to the kitchen where the elderly couple spent their days, though he couldn't say what they did.

Mr. Barret looked up at Hugh's entrance. "Couldn't have left it much later, could you?" The old man was reed thin, white haired—what was left of it—and wore a permanent scowl.

"There's still one more day in the week."

"And a whole bushel of excuses, I've no doubt."

Hugh didn't wait for an invitation to sit because he'd learned there wouldn't be one. He chose a chair that allowed him to face the elderly man. "How are you faring in this cold weather?"

"Surviving, which is all we can hope for. What's this I hear about you taking a young woman to live with you? What's this world coming to that a preacher would live in sin?"

Hugh's ear tips grew hot. He had no intention of arguing with the old man but he wanted to defend himself. Before he could speak, Mr. Barret rushed on.

"The young Marshall gal is what I hear. The old man must be getting doddering in his old age to allow such a thing."

Hugh understood him to mean Grandfather Marshall.

Mr. Barret rushed on with his sister tsking disapproval in the background. "And Bud and his fine sons. Have they all taken leave of their senses?" Mr. Barret leaned forward. "What have you got to say for yourself, young man?"

How had the troublesome old man become aware of this already? Then Hugh recalled that the pair paid a young lad to bring their groceries every week. Likely they'd hear the news from him and had assumed and embellished it on their own. "Have you heard I found my son?"

"Mrs. Ross says the boy is addled in his head." Mrs. Ross must have been the boy's source of information and he'd simply repeated it to the Barrets.

Hugh doubted Mrs. Ross had used those sort of words but how like Mr. Barret to put an ugly twist to the whole situation.

"He's been mistreated but I will take care of him, whatever it takes."

"Even living in sin with an innocent gal?"

"Certainly not. She has her own quarters."

Mr. Barret's snort carried a whole world of doubt.

"Grandfather Marshall is staying at the parsonage as well and he makes sure things are appropriate." Hugh had the satisfaction of seeing Mr. Barret momentarily stalled…briefly.

"It's still mighty suspicious looking."

Hugh understood the old man's concerns. All the more reason to hope someone older would answer his ad. He knew it didn't make sense but someone more mature and less attractive than Annie would invite less speculation. For Annie's sake he should tell her to go home. But then who would look after Evan? Seemed he had no choice but to accept her help for the time being. *Lord, protect her from gossip and send a more suitable woman.*

He turned his thoughts back to the room he sat in. "You asked me to call. Was there a special reason?"

"Just figured you should be doing your job as the preacher and paying us poor old folk a visit more regularly."

Of all the people Hugh served, this man made him feel the most inadequate. He supposed God had put the old man in his life to remind him of his failings and shortcomings.

He shared a Bible verse with Mr. Barret and prayed for his well-being before he took his departure. Back on the street, he turned immediately back toward home, anxious to know how Annie had managed without him.

Not that he had any real doubts about her abilities. At least until she was distracted by something beyond the four walls of his house. No, his concern was more because of not knowing how Evan would react to any given situation.

He slipped into the house through the office door, hung his coat on the nearby hook and hurried across the room. He ground to a halt at the sound of laughter. The deeper chuckle must be Grandfather, the light-hearted merry sound that drew longing and happiness from his heart would be Annie.

How long since he'd heard laughter in his home? Had he ever heard it? Not in this house where, until a few days ago, he had lived alone in somber silence. Perhaps before his brother Kenny died he'd heard it in his childhood home. Certainly not after that unfortunate day. There had been smiles and chuckles at the Caldwell house but not this kind of overflowing amusement.

He remained at the door, purposely eavesdropping on the moment. What were they laughing about?

"My turn," Annie said and silence followed her words.

Hugh tiptoed into the next room, drawn by something stronger than he could explain. A need, a desire to witness what made her laugh.

She leaned over the table, the picture of concentration as she studied a pile of thin straw-like sticks stacked in the middle of the surface. They were playing pick-up sticks. Angled away from where Hugh stood, she did not notice him watching. Grandfather sat with his back to him.

"You know I'm better at this game than you are," the old man said. "Always have been." He turned to his right. "She thinks because I'm an old man she can beat me." He chuckled. "You watch me prove her wrong."

Hugh realized Grandfather talked to Evan. The boy pressed his back into the corner but had shifted about so he could watch the game.

Hugh's heart warmed to see his son responding even this much. Up until now, he had avoided looking at anyone. Not wanting to spoil the moment, Hugh remained motionless.

Evan's attention shifted to Annie whose hand hovered over the sticks. With poised finger and thumb she gingerly touched a stick and the whole pile shifted.

"Well, phooey." She leaned back, her arms crossed in disgust.

Grandfather chuckled. "Tried to warn you." He rubbed his hands in glee. "Now my turn. What do you think, Evan? Can I get a stick? Which one would you choose?"

Hugh held his breath, waiting, praying for some indication the boy understood and wished to participate. But Evan turned his head away and Hugh swallowed hard as disappointment and discouragement clawed at his insides.

Grandfather studied the pile, chose a stick and

slowly lifted it off the stack. He crowed with victory when none of the sticks moved. "Beat that, young missy."

She ticked her finger on the old man's elbow. "Don't be a gloating winner. Isn't that what you and Pa and Mama always told us?"

Evan was again watching them and Hugh thought he saw a flicker of amusement in the boy's eyes and then he noticed Hugh in the shadows and jerked back so quickly that Annie turned to see what had startled the boy.

"You're back." She pushed to her feet. "How was your visit? Do you want tea or coffee or did they serve you some?" She glanced back to the table, pink rushing up her neck and stalling at her chin. "We were playing a game. Supper is in the oven. It will be ready on time."

She thought he would disapprove of how she spent her time? She couldn't be more wrong. "Annie, you're free to do what you like. I'm not judging you."

Her eyes darkened. "Ah, but you are." Before he could argue otherwise, she turned to fill the kettle and set it on the hottest part of the stove. "Tea or coffee?"

"Thank you. I'll have whatever you and your grandfather want."

"I feel like coffee," Grandfather said. "I take it the Barrets didn't offer you anything?" He must have meant the question to be rhetorical because he didn't wait for Hugh to answer. "How are they?"

Hugh gave a few details of his visit, reminded again of how unfair this arrangement was to Annie. He should end it now, but how could he? He needed someone. And not just anyone. Someone who related to Evan as well as Annie and her grandfather did.

Annie swept the pile of sticks off the table and dropped them into a tin. Why should she feel guilty to be seen playing a game with Grandfather, especially when it created another way to draw out Evan? And yet she did because he was judging her. Four weeks—minus a day—to prove to him that she was right for this job. Only it wasn't a job. If he found her satisfactory, it was a lifetime agreement. For better or worse. For richer or poorer. In sickness and in health. That would include the sickness or health of his son. Poor little Evan who had watched her and Grandfather play pick-up sticks. She considered that well worth any censure with which Hugh viewed the pasttime.

Perhaps she needed to be less critical of herself too.

She made coffee and served it with cookies she had baked that very afternoon while Hugh had gone to visit the Barrets. Grandfather finished his coffee and retired to his chair with a book but soon the book fell to his lap and his head tipped to one side as he napped.

Annie watched him for a moment. She hated to think that he was getting old but last year he had gone out every day in the winter to check on the ranch activities. This year he seemed content, maybe even relieved, to stay indoors, close to the fire.

"You're worried about him?" Hugh's softly spoken words drew her attention. His kindly expression caused her throat to tighten.

"I suppose I am," she murmured, not wanting to disturb her grandfather. "He isn't as active as he was last winter." She told him how things had been a year ago. Her throat tightened. "I can't bear to think of losing him." Her voice broke and she ducked her head.

"It hurts to lose those we love. Sometimes…" He paused and she clung to that moment of silence, hoping for something that would help her know how to deal with loss—other than to pull the edges of herself closed.

He continued. "Sometimes I wonder if it takes a special person to cope with a profound loss." He looked away—past her, his gaze on something beyond the walls of the house. She wondered if he still talked about her and Grandfather or if he referred to his own life.

How deeply had he loved Bernice? Had her loss left him empty and hurting?

His attention shifted to Evan.

Perhaps, she thought with startling clarity, he wondered about his son, wondered if the poor child would recover from his loss and mistreatment. A fierceness filled her.

"We must never give up on him. We must believe the best for him, secure the best for him."

His look was somewhat startled and then he smiled. His smile gave way to a chuckle. "And if a Marshall decrees it, it will be so?" He sobered so suddenly it left her dizzy. "I hope I can live up to that standard. That I don't fail my son."

"Failure is not in my vocabulary," she said with so much conviction his eyebrows headed for his hairline. She rose, her intention to go to the stove and finish supper preparations.

"That's an ominous thought."

She turned and faced him. She'd hoped he would

understand that she meant to prove her worth so he would see that marriage was in the best interests of him and his son. And her, of course. He seemed to have thought her words carried a warning. "When I set my mind to something, I generally manage to do it."

Grandfather jerked awake in time to hear her words. "The Marshalls are a stubborn bunch," he said.

"Not stubborn," she corrected. "Determined, strong-minded…" And then the perfect word came to mind. "Committed." Feeling she'd made herself clear, she continued with supper preparations.

Not until she turned to set the table did she see that Hugh still watched her. She wished she could say he looked thoughtful. Even grateful that a woman with such strong ideals was willing to be his helpmate. The look in his eyes could best be described as bleak.

Her insides faltered though she determined she would not reveal it. Did he find the prospect of sharing his life with her so unappealing? Was there something wrong with her? Was that why Rudy had left? Her confidence wavered then she lifted her chin and reminded herself she could out-bake, out-clean, out-take-care-of anyone near or far. And she had four weeks to prove it to him.

She served up a meal that would have made her brothers express gratitude—mounds of creamy mashed potatoes, smooth rich gravy, tender roast beef from the supply of meat in the woodshed and a colorful array of carrots and winter turnips. Hugh ate distractedly as if the food meant nothing to him.

Huh. Wait until she served the chocolate pudding she'd made. A recipe handed down from her mother.

Mama said her own mother had taught her to make it. She dished out servings of the pudding to everyone. Again, Hugh ate without comment, almost without conscious thought of what filled his spoon. Little Evan, at least, gave a barely audible sigh of pleasure.

Grandfather pushed away his clean bowl. "Thank you for the great meal."

"You're welcome."

She vowed she would not look at Hugh, would not expect a comment from him.

He sucked in air and sat up like a man waking from a dream. "Yes, thank you. A lovely meal."

She smiled. "You're welcome."

He leaned back in his chair and stared into the distance as she cleaned up.

Grandfather had moved to his chair, a book open on his lap. She expected he had dozed again but his eyes were open and he watched Hugh then looked at Annie.

She knew him well enough to see the warning in his gaze and wondered what he meant to warn her against. However, she would not ask because she had no intention of changing her mind.

Hugh stirred himself. "It's time for bed." He tipped his head to indicate he meant for Evan. Perhaps the prospect of the scene that would ensue explained his contemplative silence.

Annie sat at the table with the storybook and spoke to Evan. "It's time for a bedtime story. Do you want to hear about the bear or the fox?"

He stared at the wall.

"The bear?" She paused, allowing him time to indicate his preference.

Nothing.

"The fox?"

The slightest twitch of his shoulders.

"The fox it is, then." She read a story about an inquisitive little fox who liked to run ahead of his mama fox. The mother fox was always warning him to wait for her but he was in a hurry and rushed onward, never looking to the right or the left for danger. One day he ran right into a trap. The hunter would have gotten him except a kindly little boy came and set him free. The moral of the story was we do things that trap us in sin but Jesus sets us free.

Annie didn't think the moral applied to Evan's situation. *Please God, give me the right words for him.*

She thought of something her mama had said a long time ago. "My big brother Dawson once teased me and made me so angry I took the china doll he'd given me and smashed its head."

Both Hugh and Evan regarded her with shock.

"I was immediately sorry but I couldn't undo what I'd done. Mama was not happy with me but I told her it was Dawson's fault because he teased me so much." As she looked back she wondered how she could have been so upset. Far as she could remember, Dawson had only said she was too little to go with him and her other brothers. They didn't need a little tagalong sister following them.

"You know what my mama said? *Dawson is hurt that you destroyed something he gave you but you hurt yourself much worse than you hurt Dawson.* She went on to say, *You can't control what others do but you can trust that God cares for you and sees how*

*much your brother's teasing hurts you. When things
like this happen, remember what God says.*"

She let the comfort of her mother's advice fill her
thoughts before she finished. "'I will fear no evil: for
thou art with me.'"

She spoke directly to Evan, pleased when he didn't
turn away from her. "God helped your papa find you.
Now you are safe. You're free from bad people who
wanted to treat you wrong. You don't need to be
afraid."

Evan ducked his head but she knew he heard every
word and prayed they would begin a healing process
in him.

One word from Annie's story stood out in Hugh's
mind. *Trapped.* A certain, sure warning to him. Annie
was eager now for this position. It was new, exciting, challenging. How long before she felt trapped?
He couldn't find an answer. Didn't care for the one
that said it wouldn't be long. But for now he appreciated her attempt to help Evan see he didn't need to
be afraid any longer.

"I'll say our bedtime prayers." He asked a simple prayer though inside, where God alone heard, he
asked for Evan to be normal and for a woman who
wouldn't feel trapped in his life.

And then it was time for the dreaded going-to-
bed routine.

Annie pushed to her feet. "Bedtime, Evan." She
gave Hugh an encouraging smile.

Evan crowded into his corner and began to pump
his legs in an attempt to keep Hugh away.

Knowing he must do so, Hugh scooped the boy

up, restraining his arms and legs and holding him so he couldn't bite.

Annie stayed at Hugh's side. "You're safe, Evan," she murmured. "You don't need to be afraid. No one is going to hurt you." She followed to the bedroom, crooning words of comfort and encouragement all the way.

Hugh lowered Evan to the mattress and he scurried into the corner, his gaze wary.

Annie started to sing softly. "The Lord's my shepherd, I'll not want."

Evan shifted his attention to her, openly watching. He pulled the quilt around him.

She sang the song through three times as Evan's eyes slowly drooped.

"I think he's almost asleep," Hugh whispered.

"I'll tiptoe out."

Evan's eyes jerked open and he watched her but before she made it out the door, his eyes closed again.

Hugh stared at him a moment. This was a vast improvement over the last few days. It was all due to Annie and for a moment wishing and warning warred in his heart. It was too early to go to bed. Besides, he had things he needed to say and he tiptoed after Annie.

She turned at the sound of his footsteps. "Is he okay?"

"Almost asleep. I'll be able to watch the door from the sitting room. Are you anxious to go to bed or do you want to visit for a while?"

"Visit? That sounds nice."

He heard the warning note in her voice but whether or not she welcomed it there were matters that needed to be cleared up. He waved her to a big armchair and chose one that allowed him a clear view of the bedroom. He had only to shift his attention to his right to see Annie.

She watched him but as soon as she saw his gaze on her, she shifted to look through to the kitchen where her grandfather slept by the warm stove.

"If you're cold I could light the fire." He indicated the fireplace.

"No. This is fine." Someone had left an afghan draped over the arm of the chair and she pulled it across her knees.

Satisfied she was comfortable for the time being he said, "Those are good stories you read. They have excellent teaching points."

She smiled. "No doubt that's why my mother choose that book. She believed in using every available teaching moment." She looked thoughtful. "I'm hoping I can do the same for Evan."

He gave her time to muse before he brought up one of the subjects on his mind. "I couldn't help thinking we could all learn something from that fox."

"I doubt you're referring to our Savior freeing us from sin's trap." Her eyes were guarded.

"You're right. I don't want to see you trapped by a decision you've made in haste." He detected a slight narrowing of her eyes.

"And what decision would that be?"

He chose to ignore the warning note in her voice. "For some reason, right now, you feel you want a future like this." He waved his arm around hoping she understood what he meant—him, a loveless marriage, a troubled child.

"You're suggesting I'm like Freddie Fox—running into danger, not heeding warnings?"

"I've tried to warn you."

She held his gaze in wordless resistance, not relenting one inch.

He glanced down the hall to make sure Evan hadn't wandered out of the bedroom then he leaned forward to meet her gaze.

"Annie, who is Rudy?"

It gave him no pleasure to see shock and pain cross her features before she covered them with a mask of indifference.

Chapter Five

Annie jerked back, his question like a slap. "Who told you about Rudy?" She never spoke of the man, never admitted to anyone how much his leaving had hurt.

"I didn't mean to eavesdrop but I heard Logan and your grandfather mention him."

If he'd heard the conversation he knew that Logan didn't like Rudy and Grandfather thought she cared too much for the man. None of them knew how foolishly, desperately, she'd seen him as an answer to her insecurities and fears. She'd given him her heart completely and wholly.

Even at the time she'd recognized the wrongness of letting him take a place in her heart that belonged to God. Only trusting God could enable her to overcome her fears. That had been a trap she should have fled. A mistake she didn't mean to repeat. This unimpassioned arrangement with Hugh was totally different. Her heart was guarded, protected.

"He's of no concern to you."

"A ricocheting bullet is a dangerous thing."

He was worried Rudy might return and resume where they'd left off? Even if Rudy came back—and that was highly unlikely—she knew better than to ever trust him again.

Filled with raw hurt, she sprang to her feet. "That shell is spent. It will never be a danger to you or me or Evan." She hurried to the kitchen and shook Grandfather's shoulder. "Wake up. It's time for bed."

The old man pulled himself from his chair, grabbing Annie's arm for assistance. He was weaker than normal and it concerned her.

She turned her gaze to Hugh as they passed. "Good night."

He must have read more than her anger, must have seen her worry. He patted her on the shoulder. "Perhaps the cold is bothering him."

She didn't want to be touched by his concern. Didn't want to find his gentle hand comforting. Did not want to feel anything toward this man but—

What? Indifference? Coldness?

Nothing.

However she could not ignore the thought. How could she hope to offer anything to Evan—and Hugh—if she turned into a cold, unfeeling person?

At the moment she could see no alternative.

By morning, her hurt had abated. Rudy was over and done with. A closed book. Making a home for herself with Hugh and Evan shaped her future. She looked forward to proving herself and hurried to the kitchen.

The coffee was ready when Hugh followed Evan into the room. Evan went immediately to his customary corner. She'd placed a thick mat there and a warm blanket to ensure the boy was as comfortable as his position allowed.

How could she remain distant in light of the little boy huddled in the corner?

She poured Hugh a cup of coffee and set it before him. "Good morning."

"Morning." He downed a mouthful of the hot liquid.

Annie smiled to herself as she turned back to the stove. Hugh was obviously not a morning person. "Today," she said for Evan's benefit. "I'm going to make pancakes just like my mama used to make. Do you like pancakes?" She watched Evan for some signal.

He sat motionless but she could tell by the way he tipped his head that he listened. So she talked some more. "My pa always gets a sad look on his face when I make them for breakfast. I know he's missing Mama just like I do." She let out a little sigh. "Guess maybe I'll never stop missing her." She brightened. "But I have so many good memories of her that she'll always be with me."

She felt both Evan's and Hugh's interest which encouraged her to continue. "I suppose being the only girl and the youngest meant I spent lots of time with Mama. And like I told your papa yesterday, Mama never missed an opportunity to teach. She would take the smallest thing—like a wildflower—and point out the tiny little details—saying it proved how completely God is in control. The Master Planner, she called him." She paused and stared out the window, seeing nothing as, in her thoughts, she sat at her mother's side listening to her words. *There isn't one detail of our lives that God has not designed to create beauty.* She'd been taught that from a young age. Sometimes it was hard to see the truth in her own experience. But to come right out and say that God must have made a mistake in letting her mama die so young seemed to besmirch her mother's memory. As to Rudy, well that was Annie's own foolish decision. She wasn't ever going to repeat the lesson she'd learned with him. Her gaze turned to Hugh and she met his dark brown eyes watching her.

Grandfather hobbled into the room and sat at the table. Annie poured him coffee and then fried pancakes. She made a rabbit-shaped one for Evan and was rewarded with a flicker of amusement in his eyes before he ducked his head.

She joined the others at the table for breakfast.

Grandfather ate heartily then leaned back. "Annie, you are a fine cook. Every bit as good as your mother or even your grandmother."

Annie beamed at him. "Thank you." Being favorably compared to the grandmother she'd never met was highest praise.

Grandfather seemed bright and cheerful this morning and it eased a tension Annie hadn't realized she carried.

They finished the meal and she began to gather up the used dishes. She lifted the lid on the stove to add more wood, saw she was down to her last two pieces. "I have to go out for more wood."

Not giving Hugh a chance to say he'd do it, as he had been doing prior to this, she put on the old coat of Logan's and slipped outside. A brisk wind pulled her skirts tight about her legs. She shivered in the cold. One good thing about it: she couldn't see a woman traveling to Bella Creek in response to Hugh's ad in this weather.

She squared her shoulders. The last of her stiffness from his comments the night before disappeared. He would not find anyone more suitable than she.

A movement at the corner of the woodshed caught her attention. A dog pressed to the wall, seeking protection from the wind. A smallish dog, perhaps the runt of a litter. Barely more than a pup.

She squatted down. "Poor little guy. You're cold and hungry, aren't you?"

The pup wriggled happily at the attention. Big floppy ears flapped across his face.

"Aren't you sweet?"

The little animal had matching brown spots around each eye, a matted brown-and-black hide that might be curly if it was clean, and a white-tipped tail.

"You stay right there and I'll bring you something to eat." She gathered an armload of wood, hurried into the kitchen to deposit it in the woodbox then dumped all the kitchen scrapes into a tin bowl.

Aware of both her grandfather's and Hugh's watchful interest, she took the slop bucket, hoping they would think she only meant to dump it out. She hurried outside and emptied the bucket before she set the bowl of food down a few feet from where the pup sat watching. She hoped he would trust her enough to come close to eat. He wriggled so much he almost lost his balance and she laughed.

"Come on. This is for you."

The pup edged closer, wary, ready to retreat if she did anything to indicate she posed a risk.

She kept very still, waiting. The pup reached the bowl and ate eagerly. She patted his head, pleased when he didn't shy away. "I wonder if someone is missing their pet." Perhaps she'd slip away and leave a message with Uncle George who ran the store. He'd find out if the pup belonged to anyone.

In the meantime, she'd see that the animal was cared for.

She glanced toward the house. How did Hugh feel about dogs indoors? She had no idea. How would Evan react? She couldn't begin to guess.

"I think it would be best if you stay outside for now but I'll leave the door to the shed open and you can get out of the wind."

She got him to follow her into the shed by taking the bowl inside. She found a horse blanket and put it on the floor. The puppy sniffed at it then sank down with a sigh. A grateful sigh, she thought.

She filled her arms with more wood, grabbed the empty bucket and returned to the kitchen.

Hugh waited until she'd unloaded her arms then pushed to his feet. "I'll be in my office."

She watched him out of sight then released a long, soft sigh.

"Annie, have you two fought?" Grandfather barely waited until Hugh was behind his door to speak.

"Of course not. Why would you think so?"

"He barely spoke a word this morning. And you're very quiet too."

"Me? I talked the whole time."

"Not to each other. Girl, if you plan to marry him

you need to learn to talk to him." He sat back and gave her squinty-eyed consideration. "Could it be you are already seeing the foolishness of such an arrangement?"

She gave him look for look. "I believe I am needed here." She indicated Evan whom she knew would be listening to every word and perhaps wondering if she planned to stay. "Besides, the arrangement suits me."

Grandfather leaned back and rumbled his lips in despair. "Girl, it ain't healthy to deny yourself love."

Not prepared to argue with the man she respected so much, she tried to ignore him.

Not that she could hope he'd let it go.

"Annie, what are you up to?"

"I thought I'd wash up the dishes."

Grandfather grunted. "I think we've been guilty of spoiling you so that you can't see past this momentary whim."

His assessment of her stung. How could he see this as a selfish desire? She could—and would—take very good care of Hugh and Evan. She responded to something else he said. "Spoiling me? Is that what you call it when I cooked and cleaned and did laundry for five men and a little girl?"

He looked slightly uncomfortable at that. "You know what I mean. You were allowed to run free with Carly. You'll not have the same kind of freedom here. Hugh's the preacher and has a certain reputation to maintain."

She let out a gusty breath. "You made it sound like I was wild and crazy."

"Who is outside?"

She glanced at the window to see who had come

up the walk then realized he had noticed the bowl of food she'd taken out. She could honestly say, "No one." To signal the conversation was over, she began to wash the dishes, her back to him.

Evan shifted. What did the poor little guy think of all this? If only she could tell.

Recalling the puppy outside gave her an idea and she began to tell a story for Evan's sake.

"Once upon a time, there was a little black-and-white puppy with big floppy ears and a spot over his right eye. His name was Spot." How was that for original? "Spot was an unusual dog. You see, he thought he was a little boy." She glanced out of the corner of her eye to see if she had Evan's interest. He looked at the floor by her feet, his whole body alert.

Satisfied that he listened, she continued. "Spot sat at the table just like a boy. He couldn't use the fork and knife, but he put a paw on each and pretended he could." She continued spinning a yarn about a dog pretending to be a boy, hoping Evan would see how a little boy should act.

Hugh tried to concentrate on his notes. He must. Tomorrow, he would need to deliver a well-prepared sermon. But his mind kept hurrying back to the kitchen. And Annie. The girl left him so confused he couldn't sort out his thoughts.

She'd been upset that he asked about Rudy. Had refused to talk about the man. Said Rudy would not be a threat. In his experience, the more a person avoided a subject, the more it mattered and that concerned Hugh. Bernice had run off and look at the harm it had done Evan. If he allowed Annie to stay and Rudy returned, wouldn't she suddenly realize how much she cared for the man and see how much he had to offer?

He must spare Evan another heartrending separation.

Annie's soft voice came to him. He unashamedly listened as she told Evan a story about a dog. Which reminded him of her trying to take that bowl of food outside without anyone seeing it. He'd watched out the window as she fed a stray dog. He had no objection to her doing so. He didn't care to stand by when animals were neglected. His smile of amusement fled. Much less when people—and especially children—were neglected or worse.

The sweet sound of a chuckle drew his attention back to Annie's voice.

"What do you think, Evan? Should the mama let Spot sit at the table just because he thought he was a boy?"

A moment of silence.

"You're right. Dogs belong on the floor."

Had she answered on Evan's behalf or had he—as she seemed to believe—given her a clue as to his thoughts? Could she be right?

Already Annie had given him hope regarding his son. He pressed his hand to his forehead. He didn't want to grow to depend on her. She was too young. Too eager for life. And there was Rudy. And if not Rudy, there would be some other young, fun-loving man.

He closed the door gently and forced his attention to sermon preparation.

Even through the door, he heard the murmur of her

voice and the occasional low rumble of her grandfather's. He wished he could be in the same room, listening to what she said and observing Evan's reaction.

Lord, God, I must concentrate. Show me what I need to say to the congregation tomorrow. And please reinforce the walls around my heart and those around Evan's that neither of us will grow too dependent on Annie.

Somehow he made it through the morning, though he couldn't deny that more than once or twice he glanced at the closed door, wondering, listening and then focusing his eyes back on his sermon notes.

A gentle knock came to the door between him and the rest of the house. A soft voice.

"Hugh, dinner is ready."

He almost leaped to his feet. Then exerted every ounce of his self-control and sank back to his chair. "I'll be right there." He wasn't eager. No. Just curious and concerned as to how Evan was doing.

He waited until he heard Annie's footsteps recede, waited until he thought she must have returned to the kitchen then slowly rose and made his way after her. He'd never found Mrs. Ross's food and care to be lacking but walking into the kitchen, seeing the table set with a pot of thick potato soup placed in the middle alongside a plate of golden biscuits, to be greeted by a kindly old man and a smiling young woman waiting for him, proved enough to cause his footsteps to increase in pace and his heart to do a strange little thump against his ribs.

"Brr. It's cold. The weather must have worsened." In truth the kitchen was warm and cozy. Despite the heater in his office, that far room had been chilly and silent. As it should be. He was there to work, not wish. His thoughts were making no sense and he firmly pushed them aside and sat down.

After he said grace, Annie filled the bowls and passed the biscuits. She took a bowl to Evan. "A dog can't sit at the table because he's a dog. He belongs on the floor. A boy sits at the table. Not the floor because he isn't a dog." She returned to her place without waiting for Evan's response.

However, Hugh watched the boy and for the first time saw what Annie perhaps saw that convinced her he communicated his wishes. Evan tipped his head slightly, looked at the bowl on the floor beside him and then at the chair where Annie expected him to sit. A tiny shudder raced across his thin shoulders. Hugh knew the boy understood what Annie wanted, had considered it but was afraid to join them.

For the first time since he'd found Evan, Hugh saw some basis for hope that his son would be okay. He kept his attention on his bowl of soup to hide the way his eyes stung. Annie had done this and his heart flooded with gratitude.

"Will it be okay if I leave for an hour or so this afternoon? I need to make a trip to the store," Annie said, breaking the silence and bringing Hugh back to the reality of his situation.

"Of course. I'll be here to watch Evan and keep the fire going."

Grandfather thanked him. "The cold is seeping into my bones. They tell me there will be a storm soon."

"How soon?" Was it safe for Annie to go out? Hugh looked at her, knowing his concern filled his eyes.

"I'll be fine," she assured him. She gave him a steady look. He couldn't decide if it was challenging or warning. Would she listen if he asked her not to go?

Grandfather chuckled. "Okay, you two. Stop shooting sparks at each other. Annie, you hurry home, hear. And Hugh, you have to trust her to have a little sense."

"Oh, I trust she has a *little* sense." He almost hit his forehead with the heel of his hand. What had possessed him to say such a thing? And if Grandfather thought she sparked before... Hugh almost ducked away from the brittle flashes flying from her eyes.

"Little enough to answer your ad," she reminded him. Her gaze shifted to Evan and her expression softened. She smiled at the boy. "And I don't regret it a bit. After all, look what I have here. A sweet little boy who is soon going to sit at the table like people do, a warm place for Grandfather for the winter and..." Her eyes came back to Hugh and she studied him for a heartbeat, two, three...

He held his breath, wondering how she would describe him.

"And a noble preacher."

His lungs started to work again. Noble? And preacher? They were fine words but he was disappointed in them. What more had he wanted? Nothing. Nothing at all.

"I'll clean the kitchen then go to the store." She rose, paused to look at Hugh again. "I'll be just fine."

Before he could think of an answer, she turned to Evan. "Would you like me to bring you a candy stick?"

Hugh stared as Evan's gaze jerked to Annie and

his eyes lit with eagerness. Then he ducked his head and pulled back into a tight huddle.

"Evan," Annie continued. "Look at me."

The boy kept his head down but his eyes went to her.

"If you want one, nod like this. And if you don't, shake your head like this." She illustrated and waited patiently. Evan didn't do either. "Evan," she said. "I won't buy you a candy unless you say yes." She waited, revealing nothing but patience.

She expected too much. The boy's only communication had been grunts and wild noises. When Hugh opened his mouth to speak, she held up a hand.

He was aware that Grandfather watched them with interest and a bit of pride in his eyes. He thought his granddaughter could persuade Evan to respond.

Hugh wished it could be that simple. That change would come that easily.

As he watched Evan the boy nodded his head once. So slight a movement he might have missed it. Perhaps even imagined it but no, he had not. The boy had indicated his choice.

Annie laughed softly. "Good. I'll bring you two for being such a good boy."

Hugh stared at his son, hope and gratitude welling up like an artesian well. He shifted his attention to Annie, who was making short work of cleaning up.

He could so easily fall in love with this girl.

He almost bolted from his chair. That must not happen. If he allowed it, both of them would be disappointed and worse, so would Evan. She'd be disappointed when she realized he couldn't provide her with fun and excitement. He, when she left.

She dumped the dishwater and grabbed an old coat she wore going outdoors. "I'll be back later." And with that, she slipped out the door with three people staring after her.

Grandfather eased his way to his armchair and settled in for a nap.

Hugh studied Evan. What could he do to amuse the child? Annie read to him, told him stories. "Wait here. I'll be right back." He hurried to his office and gathered up his sermon notes. Back in the kitchen he was rewarded to see that Evan watched the door for his return but as soon as Hugh appeared, the boy shifted away.

"Would you like to hear my Sunday sermon?"

The boy's shoulders twitched enough to inform Hugh that he heard. Satisfied this was a good way to pass a bit of time, he began to read his notes aloud distracted slightly by Grandfather's snores. His message was about the prodigal son. It had seemed fitting considering the return of his own son. Not that Evan was a prodigal. Merely an innocent victim. A lost son. His throat tightened as he read the Bible verse of the father's response. "'Let us eat, and be merry: For this my son was dead, and is alive again; he was lost, and is found. And they began to be merry.'" He faced Evan though the boy did not look at him. "You are my son. You were lost but now I've found you. I couldn't be happier." That gave him an idea. He should have a celebration. But his enthusiasm died—Evan was not ready for any kind of merrymaking.

Unless it was just the four of them. Perhaps he'd bring it up with Annie.

He couldn't still the little bubble of anticipation at presenting his idea to her.

What would she think? Perhaps that he wasn't old and uninteresting? He sighed. One silly suggestion wasn't likely to change anything.

Why was he so foolish to even think it might?

Chapter Six

Hugh finished reading his sermon notes aloud, half-distracted by the plans circling in his head. He supposed he should have something more to suggest than a celebration. What form would it take? Shuffling his papers together, he saw that Evan had fallen asleep on the mat Annie had provided. That didn't say much for Hugh's delivery even if the boy was only four.

He pulled the warm blanket over the boy and took the papers to his office.

He didn't return immediately to the kitchen. Instead, he went to the windows overlooking the street and scratched a hole in the frost to peer down the road. From the manse, it was impossible to see the store. He saw the church next door, the bare-limbed trees in the town square formed by the intersecting two main streets in town. He saw the hotel and the corner of Miss Daisy's Eatery but not beyond that to the mercantile where he guessed Annie had gone for her errands. A wagon rolled by. The occupants were so bundled up he didn't recognize them except to know it was a man and a woman. A cowboy rode down the street, a scarf pulled around the man's face and a fur coat protecting him from the weather.

It was cold out. Hugh knew that without leaving the house. He shouldn't have let Annie go out. He gave a little shrug. It wasn't as if he could have stopped her. He hadn't been in the area long before he understood that Annie Marshall, like the male members of her family, did not allow herself to be unduly influenced by the wishes of another. It was one of the reasons he told himself she was unsuitable. Didn't a preacher's wife have to be prepared and willing to accommodate the opinions of others rather than do things that would bring criticism down on them?

The argument seemed weak at the moment and he spun from the window, crossed the floor to the window by the back door and peered out. She'd left the woodshed door open slightly. For the dog. He had to admit he liked a woman who was tenderhearted.

How long did it take to go to the store and return?

Or had she found other amusement?

Grandfather had said to trust her but trust did not come easily for Hugh.

The old man wakened and watched Hugh. "She hasn't been gone that long, you know."

He turned from the window and, more to occupy himself than of a need, he made a fresh pot of coffee. When it was ready, he offered a cup to Grandfather. "Are you concerned about the cattle and horses in this cold?" he asked, hoping to get the old man thinking in a different direction than Hugh's worry about Annie.

Grandfather sipped the coffee before he answered. "There's plenty of Marshalls out there to take care of things. I don't mind sitting back and putting my feet up for a change."

Hugh studied the man, remembering Annie's concern. Did the older man look pale? Hard to say with his sun-leathered skin. Grandfather shifted and grimaced. A sign of pain?

"Are you warm enough?" Hugh asked.

Grandfather waved away his concern. "I'm cozy as can be."

The two of them sank back to stare at their cups.

"She's a great girl, you know."

Hugh swirled the remains of his coffee. No need to ask who Grandfather meant. Annie. "Don't suppose you're the slightest bit prejudiced?"

"No need to be. It's the plain and simple truth. Why, that girl has been running the house and taking care of the family since her ma, God rest her soul, passed away when she was barely fifteen. I daresay there isn't another young woman half as capable in the whole territory."

No doubt Grandfather thought those words should relieve any concern Hugh had regarding Annie but they only served to intensify it. Surely she'd be eager for less responsibility after all she'd dealt with. He could not, would not, believe otherwise.

"Losing her ma was hard on her. Hard on everyone in the family. Ellen was a very special woman with lots of gumption and a heart of gold. Annie takes after her ma." He chuckled. "With a good deal of Marshall grit thrown in for good measure." He sat up and leaned forward. "Me and my sons and grandsons wouldn't look kindly on her being treated poorly, if you know what I mean."

"Your message is loud and clear." Part of him wanted to stand up and firmly inform this old man that he could live up to any expectation of the Marshalls. A stronger part reminded him of how often he had failed in the past.

He turned to his sleeping son. "I only want what's best for him."

Grandfather sat back. "Then you've chosen wisely with Annie. She knows how to get through to the boy."

Hugh went again to the front window to watch for her return. She did seem to understand the boy. Was it enough?

He saw her cross the street. She huddled inside the too-large coat, a woolen scarf about her head. She carried a bundle as she hurried toward the manse. He grabbed his coat and hat and dashed out the door before he had the buttons done up. He was in front of the church before he got his gloves pulled on. The cold had a fierce bite. Annie must be about frozen. He reached her side and relieved her of her parcel, put an arm about her shoulders and pulled her close to provide shelter from the cold wind as he rushed her homeward.

It was only to make sure she was safe, he told himself by way of excuse for how he held her. Because Grandfather had warned him about her being a Marshall. And perhaps a goodly portion of his reason was because he needed her to help with Evan. Nothing more than that. Oh sure, she made good soup and biscuits and had a tender heart toward stray dogs.

He went straight through the front door and didn't

slow down until they reached the kitchen when he released her.

Grandfather watched them, approval in his eyes. Did he think his warning had sent Hugh out to bring Annie home? For his own peace of mind, he wished that was the reason but the only thing he'd been concerned about was getting her in out of the cold. For her sake. No one else's.

She shrugged out of her coat and unwound her scarf, bits of static-filled blond hair forming a crown about her head. She rubbed her hands over her head to smooth the flyaway strands.

"Brr. It's cold as the North Pole out there. Guess it won't snow while it's so cold. Right, Grandfather?"

He shook his head and looked mournful. "That's an old wives' tale." He turned to Hugh. "Some think it can't snow when it's cold. 'Taint true. I can tell you."

Hugh rubbed his hands together, resisted an urge to put his hand to the spot where her shoulder had pressed into his chest. It meant nothing. He felt nothing more than something similar to how he felt when taking care of Evan—protective, concerned. He despised himself for the lies he tried to believe. Shouldn't a man—especially a preacher—be truthful even in his thoughts? *Behold, thou desirest truth in the inward parts.* He knew the verse from Psalm chapter fifty-one. He could not face the truth…that there was something about Annie that had wormed its way—unwanted and unwelcomed—to the depths of his heart.

She warmed her hands at the stove then turned to the parcel he'd placed on the table. She untied the strings and looked at Evan. "I got you two candy sticks, like I promised." She handed Evan a red-and-white-striped candy stick and a black one. He took them from her with a shy glance.

"I got you one as well, Grandfather." She handed him a butterscotch-colored one.

"That's my girl." Grandfather stuck the end of his candy stick in his mouth.

"Uncle George says hello. He wanted to come and see you. I said that was fine." She brought her gaze to Hugh. "That's okay I hope?"

For a minute, he wondered if he had swallowed his tongue and then he found it. "Of course. You may invite anyone you like."

Something flickered through her eyes. He wished he could tell if it was surprise or approval but it was gone too suddenly.

Her hands paused over her purchases. "I got you something as well. I wasn't sure if you liked candy or what flavor but I chose this one. Green apple." She handed it to him.

"Thank you." As of this moment it was his favorite.

He couldn't tear his gaze away from her blue eyes and generous expression.

"I also saw this and thought of you." She pulled out a small book with a dark brown cover and handed it to him. "I hope you don't have a copy."

He drew his gaze from hers to read the title. "*The Morning Watches and Night Watches* by John Ross Macduff." He stroked the cover, his throat too tight to speak.

"Is it something you already have?"

He shook his head.

"Then I hope you'll enjoy it."

He had to say something and swallowed hard. "I will certainly enjoy it. I've long wanted a copy. I have to ask. Where and how did you get this?"

She grinned, pleased with his reaction. "Someone traded it to Uncle George for supplies."

"I'm so pleased you were able to get it from him."

He couldn't stop smiling, and feeling a little embarrassed by his reaction he opened the first page. "'Come near, and bless us when we wake, Ere through the world our way we take; Till, in the ocean of Thy love, We lose ourselves in heaven above!'" The words so stirred him that his voice deepened.

Her eyes shone. "That's beautiful." Her words were but a whisper.

Their gazes held, hers full of wonder, his likely full of surprise and—

He couldn't say what he felt. Awe, attraction and something that felt warm and homey in the depths of his being.

The sound of Evan slurping his candy drew them both to look at him and they laughed, their gazes again coming together. Time stood still as they looked deeply into each other's eyes. He wondered if she could see to the very most secret places of his heart, read his wants and failures.

Then she blinked and turned back to her parcel, taking out common, everyday supplies and putting them in the cupboard.

He didn't want the feeling between them to end. He wanted to celebrate. That reminded him. "My sermon is on the prodigal son—or as I am thinking of it—the lost son. When the father found the son, he celebrated. I have found my son." He smiled at Evan who had started his second candy stick. "Is there some way we can celebrate?"

She stood beside him. Close enough that the place where her shoulder had rested for a short time grew warm. She leaned in close to whisper, "You mean like giving him a bath and putting clean clothes on him?"

He whispered back. "It would take two of us. And maybe the rest of the Marshall family to get him into a tub of water."

She chuckled at his irony, her eyes flashing sunny skies as she looked at him. "One of these days it is going to have to happen but today might be a bit soon." She turned back to Evan. "I can think of ways for us to celebrate but what can we do that would include Evan?"

"I know. I guess my idea won't work right now."

She tapped her index finger on her chin. "Let's not give up quite yet." The tapping continued and then she nodded. "I know of something he might cooperate with."

If she had come up with an idea that would work for Evan he might be tempted to kiss her.

No, he wouldn't. What was he thinking?

"He likes to eat on the floor. Perhaps we can go to his level."

He pictured them all hunkered down in the corner, shoulders drawn up and backs to one another. "You think we should all sit on the floor to eat?" He knew he sounded as shocked as he felt. "Isn't that encouraging him to remain as he is?"

"Not if we turn it into an indoor picnic and sit in front of the fireplace." Slowly, she faced him, eagerness and caution chasing each other through her expression.

He decided at that very moment that he wanted to encourage the eagerness and ignore caution. "A picnic? That just might work."

They had moved as far away as possible from the other two in the room and kept their voices to a whisper so they wouldn't be overheard.

Grandfather pulled his candy stick from his mouth. "What are you two plotting?"

"A celebration," Annie said. "A party to show how happy we are that Evan has been found."

"As long as there's food." Grandfather resumed sucking his candy.

Hugh echoed the comment except his was *As long as Evan and Annie are here.*

He didn't even bother trying to correct himself.

Annie couldn't stop smiling. He liked the book she'd chosen for him at Uncle George's store. He hadn't suggested a gift was inappropriate. He seemed thrilled. She was so pleased about it that she would be secretly celebrating her success in doing something that made him happy, every bit as much as she'd celebrate Evan's safe return.

Not only that. Hugh had rushed out to escort her home.

As if he'd been watching and waiting for her return. He'd missed her. Been concerned for her safety. Only three days and he already needed her. By the end of four weeks, he would never want to let her go. Once they were married she knew she could count on permanency. Like Grandfather said, marriage was forever. Yes, Hugh's wife, even Dawson's first wife, had proved otherwise but Hugh was the preacher. He would keep his marriage vows just as she meant to.

Now to prepare a picnic. Her feet seemed to float off the floor as she sliced bread and spread butter, adding slabs of leftover roast beef. She sliced it paper-thin for Evan, having noticed last night that he had trouble chewing the meat. She packed it all into a basket she found in the pantry wondering for a moment what reason Hugh had for such a basket. She shrugged her shoulders. Likely Mrs. Ross had used it to bring home things from the store. She found a checkered tablecloth. And last she wrapped up the remaining items in the parcel she'd carried home with such anticipation. This would be part of the celebration.

While she prepared the food, she talked, doing her best to make Evan understand what would happen. When the basket was packed she turned to Hugh, Grandfather and Evan. "Let's go on a picnic."

She and Hugh would sit on the floor to be close to Evan but Hugh carried a chair in for Grandfather. The fire was bright and cheerful, the only source of light in the room.

She stood at the doorway as Hugh and Grandfather passed. Hugh gave her a questioning look. "Let's see if he comes on his own," she whispered in response to his unasked question.

"Evan, bring your mat and let's go to the other room." She waited, hoping, praying he'd do it on his own. "I have something more for you in here." She rattled the parcel. "I'll give it to you after we eat but you'll have to join us in the other room."

Please, Evan. Please. She met Hugh's eyes, saw

the same concern and hope that filled her, and clung to his gaze, searching for and finding encouragement. Strengthened, she turned back to Evan. He watched her from his lowered eyes.

If he didn't go on his own accord, Hugh would carry him but what could she say to urge him to move on his own?

"I think Spot the dog who thinks he's a boy would race you to the fireplace so he could be the little boy. If you hurry and beat him, you can make him understand he has to be a puppy."

His movements jerky, Evan shifted so he could pick up his mat and half walking, half running, never standing up fully, he scurried past her and tossed his mat to one side of the fireplace as far from Hugh as he could.

Annie met Hugh's eyes. She had to wipe a tear from hers. To most this wouldn't seem like a big step but both she and Hugh knew it was huge for Evan to do this on his own.

She followed and sat between them, at Grandfather's knees, pleased when Evan didn't shift farther to the side. Grandfather squeezed her shoulder and she understood that he was gratified by Evan's progress.

She spread the cloth and put the basket in the middle. "This is nice," she said. "It might be cold outside but we are warm and safe here." She hoped Evan understood that she meant *he* was safe.

"I'll ask the blessing." Hugh bowed his head but he didn't immediately pray and when he did, his voice was deeper than usual. "Father God, I thank You for the safe return of my son, Evan. Thank You so much for helping me find him. Help him know he is safe

and loved. Thank You for Your many blessings—
family, friends and a warm house and for the food
we are about to eat. Amen."

If she hadn't thought he would jerk away she would
have reached out that very minute and hugged Hugh.
Instead she passed around the sandwiches.

"This reminds me of when I first came out here,"
Grandfather said. She knew he was about to launch
into one of his stories about the early days and she
leaned back against his knees, content to be in this
place at this time with these people.

"I didn't have a house at the time but I had a good
solid shelter. It had frame walls up to my shoulders
and a canvas cover. I cooked outside over a fire. Sort
of like this." He sighed. "I kind of miss those days."
Then he chuckled. "Don't miss the cold though."

Annie turned to Hugh. "Grandfather says he was
the first white man here. Though I'm not sure how
that can be. There've been prospectors and explorers
since Lewis and Clark."

"Harumph. I was the first one to put down stakes."

"Oh, well that's different." She grinned at Hugh to
inform him she teased her grandfather.

"Now, don't be giving him a hard time. He's earned
every accolade he wants to own." Hugh's eyes were
full of something so warm, so *claiming* that heat
rushed up her neck and pooled in her cheeks. Thankfully Grandfather could not see.

He chuckled. "You listen to Hugh. He knows what
he's talking about. After all, he's the preacher."

"I'll get the hot chocolate." She rushed from the
room.

She fought to gain control of her tangled thoughts.

Their agreement was one of mutual convenience. There was to be no claiming involved. She slowed her breathing realizing she had no call for concern. As Grandfather said, Hugh was the preacher. He had to keep his word to keep feelings out of their arrangement.

And who, an errant voice in the distance of her thoughts asked, would make sure she stuck to her plans?

I will. I must.

"Can I help?"

She hadn't realized that Hugh had followed her and startled at his question. "Sure, you can take mugs for yourself and Grandfather." She filled two of the waiting cups, relieved that her hands didn't shake because her insides were as jumpy as a fly against a window pane. She delayed so he could return to the living room.

He stood to the side and waited for her.

That made her hand jerk so hard she almost spilled the hot liquid on herself. She cooled Evan's drink with milk and picked up the other two cups, stiffening her arms to stop any shaking.

They returned to the other room. Annie put Evan's cup of hot chocolate in front of him.

He waited until she sat down again before he took the cup.

One day soon, she decided, they would get him to start being a little boy.

They drank their hot chocolate slowly. She couldn't say what the others were thinking but Annie didn't want the evening to end. She turned to Grandfather.

"Tell about the time a bunch of desperadoes came to your camp."

Grandfather was an excellent storyteller. He knew how to make a dramatic moment more dramatic and how to drag out anticipation. He wove a tale of bad guys coming to visit him and told how they had looked at his belongings. He'd been sure they would steal everything. What was he to do?

Annie smiled as Evan shifted so he would watch Grandfather. She looked at Hugh, saw the same pleasure on his face. And something more. Or was she imagining that she saw approval?

She must not let herself grow too fond of this man. Her heart wasn't ready to take the risk of being hurt again. It would never be ready for that risk.

She forced her gaze to the fire, watching the flames leap and twist, and listened to Grandfather tell how he'd invited the bunch to join him for a meal and as they ate he told them about God's love for them.

Grandfather finished his story with a flourish. "And that's how, by showing them kindness, I outwitted the bad guys."

Evan let out a thin sigh. He looked at the parcel at Annie's side.

"I almost forgot. I've got something for you here." She brought the parcel to her lap and slowly folded back the paper, taking her time as she enjoyed watching Evan's anticipation. Unable to stop herself, she looked toward Hugh, saw the same look on his face as on Evan's and chuckled.

Hugh raised his eyebrows in silent question.

"You and Evan are wearing matching expressions."

Hugh's gaze went to Evan. Evan stared at him

for the length of the blink then lowered his head. He couldn't resist the allure of the parcel and as he watched, Annie withdrew a new shirt, white with blue stripes. "Just the right size for you," she said to Evan.

His mouth hung open and he stared at the shirt then looked at the one he wore as if comparing them.

"One more thing." Annie waited for him to look her way again and pulled out a pair of woolen trousers. "To go with the new shirt."

Again, Evan looked from the new to the old.

"New clothes to wear after you have a bath," she said.

Evan shifted, grabbed his mat and scurried back to the kitchen.

Annie called after him. "I won't make you bathe but you need one. You let me know when you're ready." She sighed. "I wasn't sure how he'd react."

Hugh shifted, folded his legs in front of him. "Don't look at it as a failure. After all, he joined us of his own accord and he's a lot more responsive than a few days ago."

"I'm going to bed," Grandfather announced. "My old bones are tired."

Annie shifted to allow him to get up and watched as he made his way down the hall. Worry about him and concern about Evan knotted inside her.

Hugh reached over and squeezed her hand. "We'll take one day at a time, letting Evan set the pace."

She shuddered. She had pulled life tight around her, closing herself to love, seeking safety and security, yet she could well lose Grandfather soon. "Everyone I care about dies or leaves." She hadn't meant to speak her fears aloud. "Seems to me the safest thing is not to let myself care anymore." She meant not to care about anyone new. "If Grandfather—" She shook her head as her throat tightened so she couldn't go on.

He squeezed her hand. "Life is full of uncertainty. I know I don't need to tell you there is only one thing we can count on. God's faithfulness. Has He not upheld you through your many losses?"

She swallowed loudly. "He has. And I know I should trust Him more but sometimes it's hard. Every time I lose someone I lose a part of my heart. How many times can a piece be torn off before I have nothing left?" Perhaps she'd already reached that point.

His hand warm and firm against hers offered something she wanted though she could not for the life of her say what it was. Nor could she explain why she turned her palm to his and gripped his hand so hard she wouldn't blame him if he withdrew. To her immense relief, he only squeezed back as if offering her a lifeline.

"Loss hurts," he said softly, his voice like a balm. "And I believe it leaves a scar but don't they say that scar tissue is stronger than untested flesh?"

"Scar tissue is ugly and inflexible."

He considered her, his eyes so probing that she wondered if he saw right to the center of her heart where she had buried secrets. And denied dreams.

"I would venture to say we can't get through life without some scarring." His words reminded her of what Pa said. *Life goes on.*

She looked at the little shirt and the pair of trousers in her lap. "We need to get Evan to bed." She pulled her hand back and got to her feet, intending to rush to the kitchen. Instead, unable to explain her actions to herself, she waited until he rose and they went side by side. He held back at the door and let her go first.

The storybook stood on the shelf and she pulled it down. There was still hot chocolate left and she divided it three ways and gave everyone two cookies then sat down to read the next story.

Her thoughts refused to obey her and concentrate on the words she read.

She did not want any more scar tissue. Did not want the wounds that led to the scars. Did not want the loving that made the wounds possible.

Except that meant she would not have known Mama's love. She couldn't regret that.

The one love she did regret was the one she'd given much too freely to Rudy.

She finished the story, knowing what it was about only because she'd heard it many times before.

Hugh prayed.

His words of blessing and trust replaced her troubled thoughts.

"Time for bed, son." Hugh spoke so gently, kindly to Evan that a yearning rose up inside Annie.

She pushed it away. No reason she should wish for that same regard. It wasn't as if she didn't know love and caring from her pa, her grandfather and her brothers.

Evan sat immobile on his mat and Hugh scooped the boy into his arms.

Evan struggled.

Annie followed the pair as far as the bedroom door then turned and fled back to the living room where she gathered up the picnic remains and took them to the kitchen. She was still there, putting away the last of things when Hugh returned.

"He's already curled up with the quilt tucked around him. Did you think he put up less of a fight tonight?" The desperate hope in his voice drew her gaze to him.

Poor Hugh. How it must hurt to see his son like this. To wonder if Evan would ever be normal.

She smiled at him. "Remember the advice you gave me."

His eyebrows went up and his eyes begged for explanation…and something more.

She swallowed hard, knowing he wanted her to offer him encouragement. "We can count on God's faithfulness." She meant *he* could. It was too late to change her words. The way his face relaxed made her not want to. "God answered our prayers in finding him. I know God's not finished yet."

"I know it too. Thanks for reminding me."

Their gazes came together in a gentle melding of hope and faith.

"God is faithful," he said.

Annie wondered why his voice sounded so distant. Why she couldn't remember that she didn't want to care about him. Why it mattered if she did.

Right now it felt like the best thing she could dream of.

He shifted his attention away. "Are you done in here?" He looked around the kitchen.

She pulled her thoughts back into order. "I'm done."

"Did you want to sit by the fire a spell?" He tilted

his head toward the living room to indicate which fire he meant.

It sounded like a fine idea. A perfect way to end the day. Then her senses returned. It was the worst idea. She must guard her heart and her mind. "I think I'll retire for the night." She slipped away before he could say anything.

Before she could change her mind.

And she wouldn't allow herself to think there was a sad note in his voice as he called, "Good night," down the hall.

Chapter Seven

Hugh cradled his hands behind his head and stared at the darkened ceiling of his bedroom. Evan snuffled in his sleep. Hugh listed all the ways the boy had shown improvement. He could thank Annie for Evan's progress. The book she'd given him lay on the table by his bed. He would turn on the lamp and read from it except he didn't want to waken Evan.

Every one of Annie's words trooped through his head. One statement stalled there. *Every time I lose someone I lose a part of my heart. How many times can a piece be torn off before I have nothing left?* Those words explained why a beautiful young woman would be so insistent on a marriage of convenience. She feared love because of the risk of loss and pain. That Rudy fellow must have hurt her deeply.

It didn't change anything. In time her heart would heal and she'd want more than Hugh could offer her. There were many things about her he admired—and he would not list them again—but it would not be fair to chain her to a man like him with a child like Evan.

Yet he fell asleep with a smile on his lips as he

thought of the many little joys she had brought into his life in only three days. And he woke with the same smile.

As he lay in the quiet stillness of morning, he reminded himself of all the reasons he must remain guarded for her sake, his sake and the sake of a little boy. He turned his thoughts to what lay ahead for the day. Sunday services. His sermon. What about Evan? He couldn't imagine dragging the little guy to church.

He heard pots rattle and bolted from his bed with the question hammering in his head. What was he going to do about Evan?

The boy stirred, opened his eyes and sat up. He took one look at his papa and scurried to the kitchen.

Hugh took his time getting dressed and followed more slowly. At the smiling welcome on Annie's face, his worries lifted. He realized he counted on her to help him find a solution regarding what to do with his son.

She poured him fresh, fragrant coffee and he sat across from Grandfather who held a half-empty cup.

"Today is Sunday," he said quite needlessly.

"Uh-huh," Grandfather grunted.

Annie hummed a tune he recognized as "Rock of Ages." A good reminder that he could trust God for the details of his life.

She turned from the stove and squatted close to Evan. "Evan, today is Sunday. Your papa is the preacher. I've heard him. He's a pretty fair speaker."

He heard the approval in her voice. She was close enough he had only to lift his hand to touch her but, instead, he gripped his cup so hard it wouldn't surprise him if the china shattered.

"Shall we go hear him preach?"

Evan drew back against the wall, pulling the mat and quilt around him like walls.

Annie rose and faced Hugh. "It's too soon. I'll stay home with him today." She squeezed Hugh's shoulder. "I'm sorry but it will take time."

Her hand was gone before he could react. It was only a gesture of sympathy. No need for him to think otherwise and he firmly closed his mind to other possibilities.

"I suppose it's for the best. You sure you don't mind?"

She chuckled, a sound so pure and sweet he wished he could catch it in a jar and keep it in his office to open and enjoy in the weeks after she left.

Was he really so convinced that she would leave? That it was the best thing? Why was it he could no longer think clearly? He downed the rest of his coffee and went to the stove to refill his cup. His elbow brushed hers and every hope of getting his thoughts under control scattered like chaff in the wind.

He hurried back to the table and hunkered over his cup. He would have rushed through breakfast and gone to his office but Annie seemed to think the Sunday morning meal should be a leisurely affair. She took her time about dishing out the food.

"I remember the first time you preached here," she said as she passed him the salt. "You were so powerful you had me on the edge of my seat the whole time."

"Sounds uncomfortable."

She laughed. "Maybe what you said made me uncomfortable."

He tried in vain to remember what his sermon had been about.

She continued. "Do you recall how you challenged us all to face the future with confidence? You said you were here, expecting God to answer your prayers. That's when you told us about—" She tipped her head toward Evan.

Hugh studied his small son, who ate eagerly but with less desperation than he had a week ago. It was another encouraging sign. "I don't know how I could have kept going without knowing I could trust God. When I learned Bernice was dead—" His throat tightened. "It was one of the worst days of my life." Seeing the way Annie's smile flattened he realized she would think he meant because of Bernice's death. "To know my son was missing—" He sucked in air. "I had no idea where he was or how to find him."

Annie again went to Evan. "I remember when your papa told us he couldn't find you. He was so concerned and asked us all to pray that God would lead him to you. God answered our prayers and here you are. We are all so happy." She patted his shoulder.

Evan did not jerk back and Annie turned to Hugh, a tear clinging to her lashes as she offered him a trembling smile. "Did you see that?" she whispered.

"I did."

Grandfather watched them but Hugh didn't care if the whole world saw as he reached out and trailed the tip of his finger across under her eyes, wiping away the tears. "God continues to answer my prayers on his behalf."

"Mine too." She blinked back the unshed tears and looked at him, so full of joy and gratitude and—

Love?

She loved Evan? Hadn't she told him she didn't

want to care about anyone again? That she feared having her heart torn to pieces?

His chest muscles constricted. He should never have agreed to this arrangement. Far too many people were going to be hurt. And yet, seeing the joy in Annie's face, acknowledging how much progress he saw in Evan and even having the kindly presence of Grandfather Marshall, he could not regret it.

Not yet.

"I must prepare for the service." He hurried to his room, changed into his black suit, brushed his dark hair into place. He went from there to his office to get his notes and his Bible, taking with him the devotional book Annie had bought for him. "Come near, and bless us when we wake, Ere through the world our way we take; Till, in the ocean of Thy love, We lose ourselves in heaven above!" The words stirred within him a desire for God's blessing and he sat down and turned the pages to the first morning reading. His heart was stirred with a noble theme. He would trust God to direct, control and suggest his every thought and action for God's honor and glory. That especially meant his feelings toward Annie.

God, help me treat her with the care and concern she deserves. Let me not seek selfish satisfaction. If it be Your will, let her presence here help Evan so that he will be strong enough to deal with a change when she leaves.

When she leaves? An errant wisp of thought intruded. *Must she leave?*

He sat back. That decision wasn't his to make but he would not hold her back…not a young, enthusiastic woman like her.

He rose and prepared to go out through the office door then reconsidered and returned to the kitchen. "Grandfather, do you wish to go to church this morning?"

"I'd like to. It's not far. I think I can bear the cold for the time it takes to cross the yard."

"Let me go ahead and get the fire going. I'll come back once the church is warm and help you."

Hugh told himself he didn't look to Annie in the hopes of seeing approval fill her eyes. And it did. He grabbed his cowboy hat from the hook, jammed it on his head and carried the warmth of her smile with him to the church where he started a fire in the big stove and glanced about to make sure everything was prepared for the service.

It would take half an hour for the cold to leave the room. Thirty minutes in which he usually sat close to the stove and prayed about his sermon. Today, his feet took him to the windows and he looked through the frost to the manse next door. He could hardly believe how much his life had changed in the space of a week. He forced himself to turn his back and make his way to his customary spot where he sank to the bench and poured out his heart to God, seeking wisdom and self-control. Guidance in how he would inform the congregation about his success in finding his son and his decision to welcome Annie into his home. Welcome? It wasn't the right word. At least not for his initial reaction and yet it was the right word for how he felt at the moment.

All he could do was pray for God's help.

A bit later, he realized how warm he'd grown sitting next to the stove with his outer coat still on, but rather than take it off, he returned to the manse. Grandfather pushed to his feet when Hugh stepped into the kitchen.

"I'm ready."

Annie held his canes as she helped him into his coat. "Now you be careful and watch for ice."

"Yes, my girl. I will be careful." He brushed his finger across her cheek. "I plan to be around to keep an eye on you for a long time yet."

She cautiously leaned forward to kiss his cheek. "I'm counting on it." She sent Hugh a look that was a little bit grateful and a whole lot warning.

He could almost hear her words. *Take good care of him.*

Grinning, he looked at Evan and then back to Annie, silently giving her the same message.

Understanding his meaning, she smiled. "We'll be just fine by ourselves."

He chuckled. "And we'll be just fine at church though I venture to say there will be any number of people who'll wonder at your absence."

"I'm sure you'll explain it. In fact, Grandfather, I want a full report of how he tells everyone that I'm living in the manse."

Hugh sobered. People would understand that he'd been forced to make arrangements for Evan's care.

Or would they?

He guided Grandfather out the front door and stayed close as they crossed the yard. It seemed to him that the older man moved much slower than he had a few weeks ago. Or was he letting Annie's worries influence his judgment?

They were the first in the door and Grandfather chose a pew where the Marshall family normally sat. "Sure hope they make it in from the ranch. Seems like a long time since I've seen them."

He patted the man's shoulder and went to the front to place his Bible and notes on the pulpit. He'd selected the hymns that he wanted and placed the list on the organ for the accompanist. Today, if he remembered correctly, it would be Mary Marshall, Annie's aunt. No doubt she would want a report on Annie. As would all the Marshalls.

For some reason, the thought of facing them didn't bother him in the least. In fact, he would suggest they all visit next door and see for themselves how Annie was. He hoped they would be pleased.

Mary and George were the first Marshalls to arrive. George went to his father and inquired as to his well-being. "You could have blown me over with a puff when I heard you and Annie were living in town. Glad you are. Saves you that trip in the cold."

Logan and Sadie with their three children were next and Logan marched right up to the pulpit. "My sister okay?"

She was doing better than okay. All Hugh said was, "She's quite fine. You're welcome to visit any time."

"I'm very protective of my little sister."

"Good to hear."

Logan barely stepped back before Dawson and Isabelle entered with little Mattie between them, holding their hands and giving them both an eager smile. On their heels came Conner and Kate with baby Ellie wrapped up warmly against the cold. Bud, Grandfather's other son and father of the Marshall boys and Annie, was away or he would be leading the pack.

They got as far as Grandfather and as a group, drew to a stop and studied Hugh.

Dawson was the first to speak. "Where's my sister?" Challenge rang from every word.

Hugh stood by the pulpit and leaned one arm on it. "She's at home with my son. He—"

Grandfather waved a hand to get everyone's attention. "Annie is at home with little Evan. He isn't ready to face the public yet. So you can all stop worrying that Hugh is being unfair to our little Annie. Far as I can see, he treats her kindly and with respect. And you can be proud of how Annie is helping Evan feel safe." With a harrumph, he leaned on his canes.

The brothers hesitated until their wives grabbed their elbows and led them to sit down.

Hugh pretended to study his notes but in reality he was chuckling to himself, feeling as if he had passed a test with flying colors. Not that he didn't hear the warning that if he should do anything to hurt Annie he would face the combined wrath of the Marshalls.

You'll never be good enough.

The familiar words came in his mother's voice. He'd tried to put her disapproval out of his life. He had only to answer to God for how he lived his life. He'd mostly succeeded in believing that was all that mattered until he married Bernice and he'd failed her.

With God's help, he would not fail his son.

But he wasn't prepared to incur the wrath of the Marshall family if he should fail Annie in any way. How else to prevent it but to find someone to replace her?

It was surely concern about his son that sent a shaft of pain through his insides.

Annie told herself she would not count the minutes until she heard people leaving the church next door. And she surely wouldn't stare out the window. Though if she did it was only to watch for her brothers and their wives and Carly Morrison. She and Carly were longtime friends. They usually spent Sunday afternoons together.

She prepared a meal, talking to Evan about Spot the dog as she did so. She hoped and prayed he would begin to see how a boy should act.

It was customary at the ranch to expect company after church. She always prepared enough to feed a crowd but things were different here. It wasn't her house. Would Hugh invite people over? Or would it only be the four of them again?

The sound of people exiting the church brought her back to the window. Finally. She wished she could have been there, heard how Hugh explained about Evan and her, and listened to his deep voice. From the first time she'd heard him speak, his voice had rumbled into her very soul pointing out places she needed to turn over to God's sovereignty. What would he have said today? Would his words have encouraged her? To do what?

She laughed as the entire Marshall family headed for the manse. Grandfather followed on their heels. She could tell that he scolded the others and wondered what he said.

Dawson led the pack exerting his position as the

eldest and stopped at the front door, waiting for them to crowd around him. She delayed until he knocked before she opened the door.

"Hi, Dawson." She greeted each of the others. The cold bit right through her. "You all best step inside before I freeze."

They trooped in, crowding the walls of the little living room.

Sammy, who was Logan's seven-year-old adopted son, and Mattie, who was Dawson's six-year-old daughter, went to the kitchen doorway and stared at the little boy huddling in the corner.

Annie followed on their heels, intent on guarding Evan against the shock of her large, noisy family. "Evan, honey, these people belong to me. My brothers and their wives." She introduced each of them. And then the children. As they were introduced the adults stood in the doorway and said hello then stepped back. The children might have stayed there, staring, but their parents drew them to their sides. Grandfather made his way to his armchair by the kitchen stove and sank into it.

She faced the rest of the family. "What can I do for you?" Did they expect her to feed them? "I'll make dinner for you all next Sunday—" That might be too soon for Evan's peace of mind. "Or soon." Hopefully Hugh wouldn't object but hadn't he said she could invite anyone she wanted?

Her brothers all spoke at once and their wives tried to make themselves heard.

Dawson held up his hand to signal silence. "Seeing as Pa isn't here, I will speak on behalf of the family. Annie, we all agree that this is a foolish decision. Change your mind and come on home."

She looked from one to the other, saw their love and concern and knew it was genuine. "In four weeks' time I expect you to all come to my wedding."

Hugh stepped in just in time to catch her words and their gazes crashed together across the room. She wasn't sure that she read his expression correctly but if she had to guess, she would say it held a great deal of promise and she drew support from the thought.

Dawson appealed to Grandfather. "Can't you talk some sense into her?"

Grandfather shrugged. "I like it here. And Annie is doing a fine job as I've already said. I think little Evan likes her. Don't you?" he asked the boy.

Evan watched the proceedings from the protection of the veil of his hair and shrank back at Grandfather's question.

Then to Annie's utter surprise he nodded his head.

She turned back to Hugh. "He nodded," she whispered.

He came to her side where he could see his son. "He did? That's wonderful. A real answer to prayer." He stayed beside her, as if to support her against her family's onslaught. "I can't say how much I appreciate all that Annie has done to help me."

His praise filled her to the brim. She dare not look at him and clasped her hands together to keep from hugging him. He had admitted he needed her. It was all she wanted.

"Would any of you like coffee before you head back to the ranch?" she asked.

Dawson shook his head. "We need to get home. I believe Kate has prepared dinner for us." He spoke to Hugh. "I trust you will bring Annie out soon."

She bristled. "Since when do I need someone to take me to the ranch? I've been going back and forth on my own for years." She jammed her fists to her hips. "Suddenly I need someone to take me? Suddenly I can't make my own decisions?"

Her brothers had the good sense to look a little uncomfortable. Sadie, Kate and Isabelle chuckled.

Sadie looked about. "Where is Jeannie?" The three-year-old was not in the room.

Annie turned to check the kitchen and saw the child. She held up a hand to signal quiet. Logan and Sadie tiptoed forward. Jeannie sat on the floor close to Evan, chatting up a storm. Evan watched her without speaking. Joy and sadness intermingled in Annie. It was good to see him allowing Jeannie to sit so close. It would be even better to hear Evan replying. However, Annie couldn't be sure Evan was able to talk.

A few minutes later as her family left, Annie overheard Sadie. "Someday you fellows will have to admit Annie is all grown up."

Dawson grunted. "She'll always be my little sister."

"I just don't want to see her make a mistake and ruin her life," Logan said.

His words tugged at Annie's heart. She had no intention of ruining her life which was why she had chosen this direction. A marriage based on need would leave her heart whole and ensure security.

Silence filled the room with her family gone. Hugh still stood close to her, his presence threatening to overwhelm her. She inhaled the scent of wood and smoke, with a hint of some kind of spice that settled right into her bones. "How was church?"

He chuckled. "Let's just say there were mixed responses to my announcements regarding this past week. Many came up to tell me how glad they were that I'd found Evan but I heard a few sniffs of disapproval when I said you were my housekeeper." He sounded faintly apologetic. "I wasn't sure how else to explain it."

"That's fine." Housekeeper? Was that all she was? How else would she explain her present situation? Wife in waiting? Prospective wife on trial? She shrugged. All that mattered was what happened in what was left of four weeks. "Dinner is ready."

"Smells good. I'll change and be right back."

She wanted to tell him to keep wearing the black suit. It looked good on him. But of course he wanted to keep it in pristine condition. She hurried to the kitchen and set the table. As she prepared to serve the hot pot, he returned wearing an off-white collarless shirt in a fabric that looked so soft she wished she could touch it.

Realizing she stared at the poor man, she waved him toward the table. "The meal is on." She'd previously filled a bowl for Evan so it could cool.

Grandfather eased himself out of his soft chair and hobbled to the table.

She watched him anxiously. When he was seated, she glanced at Hugh. She let him see her concern, found strength in the way he held her gaze so steadily.

After he'd asked the blessing and the food had been served, she turned to Grandfather. "Tell me what Hugh said."

"You want the whole sermon?" Grandfather said with a huge dose of disbelief.

"Mostly I want to know what he said about Evan and me."

Grandfather shrugged. "Didn't say a whole lot."

She leaned closer. "He said something. I want to know what."

"So ask him."

She turned to Hugh though she would have liked to hear how Grandfather viewed Hugh's remarks. "I'm asking."

He flashed a quick smile. "I just gave the facts. That I had located Evan. That he hadn't been treated well and lived in fear. I said I hoped to find an older woman who would settle for a businesslike marriage but in the meantime, you and your grandfather were living here and you were taking care of Evan."

"Thanks." She wondered if he caught the edge of sarcasm in that one word then gave her attention to her meal. He certainly never left any room for possibilities in those few words.

He spoke again. "Oh by the way, your friend Miss Morrison asked after you. I said she was welcome to visit you anytime. I understood she would come by today."

Her mood improved greatly at the news of Carly's visit.

Grandfather groaned. "You two get together and there is always some kind of mischief."

"I beg to differ. We just like to have a little fun."

"Uh-huh. Well, let me tell you." He spoke to Hugh. "There was the time Annie and Carly—"

"Grandfather, please." There had been a few foolish episodes. She didn't want Hugh to know of them. "We've both grown up since those early days." She couldn't look at Hugh. Didn't want to see his expression. One, she felt certain, that would be full of disapproval. Why did Grandfather want to tell about those things and not all the caring, helpful things she'd done for the family? She jumped up. She had the perfect way to make him remember the good and forget the not-so-good. "I made that cinnamon coffee cake you like so much."

Grandfather perked right up. "You're a girl after my own heart. You'd do any man proud."

That was more like it. She served generous slices for everyone and only when she put the dessert in front of Hugh did she finally allow herself to meet his gaze.

He watched her with a measuring study.

She gave him look for look but felt like she encountered a brick wall. He'd shut himself off to her. Her insides curled into themselves. Had the progress of the last four days been lost because of a teasing comment by her grandfather?

She sat and bent over her own dessert, suddenly unable to think of anything to say.

A knock came to the back door. She was about to answer it but this was Hugh's house and she sat back and waited for him to do so. He rose and opened the door.

"Is Annie here?"

Annie jumped up. "Carly. Am I ever glad to see you." She hugged her friend. "Have you eaten? Would you like to join us for dessert?"

Carly sniffed. "Cinnamon cake?"

"Good guess."

Carly laughed. "Your famous coffee cake if I'm not mistaken."

So overjoyed to see her friend that she couldn't stop grinning or hold back the happy laughter, Annie drew Carly toward the table.

Hugh brought in another chair from the living room and put it beside Grandfather.

Carly thanked him then turned to Grandfather. "Hello, Mr. Marshall." She winked at Annie.

Annie recognized the teasing tone and waited for the reaction.

"Hello to you, Miss Morrison."

"Miss Morrison, is it? I thought we knew each other better than that."

"I'll use your name when you stop calling me Mr. Marshall."

Carly laughed and gave the older man a sideways hug. "You know you're my favorite grandfather even if I have to borrow you from Annie. Sometimes I don't think she deserves you."

Annie laughed. She liked Carly's teasing. It took away the sting of Hugh saying he wished he could find someone else. "Grandfather knows he's well off to have me for his granddaughter."

Carly just shrugged. "I don't mind sharing with you."

Both Hugh and Grandfather chuckled.

Annie tried to think if Hugh laughed at anything she said and couldn't remember at the moment.

"And who is this handsome young fellow in the corner?" Carly asked.

"My son, Evan," Hugh said, obviously pleased by her comment.

It wasn't as if Annie hadn't showered affection on the boy. She sighed. And why was she being so critical? Just because of a careless remark from Hugh?

They finished their dessert. Grandfather moved to his chair.

Hugh leaned back, suddenly relaxed. "Is there any more coffee?"

"I'll make some." She did so and served him a cupful. Grandfather refused one.

"As soon as the dishes are done, I have a project," she told Carly.

Carly pretended to pout. "Do I have to help with dishes?"

"Of course not. You can sit and watch me do them."

Carly laughed hard and Annie joined her. Both of them knew neither of them would ever sit and watch the other work.

Carly spoke for both when she said, "I would as soon walk barefoot outside on a day like this as sit by and not help you when you need it."

Annie wondered if Carly's words should serve as a warning. It was comforting as well as frightening to think how she would need Carly in four weeks if Hugh chose a different woman.

He wouldn't, she vowed. He'd see he couldn't do better. And she would certainly keep her heart tightly wrapped up so if he did, she would not leave a portion of it behind.

Evan watched them with wide-eyed wonder. He ducked his head as soon as he realized Annie looked at him. She shifted her attention to Hugh. Why did he look so attentive? As if seeking for reasons to find fault.

She smiled gently. Silently promising he would not find any cause to disapprove. She knew many saw her and Carly as wild simply because Carly often wore trousers and rode as hard as any man. Little did they know how hard she worked to keep the Morrison ranch going. As to the riding, well, Annie knew how much fun it was to race a horse at a full gallop and feel the wind in her ears, tugging her hair into a mane to match the horse's. No one thought it risky or unseeming when her brothers did the same thing.

She and Carly had washed the dishes while she mused about her life. "Hugh, will you watch Evan while Carly and I do something?"

"He's my son. Of course I'll watch him." He looked at Evan. "Maybe I'll read to him."

Annie stared at the look that crossed Evan's face. As if Hugh's suggestion was unwelcome. "Have you read to him before?"

"Read to him last night."

"What did you read?"

He looked away, as if greatly interested in the view out the window. She knew he only meant to avoid looking at her.

He cleared his throat. "I might have read him my sermon."

She stared openmouthed.

Carly whooped then covered her mouth, trying to stifle her amusement.

Annie shook her head. Had she heard wrong? "You read him your sermon?"

He nodded, his gaze still on the window.

Amusement rushed unbridled from her and she chuckled. She looked at Carly and they both laughed, not even trying to hide the fact.

Hugh finally brought his gaze to her, his look full of self-mockery.

She sobered instantly as their gazes collided. Felt something grab her heart in a grip as firm and secure as—she remembered being very young and having a hard time staying upright on an icy path. Her pa had taken her hand and held her so she wouldn't fall. That's how her heart felt. She knew she would have to analyze this thought further. Safe and secure—wasn't that what she wanted in the marriage she hoped to gain? Safe and secure without the risk of her heart being involved. And yet, even without falling in love, it was her heart that responded.

"It was a very nice sermon," Carly said, her voice round with laughter.

He looked sheepish, his gaze never leaving Annie's. "But not for a four-year-old?"

Carly pretended to look thoughtful. "I'm just guessing here but I'm thinking many of the concepts would have been over his head."

He grinned. "Not to mention that even at thirty minutes, it's a long time for a child to concentrate."

Annie told herself to look away from his smiling eyes, the deep grooves in his cheeks, the brown eyes so dark she could lose herself in them.

Carly nudged her. "Didn't you say you had something for us to do?"

"Of course. Come to my room." She led the way.

"Something to do besides stare at the man," Carly

said half under her breath as soon as they were out of earshot of the kitchen.

"I wasn't staring!"

"And my name isn't Carly Morrison."

Annie knew better than to get involved with one of Carly's teasing arguments.

Carly had a good look around her bedroom. Picked up the picture of Annie's parents. "It looks to me like you've moved right in."

"I intend to stay and I'm getting just a little tired of telling everyone that. Hugh advertised for a woman to marry him and provide a mother for Evan and here I am."

"I'm guessing you aren't what he had in mind."

Her friend's assessment stung. "Why do you say that?"

Carly shrugged and pretended to look disinterested. "It would seem to me that a man who wants a marriage that doesn't involve love would do better to find some old maid who is willing to settle for anything. That isn't you." She gave Annie a direct look. "You need to stop running from love."

Annie shook her head. "I'm not running from anything."

Carly flopped on the bed. "So you say but Annie, I see the way you two look at each other. If you don't want to fall in love with the man, I suggest you pack your bags and return to the ranch this very afternoon."

"I am not going to fall in love." She ground out each word.

Carly shrugged. "I promise not to say I told you so." She sprang to her feet. "Now what is this project?"

Annie gladly changed the subject. "I want to make a dog."

Carly hooted. "I don't think you have that ability."

"A stuffed dog." She told about Spot and how she hoped Evan would learn some lessons from the stories she made up about a pretend dog. "I have some fabric here. I don't know why I even packed it except it was in my drawer at the ranch." It was white flannel and would do quite nicely. The girls cut and fashioned a dog with a brown spot over one of its black button eyes and stuffed it with some rags Annie had found in one of the kitchen cupboards.

They laughed a lot as they worked, making the dog do silly things.

"You really care about Evan, don't you?"

Annie nodded. "My heart goes out to him. Can you imagine losing your mother and not having a father to show you a little compassion?"

Both of them had lost their mothers and knew the sense of loss it brought.

Carly shook her head. "Poor little tyke. I hope he will be okay." They paused to listen to Hugh's deep-voiced rumble coming from the kitchen.

Carly gave Annie a troubled look. "I hope you'll be okay too."

"Why wouldn't I?"

"Because you are already half in love with Hugh. He says he would still like to find an older woman. A spinster. If he does and you have to leave, I fear you will be terribly hurt."

Annie shook her head hard, decisively. "I have no intention of falling in love. But I will prove to him that I'm the perfect woman for his need."

And if she felt a shadow of doubt concerning either of those statements, she wasn't about to admit it. Besides, she knew better than to put her heart at risk.

Chapter Eight

When Hugh heard all the laughter coming from Annie's room as she and Carly worked on whatever project they undertook, he told himself it proved this was not the place for her. How soon before she discovered how restrictive life would be as a preacher's wife? He'd set his mind to seeing her as only temporary and then she emerged with a goofy-looking stuffed dog she and Carly had made and talked to it like it was real, gaining Evan's attention.

Hugh was finding it harder and harder to remember why she was unsuitable.

On Monday morning, he made a quick trip out to get the mail. At the store, he saw an ad posted by the door describing a dog. He leaned closer and read Annie's name for the person to contact. She was trying to find the owner for the dog in the shed. Why must she continually do things that earned his admiration?

He returned home and forced himself to remain in his office with the door closed. Even so he could hear the murmur of her voice and an occasional response from her grandfather. It was all he could do not to slip out and see what she was doing. He pictured her up to her elbows in hot water as she did the laundry. Or hunkered down facing Evan and talking to him. Perhaps using that silly stuffed dog to get Evan's interest. She had managed to get through to the boy in many ways and that earned a lot of respect from him.

He closed his eyes and reminded himself to concentrate. He worked on next week's sermon in the hopes of keeping his thoughts off her and her admirable qualities.

At noon, she called him to join them for dinner. Wet garments hung from lines behind the stove filling the air with moisture that beaded on the windows where it froze into intricate patterns.

He took note of how she had filled a bowl with scraps and knew it was for the dog. And he immediately reiterated her good points—and there were many. For his peace of mind he should hurry back to his office but he preferred to spend time with his son in the warm kitchen. Spot, the stuffed dog, sat in the chair he hoped Evan would soon occupy.

Annie put a plate in front of Spot and spoke to Hugh. "I really think Spot would like to sit on the floor on a nice warm mat but I see Evan has that place. Poor Spot. He'll have to keep pretending he's a boy."

Hugh watched Evan. He shifted as if making room on his mat for the dog then looked from the chair, back to the mat. Was he considering sitting at the table?

Hugh looked to Annie, knowing his eyes brimmed with gratitude.

She smiled, looking rather pleased with herself.

Be careful how much approval you show, his brain

shouted. It was a fact he had every reason to be grateful for all she was doing. And no reason, that he could recall, not to let her know.

A short time later, the meal over, he lingered over his coffee, content to simply enjoy the warmth of the kitchen. A knock sounded on the front door. He looked at Annie. "Are you expecting someone?"

"Not me."

Reluctantly, he left the comfort of the kitchen and crossed the living room to answer the door. Six ladies with heads high faced him.

"Pastor, we need to talk to you."

His heart sank at the tone in Mrs. Shearer's voice. He stepped back to let the ladies enter. "Won't you have a seat?"

They marched in, looked about and sat down... perching on the edges of seats in the living room. He grabbed the only remaining chair and sat, certain he wasn't going to like what they had to say. They did not look like they had come offering assistance.

Mrs. Shearer appeared to be the spokeswoman. She glanced toward the kitchen. She couldn't likely see Grandfather in his armchair and if Annie had a lick of sense she would be staying out of sight.

The outer door opened and closed. Had she decided to leave so she wouldn't overhear a conversation between Hugh and some of his parishioners? Knowing she had gone outside allowed him to relax marginally.

Mrs. Shearer leaned forward, her look intense. "I speak on behalf of the entire church—"

Hugh strongly doubted that.

"When I say we find it most objectionable that you are living here with young Miss Marshall without the benefit of marriage." She sniffed and adjusted her gloves. The five other ladies imitated her.

Hugh didn't show the least reaction though inside, anger ignited. Forcing himself to speak calmly, he said, "May I ask why you object?"

Mrs. Shearer sputtered. "I would think it would be obvious, especially to a man of God."

"I'm sorry but it's not. There is adequate chaperoning. Unless you don't think Mr. Marshall is trustworthy." He let the words hang in the air.

Mrs. Shearer lifted a finger in a scolding manner. "As the preacher you must live a life above reproach. Think of the example you are setting to the unmarried boys and girls around you. Pastor Arness, you need to reconsider your actions." She pushed to her feet and her followers did the same. "By the way, I have an unmarried sister coming to visit for Christmas. I think you'd find her ideal. I expect her to arrive any day." She waited expectantly.

"I'll keep it in mind."

With her nose in the air, she steamed for the door, with five righteously indignant women in her wake.

He escorted them as far as the door and waited until they marched down the street. By exerting every ounce of self-control he managed not to bang the door shut.

Thankfully Annie didn't hear any of that.

She stormed into the living room. "You promised me four weeks."

"When did you come back inside?"

"In time to hear that woman tell you about her sister."

He slowly turned to face her. My but she was a

sight all fired up. Her eyes flashed shards of blue, her cheeks were touched with pink from being out in the cold and perhaps because of her anger. She had her fists jammed on her hips as she glowered at him.

"I also said until someone more suitable came along." Though he didn't mean to suggest that Mrs. Shearer's sister would be more suitable. There was no way of judging until he actually met the woman. She *might* be ideal. Unless she was remotely like her sister.

"Why aren't I suitable? Tell me where I've failed."

He couldn't come up with a single response. Because she had not failed in any way. Did that make her ideal?

"I'm tempted to say it would serve you right if you replaced me with someone with a sharp tongue and a critical spirit." Her anger fled, replaced with a look of regret. "But that little boy in there deserves much better." She returned to the kitchen, leaving Hugh feeling like he'd been hit by a flying boulder. He hadn't said he would replace Annie. Didn't even know if he wanted to. He didn't know what he wanted and he grabbed his coat and hat and hurried from the house, his steps not slowing until he reached the frozen creek at the edge of town. He stopped there and stared at the ice formations. Why was he letting himself get so worked up about this matter? All he needed was someone to help care for Evan. What he did not need was someone who would expect more from him than he could give.

Was Annie wanting more than he could give…or more than he *wanted* to give? She'd confessed she was afraid of love. Was he any different? Seemed to him that love came with a lot of expectations.

A galloping horse thundered toward him. He recognized John Lewis whose wife, Ida, had been ill for some time.

"Preacher, can you come right away? My wife is doing poorly and asks for you."

"I'll be glad to come. I'll need to get my horse."

"I won't wait for you." And John galloped away.

Hugh jogged back to town, pausing at the livery barn to get his horse saddled. He rode back to the church and went into the house through the office. He took his Bible in hand and went through to the kitchen.

Annie's expression shifted from welcome to studied indifference. He might have been looking into his son's eyes for all the emotion they revealed. However, he didn't have time to deal with the matter at the moment. Not that he knew of any way to do so.

"I have to go to the Lewis place. Ida is doing poorly."

"Oh, I'm sorry to hear it. Wait, I'll wrap a cake for you to take. And if I can help in any way…"

Their fingers touched as he took the cake from her. His hand froze in midair. She didn't pull back either.

"Be safe." She dropped her hand to the pocket of her apron.

"I will. I don't know when I'll be back."

"We'll be fine."

He knew they would. He went to Evan and knelt in front of him. "I have to go and help a sick lady. Grandfather and Annie will be here while I'm gone. They will take care of you." The boy didn't look at Hugh but Hugh knew he listened and understood.

He hated to leave but he didn't have a choice.

"Goodbye." He touched Evan's shoulder, grateful when the boy didn't jerk away. He said goodbye to Grandfather and last, to Annie, his gaze clinging to hers. There were things that he needed to say but now was not the time.

Nor did he know what it was he thought he should say.

Annie walked with him to the door and watched until he swung into the saddle.

He saluted then rode away. He turned for one last look and told himself he wasn't disappointed that the door had closed.

Annie leaned her head against the door. She should have told him she wasn't angry with him. No, she was angry with herself for caring so much that she was hurt to hear him say that he still considered replacing her. She had promised herself she would not care about him. And she must not. For several seconds she remained in that position, pulling every errant thought back into submission.

Only then did she return to the kitchen.

Grandfather watched her. "I'm sure he'll be okay."

"Yes, I'm sure he will." And to prove it didn't matter to her, she checked the clothes drying behind the stove, taking down the few items that were done. Determined not to feel sorry for herself, she challenged Grandfather to a game of pick-up sticks. He chortled when he won game after game.

"Could be you're not concentrating," he said. "At least not on the game." He waggled his eyebrows.

She did not reply to his teasing comment.

The afternoon trudged by on leaden feet. She was

more aware of the outside sounds than usual, hearing the wind pick up in velocity, hearing a piece of wood rattle against the side of the house, perking up at the sound of a horse passing. Not that she listened for Hugh's return.

They played the game for a bit then she announced she must make supper. She'd make something special to welcome Hugh home. Not for any other reason, she informed herself, than to make him see that she would make a perfect wife.

The chops were cooked, the potatoes done and the pie crust golden and he did not return.

"Girl, that food smells good and my stomach is kissing my backbone."

"I guess it is time to eat." She served everyone a portion.

Evan gave her a concerned look.

"He'll be back soon," she assured him, wishing she felt as cheerful as she sounded. Why was she so concerned about him? Other than he was out in a blustery wind and cold that would snap metal and she was home with his son and a grandfather who could barely walk. Pshaw. She was a big brave girl used to being alone.

Except this was different. It felt like a big hole had been left vacant.

She served Grandfather and Evan slices of pie, all the while telling herself that she had worried about this from the beginning. That she'd care too much and be the sorrier for it.

Maybe it was for the best if he found someone else.

A moan pushed at her teeth and she refused to let it pass.

Grandfather made his way back to his soft chair. "The cold surely does get into my bones."

And him indoors by a roaring fire. How must it be for Hugh if he rode homeward in that bitter cold? *Lord, protect him.* Everyone deserved to be home safe and warm in this weather.

She did up the dishes. The darkness had closed in around them and still Hugh did not return. "Evan, honey, it's time for bed."

He made a protesting noise and looked at Hugh's empty chair.

"I know he's still gone but I'm sure he's okay." She had to keep telling herself that. "Sometimes he has to stay with people who are sick and need him." In Ida's case she feared this would be her final illness. The woman had been struggling for several months now. The poor thing must be exhausted.

"I'll read to you and say your prayers then you can crawl into your bed."

He shook his head and looked directly at her, his eyes wide.

She stared at him. If only Hugh could be here to see his son communicate so clearly. "Do you want me to take you to bed?"

He nodded. And nodded again as if he wanted her to say something more.

She wasn't sure what. "I'll read to you." She picked a short story about faithfulness and then prayed with him. Another problem raised its head. How was she to get him to bed? He would fight her and maybe even bite. She didn't think she could control him as well as Hugh did.

Instead of trying, she got to her feet, held out her hand. "Let's go to bed."

He hesitated, staring at her arm. Then he got to his feet and gripped her hand so tight she could feel him vibrating.

She smiled at Grandfather as they left the room. At least she could share this victory with him.

Evan dropped her hand as soon as they entered the bedroom. He stood by his mattress and pointed to Hugh's bed.

She understood all too clearly and fought a losing war with herself. If she didn't lie down on Hugh's bed, Evan would be upset and maybe revert to a wild little animal. But to rest on the very bed that Hugh used…

It made her cheeks burn.

"Let me tell Grandfather." She went to the door and called out to him, afraid to leave Evan alone for even a moment. He hobbled to the hallway and she told him what she planned to do.

"Just until the boy falls asleep," he warned.

Her cheeks about caught on fire. "Not a moment longer."

"I'll stay up until then."

She wanted to tell him to go to bed but he was right. "Thank you. I'm sorry to make you do this."

"It's for the boy." He limped back to the kitchen and his soft chair. At least he would be able to sleep. She wasn't the least offended that he said it was because of Evan. She knew it was for her as well.

She waited as Evan settled himself on the mattress, the quilt over him. How she would have liked to kiss him good-night and tuck the quilt around his shoulders. Maybe someday soon. For a long, breathless moment she looked at Hugh's bed.

Evan wide-eyed and watchful waited for her to lie down.

She turned the lamp low, grabbed the quilt that lay folded across the foot of the bed, placed her head on the pillow and stretched out on top of the covers. A hollow in the pillow indicated where he rested his head. His scent clung to the room. She pulled the quilt up to her nose hoping to find the smell of fresh laundry but his scent clung to the quilt as well.

Stiff, silent and staring at the ceiling, she waited for Evan to fall asleep. His breathing deepened. She waited bit longer, making sure he was slumbering deeply. Quietly she slid the quilt down to her feet and tiptoed to the door. Evan didn't stir and she continued down the hall.

"Grandfather." She shook him gently. "You can go to bed now."

He came awake slowly. "He's back?"

"Not yet but for all we know he might stay overnight."

"Little Evan is asleep?"

"I left the lamp on so he wouldn't be afraid if he woke." She helped Grandfather to his feet and handed him his canes.

"Will the young one be okay?"

"I'll curl up on the couch. I'll be able to hear Evan if he wakens." She wouldn't likely sleep until she heard Hugh return.

"I suppose that's for the best. My old bones need to feel a soft bed."

She kissed him on the cheek, wished him good-night and watched him make his slow way down the hall to his room. She waited until the lamp in his room went out then hurried to stare out the dark window. Of course she could see nothing even when she scraped a hole in the frost except the lantern hanging outside the hotel to guide in any late travelers.

She had no way of knowing if Hugh was still at the Lewis's or on his way home. Or even if he'd left some time ago and fallen into some kind of trouble. She could do nothing but watch and wait.

And pray. *Lord, bring him home safely.*

After a bit, she realized how cold she'd grown and returned to put more wood on the fire. An afghan hung over the arm of one of the chairs and she plucked it up, wrapped it about herself and returned to the window.

The town lay before her, silent and still except for the moan of the wind.

Finally, accepting that he would not return until morning, she curled up on the couch and fell into a restless sleep.

Hugh had waited until morning to leave the Lewis place though even then the sky was still black. He would arrive home before dawn changed the sky to gray. Ida Lewis still clung to life. The woman was a fighter. Dr. Baker said if she pulled through this bout of pneumonia she had a good chance of a full recovery.

Hugh had been glad enough to be there and offer encouragement and prayers to the family. However, he couldn't keep from worrying about his own family. Despite every warning he'd ever uttered, he included

Annie and Grandfather in that word. And why not? he reasoned. For the time being they resided in his house and were, therefore, his responsibility.

How had they managed in his absence? Would Annie have been able to get Evan to bed? Would Evan have fought her? Were they warm enough?

Had she missed him?

He slammed the door on such thoughts. Their relationship was strictly businesslike. Both of them wanted it that way.

He stopped at the livery barn and stabled his horse, taking the time to brush him well and give instructions for feeding the animal to the sleepy young fellow tending the place then he made his way to the house. The cold had a decided bite to it, which explained his hurried stride. He passed the hotel, welcoming the lantern light to guide him on his way. From there he could see the manse. Light flickered in the front window. Like flames.

His heart kicked into a frenzy. Was the place on fire? He broke into a run, reached the door, wrenched it open and burst indoors. Flames blazed in the fireplace. He sank back on his heels, his breathing ragged. Why had he panicked? Then he noticed someone on the couch facing the fireplace. He eased forward to look over the back until he could see.

His ragged breathing returned at the sight of Annie sleeping, a hand under her cheek, her long blond hair in a braid but strands of it coiling about her face.

Had she stayed up to wait for him? The thought sent his heart into a gallop. Bernice had never waited up for him. Why, his own mother wouldn't have worried about him getting home safely. He had no right to stand gazing down at a sleeping young woman and backed up to the door and shut it with a resounding bang.

Annie grunted and sat up. She glanced around, her eyes wide and bottomless as she met his gaze. Then she blinked and focused. A slow smile wreathed her face. "You're home."

The look between them held him immobile. He knew he dreamed all the things he thought he saw—welcome, warmth, acceptance—

He jerked his gaze away.

"How is Ida?" she asked, fear creeping into her voice.

"She's got pneumonia and it was touch and go through the night but doc says she'll make it."

"I prayed for her throughout the night."

"God hears and answers." What would her prayers sound like if she prayed for him too? "Did you pray for me as well?" He had not meant to ask the question aloud. He let his gaze to return to her, watching for her reaction, pleased to see her cheeks turn rosy.

She ducked her head and whispered. "I did."

"What did you request of God?" Perhaps if he knew he could put his silly wishes to rest.

She raised her eyes to his, blue and clear and full of promise.

That's what happened to a man's common sense when he spent most of the night sitting at the bedside of a very ill woman.

Her smile trembled. "I prayed if you had left you weren't out in the cold maybe hurt or lost and if you were still at the Lewis's you would have wisdom to know how best to comfort and encourage them."

People prayed for him. People like Stewart Caldwell and his wife. People like Grandfather Marshall who had an interest in seeing that the town of Bella Creek flourished as he had planned. And other people had prayed for him to find Evan.

None mattered as much as Annie's prayers. Could it really matter to her if he got home safely? Well of course it did. She would have no reason to be here if he didn't. No other reason had been mentioned and despite his best resolve, he let himself believe she'd been concerned about *him*.

He fought a futile inner battle between the hope she would care that much about him and the fear that she would be disappointed in him. Would his mother's words never leave him? It wasn't just his mother, he reminded himself. No longer would he risk being judged a failure. All that mattered to him now was being enough for Evan.

Why did the argument sound weak to his own ears?

Chapter Nine

A nnie tried to shake off the feeling of bliss that surrounded her at Hugh's return and at the way he looked at her. It wasn't even light out yet. Had he ridden home in the dark just to be here? She knew she should rearrange her thoughts but she was so very glad to see him back safe and sound it was all she could do not to rush over and give him a hug.

She settled for wrapping her arms around herself.

"How was Evan?" he asked, bringing her back to the reality of why she was here and why he hurried home. "Did you manage to get him to bed?"

"Let's go in the kitchen and I'll tell you all about it." She hurried ahead of him, knowing if she waited she would be wrapping her arm about him and hanging on for dear life. Hearing his footsteps behind her, she rushed to the stove, added more wood and filled the coffeepot.

He sank to the chair. "I half expected to see him still there." He indicated the corner Evan huddled in throughout the day.

The coffee wasn't ready but she couldn't hold

back any longer and she faced Hugh. "You should have seen him. He let me know he missed you." She told how the boy had looked to Hugh's empty chair. "When I said it was time for bed, I simply held out my hand. He took it." She couldn't stop smiling. It was all she could do not to laugh aloud with sheer joy of recalling the moment and sharing it with Hugh. His eyes were warm, his cheeks deeply grooved by his smile.

"We walked to the bedroom and he put himself to bed." She wouldn't tell him that she'd lain on his bed until Evan fell asleep. "I couldn't believe it. I wish you'd been here to see it."

"I wish I'd been here too." He didn't say to see Evan's progress. In fact, the way his eyes sought hers and filled with the warmth of a summer evening, she allowed herself to think he might have wished he could be there because of her.

The coffee sizzled and she turned to pull it from the heat. She waited for the grounds to settle then poured him a cup and handed it to him.

His fingers touched hers. His gaze brushed her. The world seemed full of promise and possibility. She tried to tell herself she was overtired, overexcited, over everything to think such foolishness but her mind remained unchanged.

Hugh took the cup and set it on the table. He yawned. "Sorry, I was awake all night."

She stepped back, rebuked by her lack of thought. "Why don't you go lie down for a bit? Evan might feel better to wake up and find you there."

He took a huge sip of coffee and yawned again. "Maybe I will. You'll be okay?"

She'd been fine all night but it melted a corner of

her heart for him to ask. She patted his arm. "I think I can manage. You go ahead."

He grinned. "I know you can manage. That isn't what I meant at all. I only meant—" He got to his feet and shrugged. "I don't know what I meant. I'm so tired I'm not making any sense."

"Away you go." She gave him a little shove in the right direction.

He chuckled. "You're trying awfully hard to get rid of me." He faced her, sobering as he saw the look on her face.

Too late she realized she let show her longing for him to stay and keep her company. She tossed her head in an attempt to hide the truth. "I just don't want to put up with a cranky, exhausted man."

She didn't believe her explanation and from the bemused look on his face, didn't think he did either.

"Away you go before Evan wakes up."

"Yes, ma'am." He sauntered down the hall, as if pleased with himself.

Not until he ducked out of sight did she remember she'd left the quilt tossed across the bed. He'd know at once that she had been there. She could only hope he was too tired to notice or too tired to read anything into it.

Not that there was anything to read into it.

She looked at the couch and the afghan and decided she would enjoy a few more moments of sleep herself.

She didn't know how long she slept before she jerked awake trying to orientate herself. She lay on the couch with the first rays of dawn creeping across the floor. The room was cold, the fireplace having gone out. Feeling as if someone peered at her, she turned her head and stared into the watchful eyes of Evan. Had he gotten up by himself?

"Is your papa still sleeping?"

He nodded.

"Are you hungry?"

Again, he nodded.

"Good." She meant so much more than his admission of hunger. The boy was communicating so clearly and moving about of his own accord. She would have hugged him except she feared it would send him into full-out reversal. "Let me get my hair done and I'll make you breakfast."

Evan's eyes went to her hair and she thought she detected the faintest glimpse of humor. The boy was very much like his father with dark eyes and dark hair. Did he also have those deep dimples when he smiled? She couldn't wait to find out.

He followed her to her bedroom and leaned against her bed, watching as she brushed her hair and pinned it into place. His presence did not feel like an intrusion. Indeed, it felt more like a shared moment. She used to do the same with her mama.

She finished and turned to Evan. "Let's go." She held out her hand before she realized he might not welcome the gesture. When he took it, she wanted to cheer. If only Hugh could see this.

They made their way to the kitchen. He still held to her hand. She considered what to do, how to handle this. Spot, the stuffed dog, sat on the chair. "Shall I put Spot on the mat?"

Evan quivered and squeezed her hand hard. Then he shook his head and went to the mat and settled down in his customary position.

Soon, she promised herself. Soon he would choose to sit at the table and soon he'd begin to play like a normal child. Cheered by the encouragement of those thoughts, she built up the fire in the stove and moved the coffeepot over to warm up the contents.

A few minutes later, the thumping of Grandfather's canes coming down the hall informed her that he was awake. The first thing he'd want would be coffee and it was prepared and she poured him a cup. He sat at the table and consumed most of it before he said anything but good morning.

"Did Hugh get back yet?" he asked.

"Yes, earlier this morning."

"Good because my bones say we are in for a blizzard."

She glanced out the window. "Cold and blowing out there. It's not nice."

"Trust my bones. It's going to get worse."

In that case, she was doubly glad that Hugh was back, safe and sound.

She wasn't sure when to expect him to appear but prepared breakfast as usual. It was about ready to serve when he entered, yawning and stretching.

"I smell coffee and bacon."

She poured him a cup and he drank a few swallows then looked around.

"Evan, I never heard you get up," Hugh said.

Annie chuckled. "When I woke up he was standing by the couch," She jerked her gaze from Hugh's dark eyes that drew her into secret places, secret thoughts—to Evan. "Did you wonder if we were going to sleep all day?"

He nodded, met her eyes for a second then shifted

his gaze to Hugh. A fleeting, barely-there smile pulled at his mouth and then he ducked away. She hadn't imagined it. When she looked at Hugh, she knew by the way his eyes darkened and his throat worked that he had seen it as well.

She smiled. "He's going to be okay." Something thumped against the window. "Snow."

"My bones are always right," Grandfather said. "Though I wish they'd be wrong once in a while."

Annie explained to Hugh and Evan how Grandfather could tell a storm headed their way by how much his bones hurt. She went to look out the window. Hugh followed her and they stood shoulder to shoulder.

"It's really coming down out there," he said. "I can barely make out the shed."

She strained toward the window. The snow would be drifting into the shed. She needed to shut the door to keep the wood dry. Doing so would shut the pup inside. The poor thing must be freezing. Her nerves twitched and she turned to serve breakfast but before she sat down, she went to the window again. The storm was getting worse.

"Girl, sit down," Grandfather said. "You've seen lots of Montana storms. You know the only thing you can do is hunker down and wait them out."

She sat but her insides jumped. That poor little animal would be shivering.

Aware that her nervous behavior had Hugh watching her, she forced herself to sit quietly throughout the meal. Afterward, she cleaned up from breakfast and prepared a pot of soup to simmer throughout the morning.

"There's nothing like the smell of soup to make us feel warm and cozy inside."

Hugh came to her side at the stove and whispered, "What's bothering you?"

"I hope my family are all safe." Let him think that's what concerned her.

"Like your grandfather said, they are familiar with Montana weather. I venture to say they knew enough to find shelter."

She nodded. It was true.

"How do you want to spend the day?" he asked.

She should be rejoicing that he had asked, wanted her to be part of his activity. However, she couldn't relax.

"There's something I have to do." She shoved her feet into warm boots, shrugged into Logan's warm coat and grabbed the door handle.

Hugh couldn't believe she meant to go into the storm. Was it something he said? Perhaps she didn't care to do something with him. But still. It wasn't necessary to run into the jaws of a storm. She could simply say no thanks. "You can't go out in that," he protested but she ignored him and rushed out into the storm. "What pray tell?" he asked of no one in particular.

"She's got some kind of bee in her bonnet," Grandfather said. "I learned long ago to stand back and let her go when she's like that."

Shouldn't that make him remember how unsuitable she was? The words skimmed over his brain without finding a resting place. All that mattered was making sure she was safe and he grabbed his coat.

"Now wait a minute," Grandfather protested. "Don't see any sense in both of you being out in the storm. You've got to trust that she knows what she's doing."

He stood at the door undecided what he should do. Seeing the tension in Evan's shoulders, he returned his coat to the hook and went to peer through the window. Saw the dark shape that was Annie leave the wood-shed and hurry toward the house.

He threw open the door to let her in.

She stood before him, a wriggly brown-and-white dog in her arms. "I couldn't leave him out in the cold." Her eyes begged for understanding.

The pup licked her then squirmed about trying to reach Hugh and give him a sloppy kiss. He patted the dog on the head. "He's just a pup." A mixed breed about half-grown. He'd be medium-sized when he grew up. Right now he was very dirty and smelly.

Annie waited.

He wondered what she would do if he said the pup couldn't be indoors. He had no intention of doing so especially with her blue eyes beseeching him. "Put him down. Let him explore his new home."

"Thank you." She fairly beamed at him, making him feel eight feet tall and able to fell massive trees with one blow of an axe.

She released the pup and he sniffed about her feet and then about Hugh's then raced across the floor, paused by Grandfather's chair to get a pat on the head. He noticed Evan in the corner and bounded toward him.

Hugh heard Annie suck in air. His own lungs froze. What would Evan do?

The pup stopped and gave Evan a sloppy kiss then frolicked about the boy.

Evan grabbed the pup, buried his face in the fur and laughed.

"Well, I'll be," Hugh said, unashamed at how husky his voice had grown.

Annie squeezed his arm. "Praise God. I wasn't sure he knew how to use his voice."

Evan and the pup tumbled over in a tangle of limbs.

Hugh patted Annie's hand where it lay on his arm. "It appears that God has sent an answer to prayer in the form of a rambunctious puppy." Without Annie's "unsuitability" this pup would not be here. The acknowledgement kicked out every support he felt he had. He was grateful beyond words but he could not silence the warning voice in the back of his head reminding him of how unsuitable she would find him once she got to know him better. For now, with her hand warm beneath his palm he refused to let such concerns rob him of the moment.

The storm continued outside, the storm threatened in his head but they did not keep him from the joy of watching Evan and the pup playing together.

"What are we going to name him?" he asked Evan then shifted his gaze to the woman at his side.

"How about Stormy? Seeing as he came in during a storm." She smiled at him, her eyes twinkling, making him forget everything else. "Or we could call him Happy because of what he's doing for Evan."

Hugh couldn't think beyond the feeling between him and Annie.

"Let's see what Evan wants." She pulled her hand away, leaving a cold spot on his arm and a barren spot in his heart. She knelt in front of the dog and the boy and ruffled the puppy's fur. "He sure is soft, though I think he needs a bath. Just like you."

Evan studied the dirty dog then looked at himself and nodded.

"Would you like me to heat water for a bath? You could bathe and then help me bathe the pup."

Evan eyed her warily.

Hugh watched the trio. Would she succeed in getting his little son to have a bath? Somehow he felt she would. She'd already accomplished so much with him.

"Let's do that before lunch," she said as if Evan had agreed. "Now about a name. Which do you like better? Stormy or Happy?"

Hugh definitely liked the latter better but it was up to Evan. Longing to be part of this exchange, he knelt beside Annie. "Son, this dog is yours. You can choose the name. You'll also have to help take care of him. He'll need to be fed and bathed. And we must keep water down for him. I'll help you with that but first let's name him."

Evan met Hugh's gaze. At the look of trust in the child's eyes, Hugh vowed yet again that he would do everything in his power to be what the boy needed.

Even marrying someone Hugh thought unsuitable for him but perfect for Evan? Yes, it was the only reason he sought a marriage.

"Do you want to call him Stormy?"

Evan shook his head.

"Happy?"

Evan nodded and buried his face in the puppy's fur.

"Happy it is then. Shall we get water for Happy?" He held out his hand. When Evan took it, Hugh's eyes burned with joy and gratitude. He dared not look at Annie for fear his feelings would pour out unfettered.

They went to the cupboard and filled a bowl from the pump. Hugh helped Evan put the bowl on the floor next to the stove.

The puppy drank eagerly, sloshing water in a spreading puddle. Evan squatted beside the pup, watching him drink.

Annie brought a rag to mop it up then stood at Hugh's elbow. "There is not a doubt in my mind that God sent this puppy to help Evan. Happy is the perfect name for him."

Grandfather chuckled. "At least it isn't a talking donkey."

Hugh and Annie laughed at Grandfather's reference to Balaam's donkey in the Old Testament.

Annie shifted to look directly at Hugh. "Will you help me heat water to bathe that pair?"

"You sure?" He meant did she think it was possible?

"Nothing ventured nothing gained," she said. "I'll get the washtub." She went to the pantry where the tub hung from a hook on the wall.

"I suppose there's nothing to lose," he murmured and began to pump water into a pail.

"I expect everyone in the house will feel better if they remove some of the dirt they are carrying around." Grandfather was right. Both Evan and the pup were a bit ripe. Only a week ago, Evan had fought Hugh tooth and nail simply to get him home and the same to get him to bed. Yes, the boy had come a long ways but Hugh had no desire to see him retreat to those earlier days.

Annie brought the tub out and put it on the hottest part of the stove and gave Hugh an expectant look.

"Nothing ventured, nothing gained." He knew he sounded less than enthusiastic. Nevertheless, he poured water into the tub. Several times he filled the pail and added it to the contents.

"That's good," Annie said. "Now we wait for the water to heat. In the meantime…" She hurried from the room. Her footsteps receded down the hallway. Evan was too preoccupied to notice her absence but Hugh felt as if the life had been sucked from the room.

She rushed back in, holding out the new shirt and overalls she had purchased for Evan and hung them over the nearby chair.

Grandfather, normally half-asleep, sat up watching the proceedings. "I wouldn't miss this for the world," he chortled, glancing at Evan who finally noticed Annie's activities and sat back, a guarded look on his face.

"Grandfather, don't be giving him any ideas." Annie turned to Evan. "Your puppy needs a bath if he's going to be inside. I don't think he's ever had a bath so he might be a little afraid. Maybe you can show him how it's done."

Evan looked at Annie for several tense seconds then shifted his attention to Happy. The puppy's coat was soiled in many places. Evan touched them to point it out. Looked deep into Happy's eyes as if they spoke silently to each other. He looked back at Annie, a look of deep resignation.

Hugh chuckled. "I get the feeling he figures you're going to get him into the tub whether or not he wants it."

Annie tried to look as if the idea annoyed her but

her eyes gave away her amusement. "The kid is pretty smart, isn't he?"

Evan watched and listened and at her praise looked rather pleased with himself.

Annie looked about. "Let's start a fire in the fireplace and put the tub there. It will be nice and cozy."

Hugh nodded and headed for the living room where he soon had a fire blazing. Annie stood beside him as he faced the flames. Rather appropriate words, he decided, both for the room and for his life.

"I'm going to check the water." Annie turned back to the kitchen and Hugh followed her. She tested the water. "It's just right. Help me carry it into the other room."

Grandfather poured himself another cup of coffee and sat at the table where he could see the goings-on in the living room.

Hugh and Annie carried the tub through and parked it in front of the fireplace. Towels and hard yellow soap were waiting nearby. She must have brought them out at the same time as she got Evan's clothes. She rubbed her hands together.

"It's time." Her expression grew determined and she marched back to the kitchen. "Evan, are you ready?" She held out her hand to the boy.

Evan studied her and then gave a long sigh and pushed to his feet. He took Annie's hand and went with her to the other room.

Happy tumbled after them, tripping Evan in the doorway.

Hugh brought up the rear, his insides as tumbling as the puppy. This could go so very badly.

Evan stopped at the tub and stared at the water.

"You'll have to take off your clothes," Annie said. "Do you want me to help?"

Evan shook his head.

"Fine, you do it." She gave Hugh a trembling glance and he understood she was as nervous as he about how this would turn out.

Slowly Evan unbuttoned his shirt and pants, struggling often with the buttons but Annie didn't offer to help.

Nor did Hugh. The boy needed to set his own pace.

Evan was down to his undergarments. He stopped. A shudder crossed his shoulders and rippled down his body.

Annie waited.

Hugh stood motionless, uncertain what to do.

Happy lapped water from the tub.

Evan laughed and the tension in the room eased considerably.

"Do you need help?" Annie asked.

Evan turned toward her and let her peel the garment from him. It was so heavily soiled he wondered if it could even be cleaned.

Annie held it at arm's length and dropped it near the fireplace. "I'll burn it later," she murmured for Hugh's ears alone.

Evan stood shivering though the room was not cold.

"In you go." Annie held out a hand and helped Evan step into the water. "Sit down. The water is nice and warm."

Evan looked like he couldn't bend.

"You need to show Happy how to have a bath."

Evan nodded and sat down.

His head cocked to one side, Happy watched over the rim.

Annie knelt beside the tub, the bar of soap in her hands. She turned to Hugh. "You can soap him up."

"Me?" He'd thought he'd watch the proceedings from a safe distance.

Somehow, he knew to kneel beside Annie and together scrub the soil off his little son would take him further into dangerous territory.

How could he refuse the opportunity to share this joy?

Chapter Ten

Annie saw Hugh's hesitation. They would be arm to arm, shoulder to shoulder in this task. Did he object to that? No reason he should. After all, they lived in the same house. Took care of the same boy. And would be married in about three weeks. Her cheeks burned and it wasn't from the heat of the nearby fire.

Hugh rubbed his hands on his thighs and then knelt beside Annie. "What do you want me to do?"

I want you to say you'll marry me. I want a marriage based on security not love. Love offers only the fear of loss. "Soap him up and scrub him clean." She handed him the bar of soap.

"Okay, little man, it's time to get rid of that dirt." Hugh sounded strong and in control but she guessed from the way he hesitated that he wasn't.

Evan looked uncertain and shivered. He closed his eyes as Hugh began to wash him. His expression softened.

Annie nudged Hugh's arm and nodded toward the boy. She leaned close to whisper in his ear. "I think he likes it."

The flames crackled and flared. Happy flopped down before the warmth of the fire and fell asleep.

Hugh washed the soap off. "His hair needs washing."

Evan tried to scramble to his feet, the noise bringing Happy to the side of the tub.

"Whoa, there." Hugh steadied the boy. "You don't want to frighten Happy, do you? I'll hold you with your head back and Annie will wash your hair."

Annie nodded agreement at Hugh's questioning glance.

"You'll like it. I know you will," Hugh said.

Evan stared into the eyes of his father, searching for assurance.

Annie knew the moment he found it. He shuddered, his shoulders settled back to their normal position and he nodded.

While Hugh held his son steady, Annie soaped and scrubbed Evan's hair, shocked at the amount of dirty water that ran off his head. She soaped and scrubbed it again and once more until she was satisfied no more dirt remained. She grabbed a towel and rubbed his hair dry.

Hugh lifted him from the water and wrapped a towel about him, shifting around to face the fire as he dried the boy.

Happy watched with his head tipped to one side and then the other.

Annie chuckled. "Look at him, Evan. He wants to know if it's still you."

Evan touched Happy's head and the puppy squirmed with pleasure.

Hugh reached for the boy's clothing.

Annie caught his hand. "Maybe a towel about his waist until he bathes the dog."

He grinned. "You're thinking there might be lots of splashing water?"

"Something like that." Their gazes held. His smile faded and all that remained was a serious study. What did he see? What did he want to see? Why did it feel like he flipped open locks on secret thoughts and hidden wishes? She did not want him to see her inner fears. And yet she did. Perhaps hoping and dreaming that his look, a word or touch from him might heal the wounded areas of her heart.

Happy raced around the tub and tumbled into Annie, jerking her back to the task at hand. She caught the puppy and shifted him to Evan. "Do you want to put him in the bath?"

Evan nodded and Hugh unobtrusively helped lift the puppy into the water.

Happy whined and tried to claw his way out of the tub. Evan leaned over and patted the puppy's head and earned himself a wet lick.

While Hugh held the pup and the boy, Annie quickly lathered up the dog. Happy squirmed and sloshed water over the edge of the tub, soaking Annie's skirts.

Evan looked worried. As if he expected her to be cross. She laughed. "It's only water."

Reassured, he turned back to the puppy, patting his head and making soothing noises.

Annie scrubbed Happy clean, rinsing the soap out well. "Done." She handed Hugh a towel.

"Me?"

That was all the time Happy needed to escape the

clutches of these people and he jumped from the tub, sloshing water on the floor then shook himself. Water sprayed all over Hugh, Evan and Annie.

Evan laughed and wiped his face with the towel then set to work rubbing Happy dry.

Hugh looked so shocked that Annie smiled at him. "It's just water."

He frowned. "It's cold, wet and smells doggy."

She wiped her hands and face then tossed him the towel, still grinning unrepentantly.

He dried his face, all the while studying her.

Her amusement fled at the look in his eyes. She wasn't sure what he was thinking but she had three older brothers who didn't mind tossing her into the watering trough when she teased them. Surely…she swallowed hard…after all they were indoors with a snowstorm raging outside. Just to be sure, she sidled over to the window. "I see the storm hasn't let up."

A deep-throated chuckle came from the kitchen. She'd forgotten all about Grandfather. What had he seen? Nothing. There was nothing to see and no one could read her mind and see how she foolishly wished they were outdoors and he could chase her until she let him catch her.

She faced the room again and saw why Grandfather chuckled. Evan struggled to get his overalls on but Happy held one leg in his teeth. She rescued the child and straightened the buttons on his shirt.

"I think the soup is done." She hurried to the kitchen and set out the bowls. When Hugh didn't follow, she glanced back.

He stared at the tub of water.

She closed her eyes. How could she have forgotten

that? They'd have to carry it outside and dump it unless they wanted to leave it sit until the storm ended.
That wouldn't be a good idea with a little boy and a
curious pup. Someone would sooner or later play in
it and spill it.

"I'll help you carry it outside." She grabbed her
coat and boots.

He came to get his. His arm banged into her shoulder as he slipped into his coat. He halted. "Sorry. I
hope I didn't hurt you." He touched her shoulder.

She told herself it wasn't possible for him to hurt
her. Told herself she didn't want anything from him
but nevertheless, she leaned into his touch, as a hol-
lowness she refused to admit sucked at her insides.
Drawing in strength with her deep breath, she pulled
away. "I'm fine." She wrapped a scarf around her
head and marched back to the living room to grab
one side of the tub.

He followed, his gaze never leaving her face. His
eyes were dark and bottomless so she couldn't guess
what he was thinking. Finally he broke off the stare
and grabbed the other handle and they carried the tub
through to the door.

"Evan, hold your dog so he doesn't run out into
the cold."

Evan wrapped his arms about the dog's neck.

Hugh opened the door. A blast of Arctic air raced
in on the wings of snow so harsh it stung Annie's face.
Knowing they must hurry, she and Hugh carried the
tub outside. Grandfather closed the door behind them.

"Over here," he shouted and led to the corner of
the house and took three steps away. "Here." They
tipped the water to the ground, stepping back to avoid

their feet getting wet. The tub dangled from one hand; Hugh grabbed Annie's elbow and hurried them back to the door.

Inside, he dropped the tub and looked at Annie. A slow smile spread across his face and dipped deep into her heart. "You look like a snow maiden." He pulled off his gloves and wiped his thumb across her lashes. Her pulse picked up speed.

Snow clung to his lashes and his chin and she pulled off her own mittens. "I suppose that makes you a snow man." She wiped his lashes and chin.

His smile lingered but his eyes filled with something besides amusement. Something that made her tongue cleave to the roof of her mouth and her lungs refuse to work.

His thumb still rested on her cheek, warm and possessive. His gaze dropped to her mouth. Was he thinking of kissing her?

"Did I hear something about soup?" Grandfather asked, a warning note in his voice.

Annie spun away, slipped out of her coat and boots and hurried to the stove. She should thank Grandfather for his warning but it was hard to when disappointment raged through her.

How foolish. She wasn't disappointed. She did not want to fall in love. She would not allow it to happen.

Had Rudy ever looked at her like Hugh just did? Had she ever felt with him as if she hung between reality and dreams, only a gossamer thread holding her in place? She spent an inordinate amount of time stirring the soup before she could face those at the table. When she turned, she almost dropped the pot of soup.

Evan sat at the table.

"Happy needed his mat," Hugh said, his words deep with emotion.

Annie jerked her gaze from Hugh to his son. "That was very kind of you."

Evan nodded.

Annie set the pot on the table with a thud, as her arms suddenly lost their strength. If she lived to the age of one hundred she would probably never know anything that gave her more pleasure than to see the boy at the table. *Clothed and in his right mind*, she quoted a portion of a verse. She needed no other reason for seeking this marriage than that one little boy.

Certainly not love. Neither she nor Hugh wanted the complication of it.

She knew her reasons. What were his?

Hugh stared at his bowl of soup. How had helping give a boy and a dog a bath taken him so far down the road in the wrong direction? He was at a loss to explain it. However, he must find a way to correct it. As soon as the meal was over, he pushed away from the table. "I'll be in my office."

In his office he looked at his notebook without writing a thing. He opened his Bible praying for guidance. Despite the hot stove in the corner, the room was cold. Vacant. Empty.

From the other side of the closed door came sounds of Annie laughing. Was it something Evan did? Perhaps she romped with the puppy. Or Evan did. And Hugh was missing it because of his wayward, needy heart.

He leaned back in his chair, a smile on his lips. A

puppy worked wonders in Evan. *Thank You, God. And thank you, Annie, for bringing the dog into our lives.*

She was not what he'd expected. But then he couldn't say what he had expected. All he knew for certain was she deserved better than to be trapped in a loveless marriage. And he could offer her nothing else because…

He could no longer remember the reasons and sat forward, pulled his Bible close and turned to Luke chapter nine, verse sixty-two, the verse he had chosen to follow when he began his ministry. *No man, having put his hand to the plough, and looking back, is fit for the kingdom of God.* He would not turn back on his decision to put God first and keep Him there above all else. Yes there was room for his son. Nothing and no one else.

His mind firmly made up, he stared at the verse. Should he use this for the text of his next message? However, no thoughts came to mind and he opened the book Annie had given him. The words were exactly what he needed, a prayer for God to exclude frivolous, foolish thoughts. Had his mind not gone down the wrong track? It was time to pull it back to what mattered, to the choices and decisions he had purposefully made.

He bowed his head and tried to pray but the storm raged outside, distracting him. How long would it last? As long as it did, they would be shut up together. He might as well make the best of it. Perhaps it was God's way of giving him time to spend with Evan.

And Annie?

No, not Annie though of course she would be present. He forced himself to remain in the office another hour, then, with the excuse he needed to assure himself that the others were safe, he returned to the kitchen.

Grandfather sat in his soft armchair reading a book. Annie peeled potatoes and Evan sat on the floor beside Happy. Both of them examined a knot of wood.

It seemed none of them had missed him. Not that he thought they should. Nor was he disappointed. Yet his mother's voice echoed through his head. *I don't need you. The wrong boy died.*

He shook his head, trying to drive away the painful memory.

Annie had stopped peeling potatoes and studied him. She wiped her hands on a towel and came to his side. "Are you okay?" She touched his arm, her soft voice and gentle touch going a long way to erase his mother's words.

"I'm fine." He couldn't smile. Not yet. It always took a few minutes for the pain to subside after he'd remembered how little his mother valued him.

"Come. Sit down and have coffee and cookies." She led him to the table and he let her. Welcomed her guiding hand. If only he could trust her kindness to be permanent. But he feared the day she would realize he wasn't what she wanted or needed. That she'd made a mistake in wanting to marry him.

By the time she placed a cup of coffee and a plate of cookies before him, he had his feelings firmly under control.

Evan slipped to the chair kitty-corner from Hugh and eyed the cookies. "You may have two," Hugh said.

Evan took one then looked to Hugh for direction.

"One more."

Evan took it and sat eating carefully. Hugh couldn't say if it was because he feared incurring wrath if he made a mess or if it was because he was unfamiliar with eating at the table.

Hugh looked at Annie, the questions unspoken but shared.

Evan finished and slipped down. The pup raced into the living room and Evan followed at a much slower pace.

Annie took Evan's place. "I sometimes wonder what he's been through but then I'm glad I don't know. It's easier to deal with what we see than to try and undo the past."

Grandfather finished his coffee and pushed the cup aside. "God returned him to you. I gotta believe He sent Happy to help the boy heal. Seems to me the best thing you two can do is love him and you're doing a fine job of that." He looked from Annie to Hugh and Hugh knew he wasn't mistaking the look of warning in the old man's eyes. He recalled something Grandfather had said. Sometimes Annie got a bee in her bonnet and he stood by and waited for her to get it out of her system. Was that what he hoped would happen here?

Hugh expected it so he'd be okay. He knew he would. He had to be. How would Evan react?

The storm continued unabated the rest of the day and still raged as night fell.

Evan took Hugh's hand and the boy went to bed without a fuss. Happy followed them and curled up alongside the boy. Hugh watched them. Then realized Annie stood in the doorway.

He took her arm and they tiptoed down the hall. "God is good to me even when I don't deserve it."

She chuckled. "I guess none of us ever deserves it."

Grandfather had gone to bed and Hugh and Annie settled on the couch in front of the fire. Hugh wasn't wanting to go to sleep just yet and it seemed Annie wasn't either.

"It's good to see Evan doing so well," he said. "I was afraid I'd fail to help him though I suppose I did so when I let his mother leave." He hadn't meant to mention Bernice. What point was there in letting Annie know how badly he'd failed? Except perhaps to make her understand why she should run from marrying him.

She shifted to look directly at him. "You let her go? Why wouldn't you stop her?"

"Let is the wrong word. I came home one day and she was gone."

"Did you try to find her before you came here?"

He might as well tell her the whole story. That way she'd understand why he was not the man for her. "I admit I licked my wounds for a few days, believing she would come back." He let the truth come through in his own mind. "I suppose I knew from the first that she wouldn't. I had failed to live up to her expectations. Just as I have always failed."

She studied him silently for a moment. He could not look at her but stared at the flames as they twisted and turned…much like his thoughts did.

"What do you mean, you have always failed? Are you saying Bernice wasn't the first time you felt this way?"

He watched her reaction out of the corner of his

eye. "I had a brother. Kenny. He was five years older than me and I suppose he was like a father to me seeing as our pa was gone. Seems he preferred hunting and wandering to taking care of his family. It was Kenny who taught me to ride, to braid a rope, to fix things around the place. It was Kenny who taught me how to play games." He stopped as memories of Kenny washed over him. "A boy couldn't have asked for a better brother." He didn't know if he had reached out for Annie's hand or if she had reached for his but he was grateful for the comfort her grasp offered.

He drew in a steadying breath so he could go on. "Then came the winter I was eleven. Kenny went to town and I had stayed home to tend the fires. Ma would often forget to and we'd come home to an icy house. Kenny said it was too cold to leave her without heat."

His throat tightened so he had to stop a moment. "Kenny never came back." He would not let the wail clawing at his teeth escape and forced himself to speak slowly and calmly. "The preacher brought us news he had slipped on the ice and fallen under the wheels of a loaded wagon. He didn't suffer, the preacher said by way of comfort. I tried to talk to Ma but she acted like she didn't hear me. We buried him in town next to the church. To this day I find funerals hard…to hear the sound of the dirt peppering onto the coffin—" He shuddered.

Annie edged closer and rubbed his arm.

He closed his mind to everything but the story he must tell. She had to know what sort of man he really was. "I tried to take Kenny's place. About two months after Kenny's death, Ma fixed supper. I was so grateful for this return to normal. I told her I would do my best to look after things like Kenny had. She put the big spoon down with a thunk. *Boy, don't you ever think you can take Kenny's place. You don't hold a candle to him. You'll never be good enough.* She marched from the kitchen and left me alone."

He did his best to still the shudder those words still had the power to trigger.

"After that day she never again sat at the table with me, and got out of bed less and less."

The pain inside was too great to hold and he sprang to his feet and moved closer to the fireplace to stare at the licking, leaping flames, wishing they would consume the clawing memory.

When he could continue without his voice breaking, he did so. "Pa returned once, learned that Kenny had died. Saw Ma huddled in her bed. He said, *Well, that's that,* and left the next morning. Didn't even say goodbye or ask if I needed anything. Ma died a few weeks later. I was too young to be left alone, the preacher said and he took me home with him." This part of his tale contained less pain and he hurried on. "He and his wife treated me good. Preacher was kind and often read to me from the Bible and explained verses to me. He made such a difference in my life I knew I wanted to follow in his footsteps. And so here I am today."

Annie rose and stood beside him, also staring into the flames.

What was she thinking? Did she see him for the failure he was? Did she see how much the admission…the acknowledgement…burned at his insides? Would she now realize why she shouldn't marry him?

She confronted him, her face turned up to his. So close he could see the flames dancing in her eyes, see the tiny white lines at the corners of her mouth. Feel the promise of her personality.

"Hugh Arness, why would you believe such awful things about yourself? Don't you know that you are 'fearfully and wonderfully made'? That God does not make mistakes?"

He swallowed hard at her challenging look. "God's creation was perfect until sin entered. Now it's flawed. People bear a marred image."

"That's so. Yet it seems to me you are more willing to believe what your mother says about you than what God says."

"I am?" The idea both surprised him and startled him. He saw the flicker of truth in her words. "Are you saying my mother was wrong?"

She chuckled. "You know she was."

"How do I know?" He searched her gaze for more of those cleansing words.

"Because you know what the Bible says."

"Well," he said with some modesty, "not everything. In fact, I'm not sure what you're referring to."

"How about the verse in Second Corinthians that says, 'Therefore if any man be in Christ, he is a new creature: old things are passed away; behold, all things are become new.' Or 'For as he thinketh in his heart, so is he.' Aren't you thinking your mother was right when you know God doesn't agree with her?"

He wanted to argue, to say he didn't doubt God but neither did he disbelieve his mother. Her gaze was so tender, so giving, so believing, he couldn't pull the words from himself.

"Do you want Evan to believe that the way he was treated before you found him is the way he deserved to be treated?"

"Never." The word exploded from him.

"Nor does the way your mother treated you and talked to you mean it's who you are or how you should be treated." She pressed gentle fingers to his cheek. Her gaze poured into him until he felt as if some healing balm had been applied to his insides.

"You make me want to believe."

"Then choose to do so."

He caught her chin between his thumb and forefinger. Her skin was soft and warm as summer air. His heart overflowed with pleasure at her encouragement. And to think he thought her unsuitable. "You make me want to kiss you." And before he could think better of it, he lowered his head to her tipped-up face and caught her lips in the gentlest of kisses. He lingered for a long, forgetful moment, mesmerized by the warmth of her lips. Her hands clung to his arms, accepting and giving.

A log in the fireplace fell to the grate with a noisy explosion of sparks.

He jerked back. Or was she the one to move away? They stood a foot apart staring at each other. Her eyes were wide with shock. Remorse and a hundred accusing thoughts filled him.

"I'm sorry. I shouldn't have done that." He scrubbed at his hair. "I only meant to be grateful." It had started out as gratitude but shifted rather sharply to something else. Something he couldn't even identify. A feeling so intense it felt like he'd stepped too close to the fire. Those feelings lingered still though he tried to drown them in apology. "Forgive me." He should promise it would never happen again but was it a promise he could keep? Unless he could be certain of doing so, he wouldn't give it.

She shifted her gaze to the fire, leaving him feeling cold and empty. "No need to apologize. After all, if we're to be married, I expect we'll have to practice kissing."

Her airy words sucked at his insides. She spoke of marriage as if it would happen. He knew he should remind her he had almost three weeks to find someone more suitable though the days were slipping by so fast.

He had to find someone else. Someone less appealing.

Less threatening to his peace of mind.

Not so given to pointing out the flaws in his thinking.

Was that what he really wanted? He could not answer the question honestly. Instead he made preparations to go to bed, waiting only until Annie went to her own room and closed the door behind her to go to his room.

If only he could close the door to his errant thoughts as firmly.

Chapter Eleven

It took Annie a long time to fall asleep. She couldn't
say who had initiated the kiss but it didn't matter.
She had kissed him. And he had kissed her. It wasn't
her first kiss. She and Rudy had kissed a time or
two but it was nothing like this. It seemed her heart
would explode with warmth and longing. With joy and
hope. And when she'd reminded him of his promise
to marry her in three weeks, he hadn't added *unless
he could find someone more suitable*. Maybe he had
seen that she was perfectly suitable.

Suitable? What an empty word. And yet wouldn't
Hugh have rejoiced if his mother had found him at
all suitable? The poor man to have his own mother
treat him so poorly.

Perhaps God had sent her here for Hugh's sake as
much as for Evan's.

She could live with being suitable if it helped
Hugh. And if it made her needed so badly that he
would never consider anyone else.

It would provide the security she craved without
the risk of loving. She ignored the twist in the bot-

tom of her heart. The protest that it was too late. She closed the door firmly to such thoughts and returned to the idea of being suitable.

There was one more way she could prove herself invaluable and she'd broach the subject with Hugh in the morning.

The room was icy cold when she wakened and she dashed to the kitchen to start a fire in the stove. She tried to see out the window but snow crusted the outside. The wind tore at the eaves and howled around the corners. The sound made her shiver every bit as much as did the cold.

Hugh hurried into the room and held his hands out to the warmth of the stove. "I peeked out the door. I still can't see past the corner of the house. I wonder how long this will last."

Grandfather hobbled into the room. "Another day according to my bones. Maybe longer. Sure glad to be indoors where it's nice and warm." He eyed the coffeepot which had not boiled yet. "I recall a time I was outside in weather like this…" He launched into a story that Annie had heard before but Hugh hadn't and he listened with interest as Grandfather told of being caught out in a storm and how he'd fashioned a shelter out of bushes and survived. "Could've died. Sure thought I was going to but the good Lord saw fit to spare me. That coffee ready yet?"

It was and Annie poured him a cup and set it on the table. She did the same for Hugh.

Hugh met her gaze, his eyes searching hers. She gave a slight lift of her shoulders. If he thought she'd be thinking about last night's kiss he needn't worry. She had other things to consider.

Grandfather harrumphed. "God has left me here to make sure my family live good, God-honoring lives and conduct themselves appropriately."

Annie hurried back to the stove lest Grandfather see the heat rushing to her cheeks. Not that she'd done anything wrong.

Except let her heart go beyond the boundaries she had set for it. That must not happen again. Despite her mental warning, she recalled that kiss and how something inside her had burst free.

She shook her head. Her imagination was running away with her.

Evan and Happy hurried into the room. Evan stopped by the stove to get warm.

"Good morning, Evan. Did you have a good sleep?"

He eyed her a moment then nodded. Happy had circled the room and returned to Evan's side. He watched Evan and then sprang up and down on his back legs and barked.

Evan startled and then laughed.

Annie chuckled and turned to meet Hugh's eyes, intending to share joy over the child. Instead, she got lost in the warmth of his gaze. There might have been just the two of them for all she knew. Was he thinking of last night? Or was he simply grateful for Evan's progress and sharing his joy with her?

She jerked back to the stove. It was the latter. No reason to think otherwise.

She made breakfast and served it.

Evan slowly came to his chair. Spot the stuffed

dog was on it and he picked up the toy and took it to his mat, sitting it up.

Annie's throat tightened. The boy had clearly changed places with the pretend dog who thought he was a boy.

As Grandfather asked the blessing, gratitude welled up inside her. There were so many things to be thankful for—a warm house and a little boy who was doing better; a puppy who helped Evan. For Grandfather. And for Hugh. Her thoughts stalled there. She could not think, would not admit that her world tipped sideways at his name.

"Amen," Grandfather said. "Nothing like a hot breakfast to make a man forget about the weather outside." He ate with enjoyment.

Annie watched Evan. She'd noticed before how carefully he ate and he did the same this morning as he struggled to use a fork.

Her insides ached at the neglect and abuse this child had endured. She shifted her gaze to Hugh. Saw a reflection of her pain and something more. The best way she could describe it was to say it made her feel like he saw a shared future with them both dedicated to making life good for Evan.

Making life good. The idea held great appeal. However, it wasn't security that accompanied that thought. It was happiness and belonging.

She jerked her attention to her food and her mind to her plans for the day.

As soon as the meal had been cleaned up, she sat back at the table where Hugh remained. Grandfather had gone to his soft chair and Evan played on the mat with Spot and Happy.

"It's not long until Christmas," she said.

"I know. The children at Sunday school are already learning parts for the concert."

"Let's talk about what we'll do for Christmas."

Hugh sat up straight, looking confused. "Isn't the Christmas concert enough? I understand oranges and small gifts are distributed to the children."

"I don't mean how the church will celebrate. I mean how we, as a family, will." She watched as the implications of what she said sank in.

He rocked his head back and forth, clearly confused.

She pressed on. "What did your family do to make it special?"

His eyes darkened and he looked past her. "My ma didn't celebrate anything after Kenny died."

She guessed as much. "What about before? Surely Christmas meant more than another day."

A smile tugged at his mouth. "I remember one year when I was maybe nine or ten. Kenny announced to Ma that it was Christmas and we should do something special. She said to do whatever he wanted. He told me to put on my outer clothes and he grabbed the axe. I remember thinking he was so big and brave with the axe over his shoulder. We marched down the road to the nearby river.

"*We need a Christmas tree*, Kenny said. *Not too big but something nice and green to remind us that Jesus came to give us new life.*

"*Will Mama be happy?* I asked.

"Kenny squatted down to face me and patted my shoulder. *Hugh, Mama isn't happy very often. That's just the way it is.*"

Annie wondered if Hugh realized he put his hand on his shoulder as if recalling how his brother had touched him.

"We found a tree." Hugh smiled. "Kenny insisted we look at it from every angle and made a great deal out of pointing out how perfect it was. He told me to stand back while he chopped it down and then together we dragged it home and set it in a pail of sand in the corner of the living room. Kenny produced some bits of yarn—" Hugh grew thoughtful. "He must have gathered it up for weeks. He showed me how to tie it into bows and we hung them on the tree." He smiled and then chuckled. "I expect it looked pretty crude but we were happy with it."

Annie pictured two young boys doing their best to make the season special. She saw love and tenderness in every action.

"Kenny helped me make a star out of brown paper and tied it to the top of the tree. Kenny opened the big family Bible and found the Christmas story and read it. He wasn't a good reader but I didn't know and if I had, I wouldn't have cared. All that counted was this feeling of sharing something special with my brother. I felt like I mattered to him. Ma patted Kenny's head and said, *You are such a dear boy.*"

His voice grew husky. "She never said anything to me but Kenny squeezed my shoulder and said I was a dear boy too. Then he gave me a present wrapped in a bit of cloth."

Hugh again got that faraway look in his eyes and Annie knew he had gone back in his memories to that day.

"It was a wooden whistle he had carved. Best gift

I ever got." He grew quiet, thoughtful. "Best Christmas I ever had."

Annie realized that it was likely the last Christmas Kenny had been alive. Hugh had lost so much when he lost his brother. She decided right then and there she would make this Christmas one to rival that one. Both Evan and Hugh would have memories of this year that would stay with them the rest of their lives.

"Nothing special about your Christmases with the Stewarts?"

"They were older and thought a quiet time of reading and a new shirt were enough."

She chuckled, hoping to draw him away from the darkness that filled his eyes. "Surely different than a Marshall Christmas. Ours have always been full of fun and activity."

She was rewarded by the flare of interest in his eyes. A glance at Evan and she knew he listened to every word.

"What is a Marshall Christmas like?" Hugh asked.

"When Ma was alive she always found something special for each of us. I remember the year she bought me a hairbrush and hand mirror set with English roses painted on the back." She still had them and cherished them.

"Go on."

"We have a special breakfast—everyone's favorites. Then Pa and the boys do chores. When they come in, we open presents." She grinned. "It's very noisy. We play games and then have a big dinner in the middle of the afternoon."

"Sure is different than mine, isn't it?"

"I think we both have special memories and I think

we should combine them to make our first Christmas memorable." She held her breath hoping he wouldn't point out that he might find someone else before then.

He looked to Evan. He couldn't possibly miss the eagerness in the boy's eyes. He turned back to Annie. "That sounds like a wonderful plan. You'll have to tell me what to do though."

"We'll all work together." Her mind whirled with what they could do. She thought of how Kenny had read Hugh the Christmas story. They could make figures to illustrate that. "We can start today if you like."

"It's almost a month away."

"I know but think how much fun we can have for a whole month."

His expression could be best described as doubtful but Evan's was so hopeful she knew it was the right thing.

"What are we doing today?" Hugh asked.

"The Christmas story. Wait here." She hurried through the cold living room and realized the storm still blasted outside. She chose to believe that God had given them this interlude so they could grow together as a family.

She returned with paper, pencils and scissors. "Let's draw the figures of those involved in the Christmas story."

Hugh snorted. "You don't want to see my drawing."

"It's not for public viewing. It's for us. And making it is half the fun. What do you want to do? The wise men, the shepherds, sheep…?"

He stared at her. "You're not joshing?"

"Nope. I'm perfectly serious." Did he catch the referral to perfect? She wanted him to acknowledge she was perfect in her role of mother, and would be equally perfect as wife.

"Evan, why don't you come and join us? Grandfather?"

"I've got a better idea. I'll carve some animals. Can you find me a scrap of wood that I can carve?"

"I can do it." Hugh jumped up, just a little too eagerly in Annie's view. He found several pieces of wood and took them to Grandfather. "Can you teach me how to do it?"

Annie rolled her eyes. "So much for drawing the figures."

"This is even better. They'll last."

"There's that." She liked the idea of something they could cherish in the years to come. "Evan?"

The boy looked from his papa to Annie. While he made up his mind, she quickly sketched out the outline of a sheep. "You can color this and then I'll find some wool and you can glue it on to make a real sheep."

"A real pretend sheep?" Hugh asked.

She laughed. "I'll glue the figure to a piece of wood so it will last."

Evan climbed to his chair and took the colored crayon she handed him. The set had been a gift from Annie's mother two years before her death and although Annie cherished them she couldn't think of a way she would sooner see them used than in Evan's little hands. He held the crayon awkwardly. She wrapped her hand about his and showed him how to make blue marks on the paper. It didn't matter if he scribbled. As she'd said, she would later cut out the sheep and glue it to wood.

The tip of Evan's tongue poked out the corner of his mouth as he concentrated on his task.

She drew three more sheep then turned to see what Grandfather and Hugh were doing. Grandfather had the rough shape of a camel. Hugh might have been making the same animal but it was hard to tell.

He glanced up and saw her watching. "It's harder than it looks."

She knew her eyes revealed her amusement and hoped he wouldn't be offended. She knew he wasn't when he chuckled and turned the bit of wood round and round.

"I can't tell which is up or down."

They both laughed; their gazes caught and held and she couldn't remember what she meant to be doing.

Grandfather touched Hugh's hands. "If you whittle away a bit here and here..." Hugh blinked and looked at what Grandfather showed him.

Throughout the day they continued work on the animals, pausing for soup at dinnertime. Evan colored a bit after the meal and then wandered off to play with Happy but always returned to see what Annie was doing.

She'd decided to make human figures of those in the Christmas story out of fabric and sticks. She didn't rush the project. It was too pleasant to be working together on something, anticipating the pride and joy of the finished product. As they worked, they talked. Grandfather always had lots of stories and they seemed to draw out Hugh who shared stories of his early days when he'd first begun his ministry.

"I remember getting lost on a hot summer day when I had set out to visit a family with a dying grandfather. I had run out of water. Could see no rescue, no help, nothing to direct me."

She held her breath. Obviously he'd survived but still it frightened her to think of his situation.

Grandfather's hands had grown still as he listened to Hugh. "How'd you find your way out?"

"I took shelter under a lone tree and sat down to think and pray. I was pretty discouraged. Things had not been going well for me." He shrugged. "I suppose you could say I was a little like Elijah sitting under the juniper tree waiting to die."

Annie knew the story. How the prophet had been fleeing for his life and begged to die. "What happened?"

He gave her a grin. "I fell asleep just like Elijah did and…" He trailed off, the gleam in his eye informing her that he meant to tease her. She remembered Elijah had been visited by an angel but didn't think Hugh would have had the same experience.

She turned back to her drawing, pretending it didn't matter.

Grandfather chuckled. "Put the poor girl out of her misery. You realize she's holding her breath, don't you?"

Annie sucked in air.

"Dusk had fallen when I woke up. I saw a campfire in the distance and rode to it. A weathered old man watched me ride up and demanded to know if I was lost. I said I was and told him where I wanted to be. He said I was ten miles off course and he would take me there in the morning." He sat back with a pleased look on his face. "Turned out he was the man I was supposed to go visit. He said reports of his fatal illness were greatly exaggerated."

Annie laughed, as much from sheer relief at Hugh's safe rescue as from amusement.

At suppertime, she gathered all the supplies into a basket. The day had passed in a pleasant glow of togetherness. This was exactly what she hoped would happen. "We'll work on it again later." She'd save it for times when they could all be together.

Hugh woke up the next morning and lay listening. When he heard the wind still battering the house and the snow pelting against the walls, he smiled. It still stormed, shutting them in. Perhaps it was wrong to be glad of a dangerous storm and he prayed that God would keep everyone safe.

Being together like this offered something he knew wouldn't have been possible under normal circumstances.

An opportunity to kiss Annie? Though it seemed not to have held much meaning for her. She hadn't even mentioned it.

Yesterday, her enthusiasm for Christmas had proven to be contagious. He wanted a Christmas to remember. And one for Evan to remember just as Hugh had one with Kenny that he would never forget.

He'd ended up with a carving that almost resembled a camel. It had only taken Grandfather a few minutes to make it believable.

Hugh lay in the cold dark, feeling rather pleased with life at the moment. He knew the feeling couldn't last. Knew he should be resisting it. But that was the thing about the storm…it made impossible dreams possible.

Doggy breath and a wet kiss startled him from his daydreams. "Happy, do you want out?"

The puppy whined.

Evan scrambled to his feet and into his clothes. Since his bath he had changed into a nightshirt at bedtime. He rushed to the little room at the end of the hall to relieve himself and Hugh hurriedly dressed and took Happy to the door to let him out. He waited with the door closed until he heard the puppy whine then let him in. Happy's icy feet clattered on the floor as he raced to the mat and sat shivering, giving Hugh accusing looks.

"Hey, it's not my fault it's storming out. But okay. I'll get the fire going." He stirred up the embers and added wood.

Annie stepped into the room, shivering. "You beat me up this morning." She usually had the fire going when he staggered to the kitchen. She quickly prepared a pot of coffee and put it on the stove.

"Thanks to Happy who wanted out. Now look at him, sitting there with big sad eyes because he blames me for turning him out in the cold."

"Poor puppy," she crooned, rubbing Happy's neck and patting his head. Happy wriggled with joy.

"Poor puppy? He has it pretty good I would say. He could be out in the woodshed."

She patted his arm. "Poor Hugh. Are you feeling sorry for yourself?"

"Of course not." Except maybe he was. Why should Happy get that kind of attention? He stared at the coffeepot, willing it to boil. Once he had a hot drink he wouldn't be jealous of an innocent puppy.

Grandfather limped into the kitchen just as the coffee boiled. Hugh poured two cups of the hot liquid and carried them to the table.

"Storm will last another day," Grandfather announced.

"Huh." Hugh didn't dare put any sort of emotion into his grunt. Another day of storm. He couldn't complain.

Annie hummed as she prepared breakfast. Evan and Happy had heads together looking at the little stuffed dog that Annie had made. He saw Evan's lips moving but the boy didn't speak. He'd never heard Evan say a word. Would he ever talk? A great sense of failure swept through him. Was it his fault, his failure that affected the boy rather than his recent conditions? He kept his eyes on the contents of his coffee though he ached to look to Annie seeking some kind of reassurance.

He drained the cup and forced his thoughts to a different direction. It struck him how both he and Evan had suffered because of the failure of their parents and he vowed he would somehow make it up to his son. Exactly how he'd do that he couldn't say but having Annie here seemed like a good start. What would he do if someone more suitable showed up on his doorstep?

He slowly filled his lungs, filling his heart with courage and strength. He would do what he must and send Annie away. She could do far better than settle for him.

His mind clear on the matter, he ate the breakfast

she set before him. Would they do more Christmas preparations today?

Annie was awfully cheerful and he wondered why. She saw his look of curiosity.

She bounced forward in her chair. "I remembered something my mother did with me when I was little. She made me dough to play with. I think I can remember how to make it. We can roll it out and cut out shapes to hang on our Christmas tree. Won't that be fun?"

For the space of two seconds, he clung to his desire to keep things businesslike between them. Then he turned to Evan. "What do you think, son, does that sound like fun?"

Evan looked hard at Hugh. He realized the boy was trying to guess how Hugh felt about it. Hugh smiled letting some of his hesitant eagerness show.

Evan smiled and nodded.

"Good," Annie said. As soon as she finished the dishes she mixed up flour and salt and water until she declared it the right consistency. They spent the rest of the morning rolling it out and cutting out star, Christmas tree and cross shapes. She poked a hole in the top of each. "So we can put a string through to hang them," she explained. She carefully arranged them on a tray and set it in the warming oven to dry.

He wondered what they would do in the afternoon. Would she continue to plan activities that kept them together? He soon had his answer.

"I'm going to make some more dough and we can make whatever we want with it. Not just stuff for Christmas."

They spent the afternoon rolling and punching and shaping the dough.

Evan had made something and looked from Annie to Hugh as if seeking approval.

"What have you made?" Annie asked.

Evan pointed to it.

Annie looked at Hugh, silently pleading for help. Something about the way she looked at him slipped between the cracks of his inner barriers and exploded like a burst of sparks from a burning log.

He couldn't tear his gaze from her warm smile and trusting eyes.

"What do you think it is, Hugh?"

His breath rushed out and he looked at Evan's creation. "I'd say it was a dog. Am I right?"

Evan nodded and gave him a pleased smile. The boy carefully carried the dough dog to the mat in the corner and placed it beside the stuffed dog.

"How'd you know it was a dog?" Annie whispered.

"It looks almost like Spot."

"It does not!" She huffed her shock.

"It does except for the ears and the eyes and the nose and the tail and the—" He laughed, pleased when she joined him. Her amusement filled her eyes and flooded his heart.

It had become harder and harder to guard his thoughts.

He sobered. He must be careful. Not only was his future peace of mind at stake, so was Evan's.

That night, Annie read a story to Evan. Hugh wondered if the boy enjoyed the sense of routine as much as he did. Hugh said prayers with the boy, feeling peace enfold them. Then he took Evan and the pup to the bedroom. They both curled up, next to each other and sighed their contentment. Knowing they were settled for the night, Hugh returned to the living room where he had built a fire.

Annie sat on the couch staring into the flames.

And waiting for him?

Of course not. She was simply enjoying the warmth of the fire.

She turned to him as he sat beside her. "Evan is doing really well, don't you think?"

"He's come a long ways." He didn't point out that he had a long ways yet to go. He was only four. He had plenty of time.

"I've been thinking of what you told me about your mother."

He stiffened at her words. Any talk or thought of her made his insides hurt.

"Correct me if I'm wrong but I get the feeling that you think you are to blame for how she treated you. As if you somehow deserved it."

He didn't correct her.

"How can you believe that?" Her voice rang with passion. "A mother is supposed to love her children. If she doesn't she must have something wrong with her. I know if I had children I would love them so fiercely I would fight a band of marauding murderers to protect them. Evan isn't my own child but I would do anything for him."

"You love him." He meant it as a fact.

She didn't deny it but looked away, a troubled expression on her face.

"You said you didn't want to love."

Her voice fell to a whisper. "I don't but sometimes

I can't help it." She gave him a look of such agony that he couldn't stop himself from putting an arm around her and drawing her to his chest.

"I'm sorry you've been hurt by love."

She shuddered and leaned into him. For a moment she didn't speak. "Everything I love is ripped from me. My mother died. My brothers married. Not that I'm not happy for them but they've moved on. My pa is off to see the ocean. And Grandfather—" The word choked from her and she couldn't go on.

"Your grandfather is getting old."

"And tired. I know. But to think of losing him…" She rocked her head back and forth, her agony apparent.

Hugh sought for words of comfort. He prayed for wisdom. It was his job as the preacher to offer up such things to those with troubled souls but this was Annie. He felt completely inadequate with her. One thing he knew though. "Annie, it's your kind, loving spirit that makes you who you are. It enables you to give those around you the care they need and deserve. You could not have reached into Evan's frightened little heart without love."

She stayed resting in his arms. He hoped she believed him, believed that love gave her the power to be who she was.

She sat up, jerked to her feet and faced him. "I can be who I need to be without opening my heart to the pain of love." Her eyes were wide with emotion.

He stood up, close enough to touch her arms, to pull her close and hold her tight but something in her stance kept him from doing so.

"Was it Rudy who hurt you so badly that love frightens you?"

"Good night." She spun away and headed down the hall in a great rush.

He stared after her.

What had the man done to her to leave such a scar?

Chapter Twelve

Annie rose the next morning, determined to go back to her initial decision to enter into a loveless marriage. She wanted nothing more than security with her heart locked firmly behind thick barriers.

She had coffee prepared when Grandfather shuffled into the kitchen.

"Storm's over," he announced.

She glanced at the window. Dawn turned the frost covering the glass to a blushing pink. She hadn't even noticed the change in the weather.

And just in time. No more being shut up together as if the rest of the world didn't exist.

Hugh, Evan and Happy hurried into the room. Happy went directly to the door and waited to be let out. He ran around snapping at the snow and yapping.

Hugh, his hand resting on Evan's shoulder, laughed. "Silly dog thinks snow is fun."

Annie watched father and son, feelings she didn't want to acknowledge tugging at her heart. Determined to keep her emotions firmly in control, she turned to the stove, stirring the scrambled eggs with more vigor than was necessary.

Hugh whistled and Happy bounced into the house, circling the room at a gallop.

Evan laughed as the pup bumped into him, knocking him to his bottom.

Annie looked at Hugh—to share enjoyment of this boy, nothing else—but at the warm, claiming look in his eyes, her heart revolted and burst free.

Claiming? She shook her head and returned to breakfast preparations. It took every ounce of her determination to push her heart back behind the barriers she'd once thought solid and impenetrable.

A few minutes later she was able to speak without any trembling in her voice. "Breakfast is ready." She served it up and sat down, keeping her head bowed as if waiting for the blessing to be asked when in truth, she didn't know if she could look at Hugh and keep her feelings under control.

Grandfather asked the blessing and for a few minutes, attention was on the food.

"I need to check on the Barrets this morning," Hugh announced. "They might have run out of wood."

He finished his breakfast, drained his coffee and pulled on his heavy outerwear. "I'll shovel a path to the woodshed and the church before I leave."

Silence followed his departure. The room seemed empty, hollow even.

She would not let herself think it might only be her heart that had that feeling and turned to Evan. "What would you like to do today?"

The boy's eyes went toward the door.

"You want to play outside?"

He nodded.

"That's a good idea. I'll take you out as soon as I have the kitchen cleaned." She washed the dishes and tossed leftovers into a pot to make soup. The delay would ensure that Hugh had left by the time they went out.

Evan was almost as excited as Happy and squirmed as she helped him put on warm clothing. Outside, the snow sparkled with shards of light in the bright, warm sunshine. The wind had pushed the snow into drifts and odd shapes.

Happy raced about and Evan did his best to keep up.

While they played, Annie took in several armloads of wood to the kitchen then restocked the supply next to the storeroom that could be accessed from indoors and had been seriously depleted during the storm.

Her task finished, she leaned against the wall of the house, enjoying the sun and watching Happy and Evan. They had tired of running about. Evan found a stick and dug at one of the snowdrifts, creating a hole.

Annie's gaze went beyond the yard. How had her family managed during the storm? Was everyone safe? Was Pa safe? Had he seen the ocean? She missed them all.

Logan and Sadie lived in town though they hoped to build a house next spring and move to the ranch. She could visit them. What would she do with Evan? She'd ask Hugh.

She heard the sound of the front door opening and closing. Had Hugh returned? She realized how long they'd been outside. "Evan, Happy, come along. It's time to go in."

Evan carefully stuck his stick into the snowbank and then he and the pup followed her inside.

Happy flopped on the mat in the corner for a nap.

Annie looked about. "I thought I heard someone at the front door."

"It was Hugh," Grandfather said. "He's in his office."

"Oh, I wonder how the Barrets are." She helped Evan take off his coat, his woolen outer pants and boots. Along with his snow-crusted mittens, she hung everything behind the stove to dry. The smell of wet wool soon filled the air and water dripped to the floor as the snow melted from the clothing.

She spared a glance at the closed office door hoping it didn't signify bad news then stirred the soup. A glance at the clock informed her she had an hour before lunch. Time enough to make biscuits.

A little later, she went to the office door and tapped on it. "Dinner is ready."

"I'll be right there."

She waited but when she didn't hear a chair scuff or boots on the floor, she returned to the kitchen and set out the food.

Hugh slipped into the room and sat at the table.

She met his gaze, knowing hers expressed concern. "Was everything okay?"

He looked confused.

"With the Barrets?"

"They were down to their last stick of wood. Other than that, still feisty as ever. I carried in a bunch of wood for them."

"Good to hear."

"I was working on my sermon for Sunday. Here it is Friday and I don't have anything prepared. I'll be in there all afternoon if anyone is looking for me."

That meant she couldn't ask him to watch Evan. Perhaps she'd take him with her but was he ready to go out? She had no wish to push him harder than he was prepared for.

She waited until the meal was over and Hugh headed back to his office and then she hurried after him. "Do you have any objection to me taking Evan out to visit Logan and Sadie?"

"Do you think he'll be okay with that? It's only a few days ago that he was about as social as a feral cat."

"I thought it would be worth seeing how he reacts. If he doesn't do well, I'll simply bring him home."

He studied her, searching her gaze.

She couldn't guess what he looked for, didn't know if he found it, but he nodded. "I trust you to do what's best for my son."

"Thank you." And she meant more than permission to take Evan out. Trust. A far better basis for their marriage than love. Even if it did feel a little lackluster.

She returned to clean up the kitchen. As she worked, she prayed for wisdom in presenting her idea to Evan. Before she could think of what to say, a knock came to the back door.

She opened the door to Sadie with little Jeannie at her side. The girl was less than a year younger than Evan. Perhaps she would be a good playmate for him.

"I couldn't take another day shut in like that," Sadie said.

"Come on in. I was just thinking of going to visit

you but thought it might be too soon for an outing."
She tipped her head toward Evan who had backed
into the corner and stood with his hand on Happy's
head. Somehow the pup seemed to know he needed
to remain at Evan's side.

"I left the others at home," Sadie said. "They're
a bit much all at once." She smiled at Evan. "Hello,
Evan. We met before. Do you remember me? I'm Aunt
Sadie and this is Jeannie."

Annie could have hugged her sister-in-law at intro-
ducing herself as Evan's aunt. At least she took Annie's plans seriously.

Sadie turned to Grandfather. "Hello, Grandfather.
I see you survived the storm."

"We're fine," he said.

Jeannie hugged Grandfather then stood by his side,
studying Evan.

Hoping to make it possible for the two little ones
to become friends, Annie introduced Happy. "He's
Evan's dog. You may say hello to him." She meant
Evan as much as Happy.

Jeannie edged closer. "Hello, Happy. Hello, Evan."
She touched the top of the dog's head then drew her
hand back and stood as if waiting for Evan to make
the next move.

Annie tried to think how best to help them. "Evan,
why don't you show Jeannie your pretend puppy?"

Evan looked at Spot near his foot and nudged it
forward.

"Can I play with it?" Jeannie asked and waited
until Evan nodded before she picked it up.

"I like this puppy." Jeannie sat on the floor close

to Evan's mat and began to talk to the stuffed toy, telling it all about the things she and her brother and sister had done during the storm.

Annie saw the tension leave Evan's shoulders and he sat on his mat, Happy crowded close to his knee.

"They'll be okay," Sadie said, and Annie was inclined to believe her. "I see a lot of improvement since I last saw him. Was that just a week ago? Hard to believe it's only been that long. The last three days seemed to go on forever."

Annie decided not to say she'd felt quite the opposite. "Have you heard anything from the ranch? I've been wondering if everyone was safe."

"Logan was out there during the storm. He returned this morning to let me know he was okay." She twisted her wedding ring round and round. "You can't imagine how worried I was not knowing." She shuddered.

Annie squeezed Sadie's hands. "That must have been terrible." She would not think how she would have felt if Hugh had been absent during the storm. Would not let herself shiver.

"Anyway. He already went back to the ranch. Said he had to help check on the herd. Everyone safely hunkered down at the ranch for the storm. Logan said Kate did her best to keep everyone occupied but he couldn't stop worrying about me."

"I'm glad everyone is safe and sound. That's an answer to prayer."

Sadie gave Annie a piercing look. "How are you doing? And I don't mean because of the storm."

"I'm perfectly fine." If Grandfather hadn't been there listening she might have been tempted to ask

Sadie about love. No. She immediately retracted the thought. She meant she'd ask her about marriage. She could do that even with grandfather listening.

"I expect we'll be married by Christmas. It would be convenient for everyone to have this settled. It would give Evan the home and stability he needs. There's no need for Hugh to look further for someone to marry him and provide a home for his son." She knew she rattled on but she couldn't help it.

Grandfather bolted from his chair, grabbed his canes and thumped over to Annie's side. "I've no reason to object to you marrying Hugh. He's a fine man. But you both need to be honest about what you need from a marriage."

"I think we are pretty clear about it."

"You aren't being honest with yourselves." He thumped back to his chair.

Sadie studied her with knowing eyes. "What aren't you being honest about?"

Annie shook her head. "I have no idea what he means."

Grandfather harrumphed. "She's probably telling the truth. More's the pity. I never thought I'd see the day a Marshall couldn't see what was as plain as the nose on their face."

Sadie chuckled. "So that's the way it is."

Annie's cheeks burned and she turned away, preparing tea and cookies. She was pleased when Evan sat at the table with them. And grateful that the topic of her marrying Hugh had been dropped though Sadie wore a funny little grin when she looked at Grandfather.

* * *

Hugh sat with his head in the palms of his hands. He had a sermon to prepare but his thoughts wandered willfully. Annie wanted to go out. He could hardly forbid it. Was she already feeling trapped by the confines of his house, his life…him?

He heard the outside door open and close and assumed she had left until he heard talking. He strained to hear who it was and recognized Sadie's voice. Perhaps a visit from Annie's sister-in-law would make her feel less like running.

Running? Is that what he expected of her? He sat back and stared at the far wall. Annie wasn't the running type. She was the sticking type. He didn't want her to be stuck. Wasn't that what happened to his mother? And it sucked the life right out of her.

No. He did not want that for Annie. He would not like to see her spirit quenched. Which left him right back where they'd started. He needed someone older, someone with less zest for life who would be satisfied with what he had to offer…a marriage in name only.

He jerked forward. He had not made that clear to Annie. Was she expecting a real marriage even if a loveless one?

How was he to clear up that notion?

And he must. At his earliest opportunity.

Just as he must prepare a sermon to deliver in two days and he bent his head over the scriptures seeking guidance as to what he should say. *Lord, show me Your truth from Your word.* His gaze fell to the passage before him. Ephesians chapter five. *He that loveth his wife loveth himself.* The words flashed like a beacon. Did he love himself? That seemed selfish, even evil. And yet it was in God's word.

He closed his Bible. He could not preach a sermon based on this verse because he didn't believe it.

His heart twisted and turned and he called out to God for forgiveness as he acknowledged his lack of faith. God loved him. He didn't doubt that. But his mother hadn't. Nor had his wife. In his mind, had he let that make him think himself unlovable? Except for God. Could he love another human besides his son? That was a good place to start and he smiled. *Thank you, God, for the gift of my son and the love I have for him.*

And for Annie.

Those were not his thoughts. Yes, he was grateful for Annie but he didn't love her. He would not let himself.

He compelled his mind back to sermon preparation. He knew he had a reputation for delivering the truth in a forceful way but what truth could he deliver when he couldn't find it for himself?

Christmas. God sent His Son. He could speak truth from those thoughts having almost lost his son.

By the time Annie knocked to announce supper, he felt he had a sermon he could deliver.

And a truth he must make plain to Annie.

He waited until Evan was in bed and Grandfather had gone to his room then joined Annie in the living room before the fire.

She began to speak before he could. "Poor Sadie. Logan wasn't able to get home before the storm broke and she sat through it not knowing if he was safe or not. I almost feel guilty because we had such a pleasant time."

He knew he should interrupt her and tell her what marriage to him would involve but she faced him, her eyes alive with joy.

"Mama used to say that counting one's blessings was the surest way to happiness and I've been thinking of all mine." She held up her fingers and ticked them off one by one. "My family was kept safe throughout the storm. For my family, of course and especially sisters-in-law. Now I'm not the only female adult in the family. And all my nieces and nephews. There's something very special about being an aunt. I can play with the kids and tell them stories and enjoy them without the same worry."

He wanted to know if she worried about Evan but he would ask her later after she'd done counting off her blessings.

"For Grandfather's health. He seems much better today. I suppose it was the stormy weather that had him feeling poorly. Then there's Evan. He's such a sweet boy and to see him becoming more normal every day is such a joy. And Happy. He's done a lot to help Evan." She bounced about so she faced him more fully. "I have saved the best for last."

He hardly dared to breathe. Was she about to mention him as the best? His chest hurt with anticipation.

"Hugh, you'll never guess what happened."

He managed to shake his head.

"When Jeannie was here she picked up the book I read from for Evan's bedtime stories. And Evan marched to her side, took the book and said, *Mine*."

Annie beamed.

It took Hugh several seconds to take in the meaning of her words. "He spoke?"

She nodded. "He can talk." She sniffed and closed her eyes. "I'm sorry." The words were strangled. Tears dribbled down her cheeks.

He tried to think what to do. His heart, not his head, guided his actions and he pulled her to his chest. "Don't cry. Please don't cry." His throat tightened until he could hardly get his words out. "I'm thrilled to know he can talk."

"Me too." She leaned back to look up at him. "These are happy tears."

"Oh. Good." He pulled a clean handkerchief out of his pocket and gently dried her cheeks and wiped the silvery drops from her lashes.

She watched him, her eyes dark and full of promise.

His fingers trailed down her cheek and lingered on her chin. "You have made such a difference in Evan's life." He lost himself in the depths of her look. He couldn't say who made the first move but again drawn by his heart, he lowered his head and claimed her lips, tasting the sweetness of dessert and the anticipation of better things to come.

He pulled back. "Thank you." Let her decide if he meant for helping Evan or for the kiss. If she asked he wouldn't have been able to answer.

They sat side by side, his arm about her shoulders and stared into the fire. The dancing flames mesmerized him so he couldn't think.

The logs burned down. She sighed. "It's time for bed." She got to her feet. "Good night. Sleep well."

It wasn't until she had gone into her bedroom that

he realized he had neglected to say the words he'd planned.

What had he meant to tell her? He vaguely recalled but why did it seem unimportant now?

Chapter Thirteen

Annie tried to explain away another kiss. Why was she being so foolhardy? The more she cared, the more chance of being hurt. She must guard against that. Nevertheless, she rose Saturday morning with a smile on her lips. And why not? The sun was shining, the air was fresh, Evan ran about like an ordinary boy, Grandfather moved easier and Hugh—

Hugh. She could not decide what to say about Hugh so pushed the name aside. Only it didn't go away. He seemed stuck dead center in her thoughts.

It meant nothing.

With a start she realized she had pressed her fingertips to her lips. She jerked them away and hurried to the kitchen to start the day. She had much to do. Make raisin pies, prepare a roast…

Her thoughts drifted off in a different direction. Perhaps after supper she could get everyone gathered around the table to work on the figures for the Christmas story. The dough ornaments had turned out rather well. All they needed was yarn or ribbons to hang them and she meant to make that a family activity.

There were gifts to prepare. Months ago, she'd started making things for her family. The Marshall family. Now she needed to make gifts for the Arness family.

Would she be Mrs. Arness by Christmas?

The coffee sputtered and Grandfather hobbled into the room, Hugh, Evan and Happy at his heels. Annie pulled her thoughts back to the here and now, determined she would concentrate on the present moment.

She poured cups of coffee for the men, carefully avoiding meeting Hugh's eyes. She didn't know what she might see and didn't want to know. *Coward*, she scolded herself as she returned to the stove. Ma and Pa would be disappointed to know she was running from a problem. They'd raised her to confront difficult tasks and overcome her fears.

She did not like having to admit that there was one fear she refused to confront. Her fear of loss. How was she to face it when it was so threatening?

With no answer to her own question, she threw herself into the activities of the day, finding it easier to think clearly when Hugh retired to his office to work on his sermon.

What would he preach on? Would she be able to hear him?

She eyed Evan. How would he handle going out in public? One way to find out.

"I need to go to the store," she announced. She needed to purchase some fabric to make Evan a new shirt and some yarn to knit mittens for him. "Evan, would you like to come with me and pick out a candy stick?"

The boy's eyes widened with eager anticipation of the candy then realizing that she'd asked him to accompany her, he shrank back, wrapping his arms about Happy's neck.

"We won't be long." She held out his coat, hoping, praying he would agree to accompany her.

Grandfather watched, his expression encouraging. "There are a dozen different flavors of candy stick," he said. "I always wonder how I can take just one." Grandfather kept talking softly as Annie waited, giving Evan plenty of time and space to make up his mind.

Finally he rose and slipped his arms into the sleeves. She buttoned the coat and gave him a woolen hat and woolen mitts to put on as, feeling rather pleased at Evan's agreement, she hurried into her own outerwear.

They reached the door.

"Happy, stay." The pup sat back with a whine.

Evan pulled on her hand and looked at the dog.

"No, he can't go. Dogs can't go in the store and Happy isn't well enough trained yet to be left outdoors to wait. He might run into the street and get hurt." She opened the door.

Evan hung back.

"You can pick out candy sticks for your papa and for Grandfather too," she said.

He nodded, squeezing her hand as hard as his little fingers could and they went outside and began the journey to the store. Thankfully it wasn't far because Evan started to quiver within ten steps. By the time they reached the intersection of the two main streets of Bella Creek, she wondered if he'd forgotten to breathe. In an attempt to ease his fear, she told him about Kate and Isabelle coming to town with the doctor earlier in the year. She didn't explain that they had come to replace the doctor who had left after a devastating fire in Bella Creek. She went on to explain how Dawson had fallen in love with the beautiful Isabelle and then Conner had fallen in love with the practical Kate. "And Aunt Sadie was the teacher. She and Logan rescued three children and ended up falling in love and becoming parents to the children."

She stared at the schoolhouse. Logan and Sadie had been thrown together because of the children. Until then, they had little interest in each other. She wondered if she remembered correctly that they had tried to avoid each other on several social occasions prior to the arrival of the children.

Had the children been the catalyst to them falling in love? Or were their feelings ripe and ready all the time and simply needed a reason to ignore their caution and reserve?

Was looking after Evan doing the same thing for her?

She shook her head. How could she think such things? Yes, she and Hugh had kissed. Twice. She hadn't minded it one bit. Truth be told, she found it rather pleasant. That didn't mean either one of them was ready for love.

She hurried onward to the store, determined to ignore such foolishness. No one was in the store but her uncle George and he greeted them warmly. "How is Grandfather?"

"Doing better now the weather has changed. You should come and see for yourself."

"I'll do that. Now what can I do for you and this handsome young man?"

Evan shrank back. A faint whimper came from him.
Please, God, don't let this drive him back into his hard little shell. "Evan would like a candy stick for himself, Grandfather and his papa. I need three yards of that fabric." She pointed it out having seen it before. "And that yarn." While Uncle George prepared her purchases, she led Evan to the colorful array of candy jars on one end of the counter.

"Which would you like?"

His shoulders were high and tight. His expression tense.

She placed her hand gently on his shoulder, the tension beneath her palm making her want to pull him into her arms and comfort him. But he'd not let any of them do more than touch him and she didn't want to push him too hard.

"See how many flavors there are to choose from? Maybe Uncle George will have a treat for Happy as well."

At the mention of his pup, Evan's eyes focused and he looked at the candy. He pointed out a red one for him, a golden one for Grandfather and a green one for Hugh.

Knowing that he remembered the flavors she'd brought home, she could barely restrain herself from hugging him.

Uncle George brought a bone from the back and wrapped it for Evan to take home to Happy.

They took their purchases and left the store. Two ladies stood on the sidewalk as they exited.

"Good morning, Miss Marshall."

Feeling Evan stiffen and hearing his faint whimper, Annie greeted them but hurried away without stopping to visit.

At home Evan gave Grandfather his candy and Happy his bone. The pup was ecstatic and bounded back to the mat where he attacked the bone with a great deal of vigor.

When Hugh joined them for dinner, Evan handed him the candy stick.

Hugh thanked him.

She waited until after the meal to indicate Hugh should go to the living room with her.

"He went to the store with me and picked out the candy himself."

Hugh blinked. Opened his mouth and closed it again.

She grinned, enjoying his surprise. Might her success earn her another kiss? Now where had that thought come from?

"He went to the store?"

"He was very brave." She described Evan's journey and behavior. Told about the two ladies on the street. "I don't think he's up to seeing a bunch of people yet."

"I'm more than pleased with this step. Thank you." Hugh squeezed her shoulder.

Heaven help her, she couldn't keep from leaning into his palm, lifting her face and wishing—

No.

She straightened. "Well, I must get back to work as I'm sure you must as well." And she practically raced to the kitchen. Her nerves felt raw. When she heard the office door close behind him, she began to relax.

The afternoon sped by as she prepared food. About four o'clock, Hugh came from his office. She expected he wanted coffee and served him some with freshly baked ginger cookies. He ate the cookies and drank his coffee but when he finished, he didn't return to his office. Her movements grew more and more jerky as he stayed and stayed. Did he have something in mind?

"How did those doughy things we rolled and cut for tree ornaments turn out?"

She tried to think if he meant to make conversation or wanted to work on the decorations? Did it mean he wanted to spend time with her? The idea sent a spiral of longing through her before she could slam the door on such thoughts. Somehow, she managed to pull a rational question from her brain. "Are you done in your office?"

"I believe I am and thought you might like to do some more Christmas preparation."

Evan jumped up and went to his father's side. There was no mistaking the eagerness in his face.

She could hardly say no to either of them and brought the tray of ornaments from the pantry.

Hugh chuckled. "I imagined misshapen unidentifiable objects but these aren't half bad."

"Half bad?" She pretended offense. "They look very nice, don't they, Evan?"

Evan looked from one to the other.

Annie watched him. Would he recognize teasing?

Then he nodded, his eyes sparkling.

She could have hugged him. Could have hugged everyone. He was a bright boy making wonderful progress.

They spent the next hour working on the Christmas ornaments and the figures for the Christmas story. It was a pleasant time creating together as a family and achieved all Annie hoped it would.

And more. It made her want to share more special moments with Hugh and Evan. It made her long to feel a part of their future. Of course, once she and Hugh married she would be a permanent part of this family. That wasn't what she meant and she wasn't about to examine what more she wanted.

Even the thought of marriage to him no longer felt like a practical arrangement and her cheeks burned as she thought of kissing him again and having the right to do so whenever she felt like it.

Her imagination was getting out of hand.

After supper, she retreated to her room when Hugh took Evan to bed. She did not want to sit before the fire with him.

Not with her wayward thoughts.

Hugh seemed distracted the next morning, which left Annie able to keep her mind from going to unwanted areas. He had little to say over breakfast and then went to his room to change.

"What do you think about taking Evan to church this morning?" he asked when he returned.

She shook her head. "I don't know if he's ready."

"I expect you're right." He turned to Grandfather. "I'll be back to get you after the church is warmed up." He touched Evan on the head and with a quick smile for Annie, departed.

She wandered about the rooms which she had dusted thoroughly yesterday, pausing to adjust the position of a book on the living room shelf, repositioning the heavy green drapes at the front window.

As she'd worked yesterday she wondered how much changing she would be allowed to do after she became Mrs. Arness.

She hugged herself and stared out the window. Was there any reason to delay discussing making their arrangement permanent? She tried not to think of what Mrs. Shearer had said about her maiden sister coming to visit. Annie knew the woman would be totally unsuitable. After all, Mrs. Shearer was known to have a harsh, critical tongue.

Her shoulders sank. It wasn't fair to judge the poor woman by her sister's behavior.

Hugh came in and hurried to Grandfather's side. Only when he turned did he see Annie at the window. "You'll be okay?"

It pleasured her some that he cared to ask. "Yes, of course."

"I'll see you after the service then."

She nodded and watched until they were out of sight.

Evan came from the kitchen and pressed to her side. "It's just you and me." A needless observation but the place felt empty.

Evan nodded and stared out the window.

If only she could read his little mind. However, she couldn't. Sighing softly, she faced the room. What was she to do? The sound of a wagon drew her attention back to the window and she watched families arriving by wagon or buggy and cowboys riding up on their horses.

She felt very alone.

She ached to see her friends and family. To take part in the singing. To hear Hugh. She eyed Evan. If they slipped in late and left before the final benediction, would he be okay? She knelt before him. "Evan, I would like to go to church. I'd like to hear your papa preach. I know you're afraid of all those strangers but would you go if we didn't stop to talk to any of them?"

He studied her several seconds, his dark, studious gaze so reminiscent of Hugh's that she wanted to hug him. One of these days soon, she would risk it for his sake as well as hers.

He nodded.

"Wonderful. Let's get ready." She brushed his hair, smoothed her own and got them both into their coats.

Hand in hand, his grasp tight, they followed in Hugh and Grandfather's footsteps. The congregation was standing and singing when she slipped into the vestibule. A couple of people turned and smiled at her but most didn't notice their entrance. She edged into the back pew, Evan pressed to her side.

Hugh saw her. Their eyes connected over the distance but it was too far for her to be able to tell what he thought. His smile flashed and then he turned his gaze back to the others.

"Please be seated," he said. He paused and Annie held her breath, wondering why. Did he have an important, earth-shattering announcement to make? She gripped the edge of the pew with her hands.

He continued. "I struggled to know what I should talk about today," he said.

Annie realized they'd arrived at the end of the song service. Perhaps for the best. She could hear the sermon then slip away before Evan got restless. What was she thinking? The boy could sit immobile by the hour. It was not something she thought was an asset.

Hugh continued. "As you all no doubt know by now, I have found my son. Praise God for that. He is so precious to me. I will never let him go. It made me realize just a fraction of how much God gave in sending His Son to earth. And then I realized something. It was wrong to live in fear." He looked about the congregation. His gaze lit on Annie and as far as she knew there were only the two of them. "It is wrong for me to fear losing him. I need to trust God to protect him. It is wrong of me to fear making a mistake. Fear is not trust." His gaze had swept the audience and returned to her. "'Perfect love casts out fear.'"

The silence in her head thundered. Perfect love. Fear cast out. She didn't know if it was possible. Even if it was, was she prepared to trust like that?

"Let me read a passage from Jeremiah chapter seventeen. 'Blessed is the man that trusteth in the Lord, and whose hope the Lord is.'"

She realized he'd announced the final hymn and she practically dragged Evan from the church, stumbling in her haste to reach the manse. Or was it because her eyes were clouded with tears that she couldn't see the ground and find safe footing?

Why did her heart reach for something his words had promised when she couldn't even say what it was?

As they stepped into the house, she swiped at her tears and helped Evan out of his coat.

She had herself firmly in control when Grandfather returned on Dawson's arm.

"Annie," Dawson said. "We'd like you to come out to the ranch for dinner. Grandfather has already said he'd come." Dawson's voice didn't suggest invitation so much as an order.

She bristled though she would not let him see it. When would her brothers ever realize she didn't need to be looked after?

Dawson waited, his expression stubborn.

A sigh rushed up her throat and she somehow managed to keep it inside. If he'd asked nicely, she would have gladly agreed except for one thing.

She glanced at Evan.

Dawson followed her gaze. "Hugh and the boy too, of course."

"I don't know. He's not been out much yet."

She wanted to say yes. She wanted to go home, be surrounded by her large loving family. Most of all, she wanted to talk to her mother. A pain as sharp as a knife stab grabbed her stomach and she barely stilled a moan. She had no mother to turn to. Nor even a father. Yes, she could talk to any of the others but still she felt the absence of her parents.

"I'll have to ask Hugh."

Dawson nodded. "You can come with or without him." He made it sound like an ultimatum and she was about to object when someone knocked and Annie opened the door to admit Isabelle and Mattie.

"Oh I see Dawson is here," Isabelle stated. She gave him a look Annie could only describe as a warning.

Before she could say anything, Kate and Conner and baby Ellie appeared behind them. Annie stepped aside to allow them to enter then stuck her head out to look one way and then the other. "This is turning into family reunion. Where're Logan and Sadie and their crew?"

Conner barely made it into the house before he spoke. "We want you to come to the ranch for dinner. How long will it take you to get ready?"

Annie's hackles rose at the way Conner issued the order.

Conner and Dawson looked at each other in complete agreement. No doubt they had discussed this thoroughly before coming to town.

She jammed her fists on her hips. "You've got it all figured out, don't you? You decided if you all came you could talk me into doing what you wanted. Or should I say you thought you could order me to do your will." She glanced over her shoulder. "I'm guessing Logan refused to join you in bullying me."

Dawson chucked her under the chin just as he had when she was four years old.

She couldn't decide whether to laugh or scream.

Hugh stepped into the house at that moment. He studied her, saw that she faced her two brothers and his eyebrows rose. "I recall your Grandfather telling me that when she got a bee in her bonnet, he just stood back and waited for her to get past it."

Her brothers had the gall to laugh.

She scowled at her brothers, spared a narrowed-eyed look at Hugh then spun to face Grandfather. "Are you suggesting that people should simply humor me?"

He gave her a tender smile that melted every ounce of her annoyance. "Annie Bell, you are so much like your grandmother. She had lots of spit and vinegar too. It's a good thing and I would never suggest otherwise. You would not have survived these big brutes of brothers without it." Grandfather glowered at his grandsons. "Annie is doing quite well at running her life without any help from you. Now extend a nice invitation or leave."

* * *

Hugh had stepped inside in time to hear Annie standing up to her brothers. The sight of her indignation amused him. Also put him in awe of her. Like her grandfather said, a woman with spit and vinegar. And she could be his.

For how long? The warning would not be silenced.

Dawson rolled his shoulders. "Annie, Hugh and Evan, would you please come to the ranch for dinner? Both Isabelle and Kate have made a nice meal."

Annie gave each of her brothers a look of stubborn consideration before she turned to Hugh. "I won't go unless you do too."

Her deference to his wishes did something unfamiliar to his insides. Not because she was acknowledging him as head of the house—that didn't concern him overly much—but because it made him feel like he mattered. His opinion mattered. Like she valued his opinion.

"I'll take you." He'd gladly take her wherever she wanted to go so long as she wanted him to. And when she didn't?

He wouldn't answer that question. Not today.

Her gaze shifted to Evan. "We can't go unless Evan wants to go." She knelt before his son who stood at the corner of the table watching the proceedings closely. She covered his hand, where it rested on the table-top, with her own. "Evan, honey, do you want to go see where I used to live? The house that Grandfather built? Jeannie will be there as well as all the other children you've met." She paused, letting him take in all in. "You wouldn't have to play with any of them if you didn't want."

He studied her a long moment. Then he lifted his free hand and touched her cheek, a gesture so tender that Hugh's eyes stung. He could see the longing in Evan's eyes to please Annie. His son gave the slightest nod then pointed at Happy.

"I'll ask." She turned to Conner. "Can he bring his dog?"

Conner nodded. "So long as he doesn't chase the livestock."

"I'll make sure he doesn't," Hugh promised. He'd been to the Marshall Five Ranch a number of times but this would be unlike that. He'd be seeing it through Annie's eyes. Seeing Annie differently.

Annie rose. "Then we accept your gracious invitation."

Dawson and Conner looked pleased with themselves then they herded their families out the door.

Hugh realized that he watched Annie with a bemused smile and hurried for the door. "I'll go arrange a buggy."

A few minutes later he returned with the rented buggy and they were on their way. On the trip out Annie and Grandfather relayed stories of life on the ranch and Hugh was happy to sit and listen, Evan pressed between him and Annie on the front seat. Grandfather sat in the back, wrapped in warm furs.

Annie was so excited he figured the only reason she didn't jump from the buggy as soon as they rolled up in front of the house was she needed help getting down. He took her hand and guided her to the ground. She smiled up at him and time stopped. He was back at church, feeling again the rush of pleasure as she entered with Evan at her side. His words took on added meaning as he spoke to her almost exclusively, though he prayed the words would encourage each of those who listened.

Fear is not trust. Blessed is he who trusts the Lord.

Seeing her listening so raptly to his sermon, he knew he wanted her to stop fearing life and its risk and trust God for her future. It was selfish to think of himself as part of that picture. As he'd said from that very first day, she deserved better. But he could not pray she would find it.

Evan tried to scramble down and Hugh was jerked back to the present moment. He let Annie hurry by to greet her brothers and sisters-in-law and hug her nieces and nephews. He lifted Evan to the ground and set Happy beside him then assisted Grandfather to the door.

Happy followed Evan indoors, clinging to his side. Evan grasped the dog's ruff.

Annie looked at the pair then brought her gaze to Hugh. "The pup understands that Evan needs him for courage."

He nodded and smiled though he longed to express his emotions in far more appropriate ways. A hug. A kiss. A shout of joy. His son was showing progress toward becoming a normal little boy and Hugh had a beautiful young woman at his side. Could he ask for anything more?

Thankfully they were ushered into the dining room and his foolish thoughts subsided. The women went to the kitchen and the men retired to the parlor. The children played in groups.

Evan and Happy stayed close to Hugh.

"You found me another chair." Grandfather headed

for the comfortable-looking armchair near the round-bellied stove. The others found seats.

Grandfather looked around. "So how have you been managing without me?"

Dawson drew his hand down his chin. "Grandfather, the place has fallen into rack and ruin. Why Conner can't seem to tear himself away from the house and Logan spends most of his days in town." Conner groaned and Logan snorted.

Dawson continued. "The work has fallen entirely on my shoulders." He sighed rather dramatically. "It's just too much."

Conner and Logan both spoke at once. Something about Dawson's share of the work was the only part that suffered and that was mostly because he managed to find a thousand excuses for running back to his house.

Grandfather held up his hand. "In other words, things are about the same as when I left. Good to know."

The brothers laughed.

Conner pulled something from the nearby desk. "A letter from Pa." He handed it to his grandfather.

The older man opened it eagerly and read it. "So he's seen enough of the ocean and is coming home. Says he'll be here for Christmas." He sat back with a contented look on his face.

The sound of an approaching wagon drew Hugh's attention to the window but he couldn't see the road from where he sat.

"It will be the Morrisons," Dawson said. "They often join us. Carly will be pleased to see Annie."

Carly and Annie. Two wild young women. Hugh tried not to remember.

Mr. Morrison came to the parlor. "I see everybody survived the storm." He spoke with a strong Scottish accent as if he made all the sounds in the back of his mouth. Hugh found it rather musical to listen to though, at times, also hard to understand.

The ladies trooped into the dining room bearing serving dishes and called the men and children to the table.

Hugh ended up sitting with Evan between him and Annie and young Beth, who was Logan's adopted daughter, on his other side. The table was crowded with the large and rapidly expanding family and yet it didn't feel the least bit awkward to be included in the family meal.

Conner, as current resident of the house, asked Grandfather to pray.

As soon as the *amen* was spoken, the noise level grew as food was passed around the table and news was shared. Baby Ellie cried and Kate took her upstairs. She returned a few minutes later.

"The little darling is sound asleep. Sundays are hard on her." She blushed. "Sorry, Hugh. No offense but the little ones don't like to wait for their meals or their naps."

Hugh chuckled. "I expect there are many adults who feel the same." He wouldn't mention the few he noticed drowsing off during the sermon. He no longer took it personally knowing that some of these individuals worked long hard hours and the mere fact of sitting still often allowed their fatigue to take over.

After a few minutes of general discussion Logan

faced Annie across the table. "Annie, are you happy living in town?"

Hugh held his breath. Felt Evan's tension.

"I'm happy looking after Evan." She wrapped her arm about Evan.

Hugh pulled in a breath, wondering if Evan would explode but he sat quietly and Hugh eased the air from his lungs.

"And Hugh." Annie brushed his shoulder and smiled at him.

Each of her brothers looked at their wives. Hugh could feel their concern but he couldn't turn from her look of tenderness. As if she truly cared about him as a man. Evan shifted, enabling Hugh to break free of Annie's gaze to stare at his plate. He knew he shouldn't wish for the kind of caring he thought he saw. The longing was there, nevertheless.

Shortly after that they finished the meal and the women took the food and dishes to the kitchen. Hugh would have liked to eavesdrop on them as there was lots of laughing. Besides it being beneath his dignity, the men sat around the table discussing the weather and various other topics. They asked him how things were in town. He was happy to report that so far as he could tell, everyone had survived the storm. "Even the Barrets made it through."

A bit later, Annie and Carly poked their heads into the dining room. "We're headed outside. We'll be back shortly."

Grandfather and Mr. Morrison waved them away but Hugh wanted to call Annie back.

She and Carly looked at each other in a way that seemed to say they had special plans that didn't include himself or Evan. She was young and full of life. Her eyes danced with anticipation. Did she ever look so free and happy at the manse? He could not live with himself if he stole that from her. How would he manage without her? More important, how would Evan manage?

The other children had scattered to play but Evan and Happy stayed at Hugh's side. He had stopped praying for God to send a suitable woman but he needed to start again. He'd do that next time he was in his office.

By the time the girls returned, their cheeks rosy from the cold and a glow of happiness on their faces, it was time to return to town.

All the way back, Hugh tried to convince himself he needed someone else. Wanted someone else. Why was it so hard to believe it?

Chapter Fourteen

Hugh could not fall asleep. In the dark, alone hours he had to face the truth. He did not want someone to take Annie's place. She'd proven pleasant to live with. And to spend the evenings with, though he'd been careful not to avail himself of any more kisses. He'd gone so far as to hint to God that if someone else didn't show up by the end of the four-week trial period he'd be quite happy about it.

He awakened the next morning with his conscience searing him. He was acting selfishly. Thinking more of his own desires than what was best for Annie.

Still he could not bring himself to say anything to her. Could not remind her that this arrangement could be temporary. Could not even bring himself to pray for a substitute.

Instead, he hurried to his office, intending to bury himself in study.

He managed to make a few notes when a knock came to the door connecting to the living room. "Yes?"

Annie opened the door. "There's someone here to see you." Her mouth puckered.

"They came to the back door?" Usually people who wanted an audience with him came to the outer office door.

"She did." The words dripped with disapproval. "Shall I show her to your office?"

She? Then it hit him like a blow to his midsection. "Someone in response to my advertisement?"

"Indeed."

He would have done anything to remove the wounded look on her face but was this God's way of making His plan plain? "Is Grandfather here?"

"Of course."

"Fine, then show her in and leave the door open." He did not want any occasion for someone to suggest inappropriate behavior.

She spun about, marched back to the kitchen and returned with a robust-looking woman with her hair in a tight black knot. He guessed her age to be at least thirty.

Wasn't he looking for an older woman?

Annie left without saying a word. He heard the outside door slap shut and guessed she had stepped out.

He hurried to his feet. "I'm Hugh Arness."

"I'm Harriet Higgins. Miss Higgins." Did she mean to tip her nose as she talked to him? "I'm Mrs. Shearer's sister. She told me you were looking for a mature woman to run your house with a view to matrimony."

They eyed each other, taking stock. She seemed the practical sort. No nonsense about her.

"I'm prepared to take over your home but I'd like to see the place, get an idea of what you need, if you don't mind."

"Of course. Well, this is my office." He waved his arm about. The book Annie had given him lay in the center of his desk. His heart clawed at his ribcage but he moved his gaze onward. "The church is next door."

"Am I to understand you are at home much of your time?"

"I work here but I often leave to visit others." Why did he feel as if he must explain himself? "Would you care to see the rest of the house?"

"Certainly." She strode from the room and he followed. They stood in the living room. He pointed out the two hallways. "My son and I share a room down there."

"I would most certainly take a room down the other hallway. I understand any union between us would be strictly for the purposes of propriety. I want nothing else."

The poor woman's face looked about to ignite with her discomfort at even hinting at anything but a marriage in name only. It had been his intent all along but sounded cold and unfriendly coming from her mouth. He couldn't imagine wanting to stay up in the evening and kiss her before the fireplace. He pulled his gaze from the unlit fire and turned to regard the rest of the room.

"As you can see, this is the living room."

She gave it careful study. "It's adequate, I suppose."

"Come and see the kitchen and meet my son." He led the way. "This is Mr. Marshall."

Grandfather struggled to his feet and shook hands with Miss Higgins then sank back to his chair, watching the woman with frank study.

Hugh would have liked to know what the older man

thought of her. However, his opinion would hardly be unbiased.

"This is Evan." The boy stood at the far end of the room, clinging to Happy's fur. Hugh was about to tell Miss Higgins the dog's name when she spoke.

"You have a dog indoors? They are dirty animals. He'll have to go outside." She made shooing motions with her hands.

Happy pressed to Evan's side as the boy withdrew and sat on the mat he had abandoned only a few days ago.

"The boy should not be sharing the dog's bed. How disgusting."

Evan whimpered and buried his face in Happy's fur.

"What did you say the boy's name was?"

"Evan."

"Shouldn't he be required to greet me?"

"Unfortunately, he does not talk. He's had rather a rough time of things in the past."

Miss Higgins drew herself up rod straight. "I will tolerate no excuses for rudeness. Evan, stand up and say hello like a good boy."

Evan's eyes widened and he looked at Hugh. The boy might not have words but he clearly communicated his fear and accusation to Hugh.

Hugh must defend and protect his son. There were a few other things he must right as well. Such as telling the congregation they should not live in fear, when he wasn't doing it.

Annie practically ran all the way to the store. Uncle George looked up at her hurried entry. His eyes widened in alarm.

"Is something wrong with Grandfather?"

"No. He's fit as a fiddle. Is Aunt Mary upstairs?"

"Yes, child. Go tell her all your troubles." He patted her back as she rushed by him.

Aunt Mary looked up as Annie burst into the room. "Annie, what's wrong?" She put aside her sewing and started to her feet.

"Grandfather is okay."

"Then who?"

"Me. I am such an idiot." She went to the window and looked out on new building across the street—the schoolhouse, the doctor's house and office, the new barber shop and lawyer's office—all replacements for those destroyed by the fire. "I believed Hugh when he said he'd give me four weeks to prove I was suitable." She gave a mirthless laugh. "I'd be perfect I said. Now with two weeks left in our agreement, he has an older woman over there. I'm sure he'll think she's ideal." She spun from the window and walked the length and breadth of the room as she talked. "She's older. Plain. And I venture a guess that some time ago, she forgot how to smile."

"And you think that makes her ideal?"

Annie ignored the amusement in her aunt's voice. "I don't. But he will. You know how foolish and stubborn men can be."

"I've always found Hugh to be both wise and amiable."

"Maybe when you meet him in public. He's sure not been that way with me." Enjoyable. Patient. Kissable. Huh. Guess the kisses meant nothing.

"What is it you want?" Aunt Mary's gentle voice eased the anger raging through Annie's veins.

"I want him to honor our agreement. Four weeks."

"And then what?"

"Marriage. Just like we discussed."

"What sort of marriage are you talking about?"

Annie drew to a halt before the window. "A marriage in name only." She could hardly get the words off her tongue and knew her warm cheeks revealed far more than she cared for her aunt to know.

"I see. Is that what Hugh wants?"

"It was his idea."

"Perhaps it is easier to consider that sort of marriage with an older, plain, unsmiling woman."

Annie stared at her aunt. "You agree with Hugh? What sort of marriage is that?" The words her brothers had spoken echoed through her head. *There is only one reason to marry...if you love the person so much it hurts to imagine a day without him.* They were wrong. There were other reasons to marry and providing a home for a child was one of them. "What about Evan? Is that what he deserves?"

"I have a different question. What about you? Is that kind of marriage what you deserve?"

Annie spun away. "It's what I want."

"Is it?" Her aunt's quiet question blasted through her.

"Yes!" She almost shouted the word.

"Annie, dear child, you have been looking for something since your mama died. And now you are running from the very thing you want."

"I wasn't running when I was with Rudy." She'd wanted so much for Rudy to give her the love and security she'd known as a child.

"Rudy was not the man for you. Too weak."

"I'm not looking for a man to give me what I need."

"Nor should you. It's not fair to expect a man to give you what only God can give."

"I know that." Annie's inside burned as she recalled the verse Hugh had quoted Sunday morning. *Blessed is the man that trusteth in the Lord, and whose hope the Lord is.* "You're right. I've been looking for security in all the wrong places. I won't find it with someone else." Her heart rent in two as she mentally walked away from Hugh. What would happen to Evan? "I don't need marriage. I don't need anything." She could go back to the ranch where she would always be welcome but she didn't belong there. "There must be somewhere I belong, where I can take care of myself."

"Annie, I believe God has prepared such a place for you. Just be careful you don't walk away from what He has offered. There's a verse in Revelation chapter three that I'd like you to look up and read. In part it says, 'Behold, I have set before thee an open door.' Be sure you don't walk away from His open door, or close it in fear."

"Fear? I'm not afraid." Even as she said the words, she knew she was. Afraid of loss of security, loss of home, loss of anything. "Sometimes it's hard to trust."

"I can't argue with that. Would you care for a cup of tea?"

"No, I need to get back. I'll have to pack and arrange for Grandfather and me to return home." She chuckled softly. "I think he quite liked living in town. Several people have stopped to visit him and he doesn't have to go out in the cold longer than it takes to walk to the church on Sundays."

"He's capable of living wherever God places him. Just as you are." Aunt Mary rose and kissed Annie on the cheek before Annie left the room.

"Feeling better?" Uncle George asked as she headed for the outer door.

"You have a very smart wife."

"I know it." Her uncle's laugh boomed.

Smiling, Annie left the store. Her smile faded as she reached the back door to the manse. She straightened her shoulders. *What time I am afraid I will trust in Thee.* Aunt Mary was right. God would guide her to the right place. She would trust Him despite the pain ripping through her.

She stepped inside and looked around. Hugh sat at the end of the table. No Miss Higgins. "When will she be back?" Grandfather's chair was empty. "Where's Grandfather? Is he packing? He doesn't need to. I'll take care of everything."

"You grandfather said he was going to have a nap."

Evan sat in the corner, his arms about Happy's neck. He seemed okay. Did that mean he had liked the woman? If so, she was grateful.

"He's not going to pack," Hugh said.

"Good. I'll do it."

"You're not going to pack either." He hesitated. "Unless you want to."

"I don't understand. What about Miss Higgins? Wasn't she suitable?"

"She probably was but she didn't suit us."

Annie shook her head trying to make sense of this.

Hugh rose, held out his hand to her. She took it because it seemed the most natural thing to do.

"Let's go to the other room where we can talk. Evan, you stay here with Happy. Okay?"

Evan nodded, his expression watchful.

Annie let Hugh lead her to the fireplace. There was no fire burning but she seemed to feel the warmth nevertheless.

"Miss Higgins had unrealistic expectations of Evan." He gave the details.

Her eyes grew damp. "She would have been cruel to him."

"I thought so."

"Now what?"

"You suit just fine." A beat of consideration. "But I don't want you to feel trapped."

Was this the open door Aunt Mary meant? If so, she would walk through boldly and confidently, trusting God for the future. "You suit me just fine."

"As your grandfather pointed out not so long ago, marriage is for keeps."

"I know."

"Won't you someday want love?"

"Like I've said a number of times, love only leads to hurt." It was time to tell him about Rudy. "I met Rudy when he came to visit his sister. He talked like he was going to settle here. He was charming and kind and courted me with utmost devotion. I trusted him. I gave him my heart. Thought he held it in the palm of his hand. But he changed his mind. Told me he'd found nothing here to suit him. He didn't even know how much his leaving hurt me. Or else he didn't care." Perhaps the latter suspicion hurt more than anything.

He brushed the backs of his fingers to her cheeks.

"I'm sorry. But I have to think the young man was shallow and likely of poor eyesight."

His words tickled her and she tipped her head to smile up at him. "Is that a fact?"

"It is indeed." He looked deep into her eyes as if searching for something. She let him look, wanting to offer anything he needed. Anything? Maybe not.

"Is there any reason to put off getting married?" he asked.

"None that I can think of."

"Annie Marshall, will you marry me?"

"I will."

His smile darkened his eyes and he bent to claim a kiss. It was quick, businesslike but wasn't that exactly what she wanted?

"Shall we tell Evan?" she asked.

"I think the boy will be relieved."

Together they returned to the kitchen and knelt side by side in front of Evan who watched them with a good deal of wariness.

Annie stuffed back another surge of anger at the things Miss Higgins had said in front of the boy. She looked to Hugh, nodding that he should relay the news.

"Evan, Annie and I are going to get married. She'll be your new mama. What do you think of that?"

Evan's wide-eyed gaze went from Hugh to Annie.

"It's true," she said, and following her heart, she held out her arms to him.

He blinked twice then scrambled to his feet and rushed into her arms with such force he would have bowled her over except Hugh caught her. He pulled her close, encircling the two of them in his arms.

Her tears flowed freely and increased in volume when Hugh pulled out his handkerchief and attempted to wipe them away. She laughed at the confusion in his face as fresh tears continued to appear.

"Happy tears," she managed to say.

"I'll take your word for it." She blinked them away and saw that Hugh's eyes glistened and she touched his cheeks.

"We have much to be happy for."

He nodded and leaned his forehead to hers, Evan held safely between them. They might have stayed that way for who knows how long except Happy started to lick them.

Both laughing at the dog, they broke apart.

Evan wrapped his arms about Happy's neck.

Annie knew he found comfort in the animal's love and couldn't imagine what would happen if someone tried to take the dog from him. Nor could she understand why anyone would want to.

"I'm so glad you told her to leave."

"Me too." He brushed his fingers along her cheek and she wondered if his reasons were the same as hers.

"We'll tell Grandfather when he wakens."

"I wonder what he'll think."

He would voice his disapproval. She did not care for going against his wishes but she knew this was what she wanted to do. She tried to hide her shiver.

Hugh bent closer to search her face. "Are you having second thoughts?"

She hadn't succeeded in hiding her concern nor did she wish to tell Hugh what made her shiver. "I suppose I'm a little nervous."

He gripped both shoulders in his big warm hands. "I don't want you doing anything you will later regret. We need to be honest with each other."

She nodded, her tongue so thick she couldn't speak. She was being as honest with him as she could.

He watched her closely, his gaze delving deep into her thoughts.

Clarity came and she found the ability to talk. "This is what I want. Is it what you want?"

"It is."

The sound of Grandfather's canes tapping on the floor alerted them to his arrival and they faced the door.

He limped into the kitchen. "Got any coffee?"

"I'll make some." Annie hurried to the stove. She'd wait until he got his coffee before she'd tell him and she sent a little warning look to Hugh.

He nodded.

The coffee boiled. She poured a cup for each of the men and pretended to be busy at the cupboard while they drank.

Grandfather's cup was half-empty when he sighed. "You might as well tell me what's on your mind."

Annie went to Hugh's side and put her hand on his shoulder, finding strength and comfort in the touch.

"We've—" she began.

Hugh reached up and covered her hand with his own. "Let me. Mr. Marshall—"

"Uh-oh, you're addressing me formally. That doesn't bode well."

Beneath her palm, Annie felt Hugh stiffen.

"Mr. Marshall, seeing as Annie's father is away,

or I'd ask him, I'm asking you. I'd like your approval to marry your granddaughter."

Grandfather gulped a mouthful of coffee then sat back and looked from Annie to Hugh. His gaze stopped at Annie and he studied her long enough to make her want to squirm. Hugh seemed to understand and he pushed his chair back to stand at her side.

After a moment, Grandfather nodded. "A marriage in name only?"

Neither Annie nor Hugh responded.

"A marriage of convenience?" Grandfather persisted. He tipped his head toward Evan who played with Happy but no doubt heard every word. "For his sake?"

"It's what we both want," Annie replied.

Grandfather again did serious study of them both.

Annie dared not look toward Hugh to see how he reacted to grandfather's scrutiny. She couldn't say if the older man looked disappointed or resigned. A trickle of worry tingled her spine. What if he refused?

Finally, accompanied with a long sigh, Grandfather nodded. "You both seem set on this."

"Yes, sir." Hugh sounded strong and sure.

"Did you have a date picked out for this wedding?"

They hadn't discussed it and Annie turned to Hugh.

"I see no need to wait," Hugh said. "Unless you do?"

"There is no reason to wait."

Grandfather shook his head back and forth. "You young people. Always in such a hurry. Annie, your pa will be here for Christmas. I ask that you wait until he is here and gives his blessing. Any objections?"

Annie held her breath. Would Hugh agree? What if someone else came in answer to his ad? Would he feel obligated to honor their agreement? Or seek to be free of it?

Chapter Fifteen

Hugh wanted to tell Grandfather there would be no waiting. Christmas was still two weeks away. What if Annie changed her mind in that time?

If that was to happen it would be best if it did so before they married. He couldn't believe she wouldn't regret this decision sooner or later and yet he wanted to marry her in the hopes it would bind her to him. Unlike Bernice to whom marriage meant nothing, he knew Annie would honor her vows.

But he didn't want her feeling trapped.

"I don't mind waiting," he said.

"Fine by me." Annie sounded a little less than enthusiastic and why that should make him feel better, he wouldn't say.

"Good," Grandfather said. "Maybe in that time you will come to your senses."

Annie's brows beetled together. "I'm not going to change my mind."

"Nor am I," Hugh said with enough conviction to make himself clear.

Grandfather shrugged. "I didn't suggest you should."

Annie let out a gusty breath. "You don't make any sense." She hurried to the stove.

"I'll be in my office." Hugh didn't look back.

The days following settled into a routine. They'd agreed not to say anything about their planned Christmas wedding until they could speak to Annie's father. At first, Hugh wasn't sure how to act around Annie or what she would expect but it soon became apparent nothing had changed.

Except for a subtle strain. She didn't linger after putting Evan to bed so there were no more quiet, intimate evenings. He wished he could ask her what her reasons were but he had his own to deal with.

He couldn't believe someone like Annie would want to marry him. Worse, that she wouldn't change her mind and so he allowed questions to remain unasked.

Perhaps the strain was in his own mind only. Annie remained cheerful. She made Evan laugh on many occasions which brought a chuckle from Hugh. One thing he could not deny was the amount of pleasure Annie's presence had brought to his home.

And slowly, as the days passed, he allowed himself to hope that this was the life he could enjoy. He found it easier to sit in his office and work if the door was open enough for him to hear the voice coming from the kitchen.

Every day, he read from the devotional book Annie had given him and found his faith expanding. One portion especially encouraged him. "Enable me to be living more from moment to moment on Thy grace— to rely on Thy guiding arm with more childlike confidence—to look with a more simple faith to Thy finished work." He discovered, he noted with a touch of irony, it easy to say these words and throw himself upon that childlike faith when his life was full of hope. That gave him an idea for his sermon and he soon had scriptures and notes outlined.

Feeling rather pleased with his life, when it was time to put Evan to bed, he turned to Annie. "Will you help me tuck him in?" She hadn't accompanied them to the bedroom since Happy had arrived and Evan went without a fight.

Her eyes flashed pleasure. "I'd like that." She reached for Evan's hand and side by side, the three of them crowded down the hall.

"Why don't we kneel by your bed and say our prayers?" she suggested.

To date, Hugh had prayed and then taken the boy to bed but at his suggestion Evan agreed. And the three of them knelt side by side, Evan in the midst. She draped her arm about Evan's shoulders. Hugh did the same, the two of them united in caring for his son. His heart burgeoned with gratitude.

"Shall I go first?" Hugh offered and prayed a simple request for safety and a good night's sleep.

As soon as he said *Amen*, Annie prayed. "God, bless each one in this house and grant us joy in Your love."

Her words brought a lump to the back of Hugh's throat.

"Me."

His eyes jerked open as Evan spoke. His glance met Annie's, as full of surprise and awe as he knew his was. He squeezed her arm. She smiled rather shakily.

"Thank you for Papa and my new mama," Evan whispered. "Amen." He bounced to his feet. Then knelt again and closed his eyes. "And Happy." The pup wriggled at his name.

Annie reached for Evan and pulled him into a hug. The boy still stiffened at this closeness but relaxed enough to press his head to Annie's shoulder. "Evan, I thank God for you. I love you." She held him a moment longer then turned him toward Hugh.

Hugh had never hugged the boy, afraid of frightening him, perhaps afraid of rejection. So far, he'd settled for squeezing the boy's shoulders or patting his head but at the way Annie nodded and pushed the boy toward him, he knew she expected he would do so.

God, help him accept my affections. He opened his arms and pulled Evan to him, not surprised when the boy stiffened. When Evan melted against him, leaning his whole frame into Hugh's chest, his heart threatened to explode.

Following Annie's example, he whispered, "I love you, Evan."

The boy rested in his arms a moment longer then scurried to his mattress.

Annie pulled the quilt over him and kissed him on the forehead.

Happy curled up beside Evan.

Annie stood up, smiling.

Hugh knelt beside the boy and his dog and kissed his son.

Evan closed his eyes, put his hand on Happy's neck and sighed.

Hugh reached for Annie's hand, pleased when she took his, and led them from the room. Wood lay ready to light in the fireplace. He waited for Annie to sit on the couch then lit the fire.

His heart was too full to allow him to sit and he walked back and forth in the space between the couch and the fireplace. "He spoke a whole sentence. He prayed out loud." The words caught in his throat and he couldn't go on.

Annie left the couch and came to his side. She took his hand and faced him. "He's going to be okay. Better than okay. I believe he will be stronger for what he's had to overcome."

"It's all thanks to you." He cupped his hand over her head as a wave of tenderness washed through him. "You've shown him it's okay to trust people."

"So have you. He knows he can trust you." He knew she had avoided being with him the last number of evenings, perhaps not wanting to cross the boundaries they had set but his gratitude toward her needed expression. He pulled her close, pressed his thumb to her bottom lip.

She closed her eyes and lifted her face to him. A clear invitation and he brought his lips to hers, kissing her with a heart so full of emotion that he could barely breathe.

She sighed and brought her hands to the back of his head. Giving as much as receiving the kiss.

He reluctantly ended the kiss and when she made no move toward leaving his arms, he pressed her head to his shoulder and his cheek to her hair. She stayed there, her arms about his waist.

"Pa should arrive any day," she murmured. "A week from now we should be getting married."

She spoke those words in a way that caused him

to know she looked forward to the day. Just when he thought his heart could hold no more, it flooded with joy unspeakable.

Annie took her time making her way to Uncle George's store. Would they be married Christmas day? She skipped once. Wouldn't that be special? And Grandfather's friend, the judge and his wife, planned to visit so there would be someone to marry them.

She had left Evan playing with Jeannie at Sadie and Logan's house so she could purchase a special gift for him. Uncle George had a Noah's ark along with pairs of many animals for sale. She'd told him she wanted to purchase it and was on her way to pick it up. Wouldn't Evan be pleased? And it was something Jeannie could play with when she came to visit him.

She rounded the corner on Mineral Avenue. Just as she passed the assay office someone jumped in front of her.

"Annie, I've been hoping to see you."

She knew that voice. She fell back three steps and stared at a familiar face. "Rudy. Where did you come from? What are you doing here?"

He grinned. So self-confident. So brash. The very qualities that had attracted her in the first place.

"I've come to spend Christmas with my sister." He leaned close as if sharing a secret. "And to see my favorite gal."

She sniffed. "And who would that be, pray tell."

"Now don't get all annoyed at me." He pretended to look repentant. "You should have known I would come back."

"I knew no such thing."

He nodded. "Yes, you did. My sister says you don't have a beau. I know you were waiting for me."

Why of all the nerve. How presumptuous and self-important could he be? Had he always been so annoying? She knew he had. How could she have been so blind?

"Why don't you accompany me to Miss Daisy's Eatery? I'm sure she'll have a special treat for us."

What he meant was she would have something for him. As if the whole town had been holding its breath waiting in hope for his return.

"I'm sorry. I have other plans." She tried to get past him.

"Let me change your plans." He grabbed her arms and pulled her close, leaning toward her. Intending to kiss her.

Anger scalded through her and she fought not to slap him right there in the middle of the street. But she didn't want to attract any more attention than she might already have done. She pushed away his arms and glanced about, saw no one watching and knew a moment of relief. She faced him, so full of indignation it was all she could do to speak calmly. What had she ever seen in this man? He was nothing but a blowhard buffoon.

"Rudy, I'm afraid your sister is mistaken. I am making plans to soon marry. I am no longer interested in you."

"You're just saying that because you're angry at me."

"I'm saying that because I'm in love with someone else." The words were out before she could filter them. She pushed past Rudy and continued on her way to the store though she hardly remembered what she meant to do.

Love was not part of their agreement and certainly not what she wanted.

She must continue to deny it, must hide it.

Hugh had made a call to an elderly widow woman two blocks from the main street. She was feeling discouraged and welcomed his visit. He'd prayed with her and he felt her spirits had lifted by the time he left.

He strode toward Mineral Avenue headed toward the Marshall store. He'd seen a pretty notebook with a flowered cover that he wanted to purchase as a Christmas gift for Annie. Might it also be a wedding gift? Her father would return any day now and give his blessing for their marriage.

He wouldn't let himself think Mr. Marshall might object or forbid it. He and Annie were perfectly suited to one another.

He neared the corner and ground to a halt. Annie stood on the sidewalk not more than fifty feet away with a young man…a tall, slender man with a smile that would likely have any number of young ladies falling at his feet. Was this Rudy?

As if hearing his question and wanting to answer it, the man pulled her into his arms right there in front of anyone who cared to watch. Like they couldn't wait to pick up where they'd left off.

Hugh ground around, a bitter taste in his mouth. Somehow he reached home and hurried inside. Evan wasn't there. He didn't worry about the boy. No matter what else was on her mind, he could trust Annie to take care of his son.

Grandfather snoozed in his chair and Hugh slipped by to the office where he sank to his chair, planted his elbows on the desk and buried his face in his up-turned palms. *Oh, God, what am I to do? I want to marry her but I can't keep her against her will. Nor do I want to hold her to a promise she regrets.*

Why do you want her?

The question trumpeted through his thoughts and he glanced around. No one else was in the room. His own mind demanded the answer.

A knock came to the outer door before he could sort through his tumbling thoughts.

Half glad for the interruption he went to open the door. "Miss Higgins." He hadn't expected she'd come calling again.

"May I speak to you a moment?"

He glanced over his shoulder. It would be inappropriate to invite her to step inside. "Do you mind if we stand here?"

Her cheeks flared with color. "Certainly. It is best if we do."

"I didn't expect to see you," he said by way of encouragement when she didn't state her reason for the visit.

She clasped her gloved hands together and lifted her head. "I'm afraid I presented myself in rather a poor light last time I was here. You see, I had decided that as a preacher you would want certain standards, perhaps had expectations above and beyond what would be expected of a normal housekeeper. In my determination to prove I could live up to those standards, I had created a rather rigid and unrealistic picture of how I should conduct myself. I apologize and ask that you give me another chance."

This woman was not the same one who had come to his door a few days ago. She looked kind and comforting.

It was the perfect solution but he did not welcome it as such.

"I appreciate your apology and your offer. I might be interested in accepting the latter but first I have some other commitments I must deal with." Namely, Annie. A stab of pain caused his knees to quiver and he grabbed the door post to steady himself. "Can I get back to you later?"

"That would be fine. Goodbye." She made her way down the walk to the street.

He stared after her until she rounded the corner then fled indoors. *Oh, Father God, what am I to do?* He knew the answer but it would be the hardest thing he'd ever done in his life.

Every breath was torture as he waited for Annie to return.

The door opened. Happy clattered across the floor. Annie spoke to her grandfather. Cupboards banged as she put things away.

He couldn't move, couldn't make his limbs obey the order to go to the kitchen and ask her to speak privately with him. He didn't know how long he would have sat there, waiting with a heart of stone.

"Hugh?"

He looked up at Annie's voice.

She stepped into the room. "Are you okay?"

"Would you come in and close the door?"

"Okaaaaay."

He didn't blame her for sounding wary. No doubt his face warned her of impending changes. He wouldn't say doom because it was likely the best thing he could offer her. "I saw you with a young man this afternoon. Am I to understand young Rudy is back in town?"

She ducked her head making it impossible to see her eyes or read her expression. "He is."

"You can assure him he is not too late."

Her head came up. She squinted at him as if she had difficulty seeing him. "I don't understand."

He had hoped this would go simply and quickly. Before he could change his mind. "You were obviously happy to see him."

Her gaze riveted his. He wanted to look away but he couldn't. The most he could hope for was to hide the pain pressing at the backs of his eyeballs.

"Perhaps you should tell me exactly what you think you saw." How did she manage to make him feel guilty as if he'd purposely spied on her or followed her?

"I saw the two of you hugging right in the middle of town. I think you were about to kiss." How could each word stab through him with unrelenting pain?

She shook her head and clasped her hands at her waist. A bottomless sigh came from her lungs. "That is not what you saw."

"I beg your pardon. I know I wasn't mistaken."

"Perhaps not in what you saw but you are mistaken in how you interpret it."

Was she telling him that a hug shared with a man meant nothing? Was that all their hugs and kisses were? Nothing. Not to be taken seriously. Of no matter. He couldn't look at her. Couldn't let her see the pain that threatened to suck out his very soul. He settled his gaze on the motto hanging by the door. "Bless all who enter this home. Grant safety and healing to those who depart and peace to those who remain." He read the words over and over without making sense of them. He knew the blessing well enough and knew he must live by the words he claimed to believe.

"Annie, I would not hold you here against your will. Nor would I expect you to keep a promise when you know it's been a mistake. You are free to leave."

She jammed her fists to her hips and he flinched knowing the gesture meant she was angry. "Hugh Arness, you did not see me kissing him. He wanted to kiss me but I wouldn't let him."

"I respect you for being so noble but I free you from our agreement. You must follow your heart."

She glowered at him. "Did you ever consider I am following my heart?"

He shook his head, trying to make sense of what she said. He failed.

"You are just like my brothers."

"I suppose that's a compliment." He sounded as doubtful as he felt.

"Not this time. Hugh, I am staying and in so doing I am following my heart. Can I be any clearer?"

"You don't want love."

"That's what I thought. I was wrong though."

He stared, his mouth gaping. He heard her words. Knew what each word meant but strung together like that, they made no sense.

"Annie?"

"Hugh."

"Is love possible?"

She smiled, enjoying his uncertainty. "Is it what you want?"

"It's what I've always wanted but never had."

"Then I would say you deserve it."

He couldn't stop shaking his head. "I don't deserve love. I don't deserve—" He couldn't bring himself to say he didn't deserve her. The hope of having her was too great to fathom, too horrific to think it wasn't possible.

She moved closer, a gentle smile upon her lips. "Hugh Arness, you are a gift from God to all of us here at Bella Creek. You are a godsend for Evan."

His eyes begged for more but he couldn't help it.

She closed the distance between them. "Most of all you are exactly what this frightened, lonely, fearful girl needs." She touched his chin with her cool fingers.

He swallowed hard. "Are you really saying what I think you are saying?" He could not bring himself to speak the words that meant the world to him. Too often his hopes had been dashed by rejection.

She pressed a palm to each side of his face. "Hugh, I love you. Yes, I said I didn't want love but you made it impossible for me to keep that decision."

He trailed his fingers along her cheeks, down to her chin. "I don't deserve your love."

"I trust my heart to you knowing it will forever more be safe." Her eyes overflowed with sweetness.

"Annie Marshall, how could you love me?"

"How could I not?"

At that moment he believed her with everything within him.

"The question is whether or not you love me." Her eyes begged for his confession.

He wrapped his arms about her without crushing her to his chest. He wanted to see her face as he told her the truth. "Annie, I loved you from the first moment I saw you the first Sunday I preached my first sermon in Bella Creek. I saw how you treated your brothers, your father and grandfather. I saw how you greeted friends and neighbors. Always with kindness, gentleness and affection. My love grew when you came here demanding to marry me. I loved you even more when you were so tender and understanding with Evan. And when you kissed me before the fireplace I thought my love would explode like sparks from one of those logs."

"You certainly hid it well."

"I couldn't believe you could love me."

She pressed her fingertips to his lips. "I know you heard many unkind things from your mother and perhaps even from your wife but I promise I will never say that you aren't good enough even when I get angry. Because you are better than good, you are everything I could ever dream of." She trailed her fingers from his mouth leaving his lips strangely hungry. "Do I make myself clear?"

"Pretty clear."

"How could I make myself any clearer?"

"I don't know. Maybe a kiss would help."

She chuckled and pulled his head down to claim his lips, her arms warm about his neck, holding him close.

He breathed in the pure sweet scent of her. He

lifted his head. "I will never grow tired of kissing you, holding you, encouraging you."

"Nor will I of you."

They kissed again. He leaned back against the desk and kept her in his arms. "So when, fair lady, did you know you loved me?"

"You know, I think it might have been the first Sunday of the first time you preached here. Though I didn't know it was love. After all, I was still insisting I didn't want love."

He thought of how she'd lost her mother to death. "Annie, I can't promise that bad things won't come into our lives. I can't guess how long either of us will live. I can't say you won't be hurt by loving me."

"But you can promise to love me 'til death part us. I'll trust God for the rest. I can thank you for teaching me that." He held her close as she told how his words had encouraged her that Sunday she'd slipped in with Evan hanging on to her hand for dear life.

"I have only one regret," she murmured.

"Already?" He tried to sound teasing but managed to hint at his worry.

"Not about us, silly. My regret is Pa is not back yet and we promised to wait until he came to get married. What if he's delayed? He has to cross the mountains in winter weather. Not that I would want him to do anything foolish like hurry home without regard for the weather."

"We'll trust God and honor our promise."

A little later they returned to the kitchen where supper waited on the stove.

"About time. I thought I was going to have to make my way to Daisy's to get some food." Grandfather gave them a jaundiced look then his eyes widened. He laughed loudly and slapped his leg. "I see you've come to your senses. About time, too, I'd say."

"I don't know what you mean," Annie protested though the look she gave Hugh suggested a bit of knowing guilt.

"I think you two were the last to realize you were madly in love. I was beginning to think I might have to write it in big plain letters across the table before you realized it." He grinned at each of them. "Glad to see you managed to figure it out without too much help from me."

"Not that he'll remember it that way when he tells others," Annie whispered to Hugh, her voice just loud enough for her grandfather to hear. "Nope. He'll make it sound like he was entirely responsible."

Grandfather chuckled. "I like a good story but I never say anything that isn't true."

Annie rolled her eyes.

It wasn't until Evan went to bed and Grandfather fell asleep in his chair, saying he wouldn't go to bed until they did, that Hugh got a chance to hold Annie again and tell her how much he loved her.

He knew he would never grow weary of hearing her say how much she loved him.

Epilogue

Christmas Day

Annie rushed from her bedroom to prepare a special breakfast for Hugh, Evan and Grandfather. She paused in the living room to admire the tree where they had hung the ornaments they'd made and tied bows of colorful yarn. The manger scene sat beneath the branches surrounded by wrapped gifts.

Evan, with Happy at his side, trotted down the hall, his eyes dancing with excitement. "Presents?" His voice seldom rose above a whisper.

"Yes. For us. We'll open them as soon as we've had breakfast."

He grabbed her hand and tugged her toward the kitchen.

She laughed. "It seems you are hungry." She knew he only wanted to get breakfast out of the way. "We'll have to wait for your papa and my grandfather."

He nodded and let Happy outside.

Annie folded her arms and leaned against the cupboard enjoying the moment. She had so much to be thankful for on this Christmas Day.

Hugh slipped into the room and pulled her into his arms, her back to his chest, his cheek pressed to hers. "Merry Christmas, Annie Bell." He'd adopted Grandfather's nickname for her, using it only for very tender moments. "Are you excited about Christmas?"

She turned within the circle of his arm to look into his face. "Our first Christmas together," she murmured.

"The first of many, many more." His smile filled his eyes, filled her heart and promised her his.

"Whatever the future may bring, of sadness or sorrow or disappointment, I will not regret one moment of the time we have together."

"Nor I." He kissed her.

Evan tugged on her elbow. "Hurry," he said in his soft voice, pointing toward the stove.

Grandfather made his way into the room. Shook the coffeepot and grunted. "No coffee?"

She laughed. "Time to get to work." Reluctant to leave Hugh's hold she didn't move.

He ducked his forehead to hers then turned her toward the stove. "More of this later."

Fueled by his promise, she hurriedly made breakfast, doing her best to keep her attention on her work but twice Hugh caught her staring into space and laughed.

She glanced at him. Saw his knowing smile and blushed.

Finally she got the food on the table and they gathered round.

"Grandfather, will you ask the blessing?" Hugh said.

"My pleasure."

They all bowed their heads. Evan clasped his hands in front of him as he had seen Jeannie do. Annie closed her eyes. How much joy could her heart hold before it exploded?

It wouldn't explode, she realized with a burst of clarity. It would expand, open up like a flower to the sun, and grow stronger with every beat of love.

"Dear Heavenly Father," Grandfather began. "This is a special day. The day we remember how great is Your love for us. A day to enjoy the love You've poured into our lives. We thank You for all Your blessings including this food that Annie's hands have lovingly prepared. May Your blessing be upon us throughout every moment of the day."

Annie kept her eyes closed after Grandfather said amen. His words felt like a benediction. His blessing meant so much to her.

They ate hurriedly in order to keep up with Evan.

She left the dishes to do later wondering if Evan could wait any longer. They gathered round the tree. Hugh read the Christmas story while his son moved the figures of the manger scene around to accompany the tale.

"And now," Hugh said to the boy, "We give gifts to each other to remind us of the greatest gift of all—baby Jesus born in a manger." He smiled at Annie. "Are we ready?"

She nodded. They had decided Evan should get his gifts first. Grandfather had bought him a storybook. Hugh had made him a pair of leather mittens. He thanked them both.

Annie handed her present to Evan. He opened it to reveal the ark and the animals.

"Noah's ark," she explained. "Like the Bible story."

He lifted up each animal for her to name and whispered the word after her. When he'd been through the entire menagerie he threw his arms about Annie's neck. "Thank you," he whispered.

"You're welcome. I love you."

He returned to the toy.

Hugh grasped her hand. He knew she longed for the day the boy would tell them he loved them. "It will come. Give it time."

"I'll wait as long as it takes."

Grandfather handed them each a gift. A scarf. "I got Mary to knit them."

After thanking him, Hugh handed her his gift.

"Oh, a beautiful notebook. Thank you. I know exactly what I'm going to use it for. I am going to keep a journal of our lives together."

He leaned over and kissed her nose. "In that case, I should have ordered in a case lot of them. You'll need many notebooks for the many years we are going to be together."

"I will cherish every moment." Whether it be short or long. She was settled with accepting whatever the Lord allowed them. No longer did she run from the risks of love knowing to do so robbed her of the joys which far outweighed the risks.

She handed him his gift.

He looked at her, his smile so warm and promising. "You have already given me so much. Thank you."

She grinned. "Open your present."

He carefully folded back the wrapping to expose a

fountain pen in a wooden box. He lifted the pen out carefully. "It's beautiful. I often thought of buying one but it seemed unnecessary." He squeezed her hand. "But you realized how much I really wanted one of these writing instruments. Thank you."

At his warm smile, she forgot everyone and everything else.

Grandfather grunted as he shifted in his chair. "Aren't we due to leave for the ranch in a couple of hours?"

She sprang to her feet. "I have much to do before then." She hurried to the kitchen and gathered up the dirty dishes. Hugh came up behind her and wrapped his arms around her. "I'll help." She leaned her head to his shoulder allowing herself just one moment of sheer pleasure before she returned to the task before her.

She washed and he dried.

"I'll go get our conveyance." He put on his winter coat and left the house.

She pressed to the window, watching until he was out of sight then rushed to her bedroom to gather together the things she would need for the day.

The rattle of harnesses warned that Hugh had returned and she helped Grandfather and Evan gather together their things.

She stepped outside to see that Hugh had a sleigh for them, with bells jingling and a big red crepe paper bow on the front. She laughed with delight.

"Merry Christmas," he called.

They were on their way, their spirits high as they made their journey to the ranch. The sky was clear, the sun trying to offer warmth. Not even the winter cold could quench her joy.

Pa stepped from the house as they drove up. He helped her to the ground. "You're ready for this?"

"As soon as I change. Thank you for your blessing." He'd returned two days ago and didn't hesitate a second when Hugh asked for his approval for their marriage.

"I can see how happy you are. Hugh has given you that. I'm grateful to him."

He led her indoors while Hugh took care of Evan and Grandfather.

Her sisters-in-law whisked her up the stairs and into her old bedroom. She looked about with a touch of sadness.

Kate must have noticed. "You'll always be welcome here."

"I will always belong with Hugh."

The three women laughed and hugged her.

Sadie turned all teacher-like. "Let's get you into your gown."

They helped her slip the dress over her head that she'd chosen to wear and did up the row of satin-covered buttons.

"Your mother would be so proud," Isabelle said.

"I'm so happy to wear her dress."

Pa waited for them at the top of the stairs. Sadie, Kate and Isabelle descended and then Annie took Pa's arm.

"You make me proud," he said, his voice catching. "If only your mother could see you now."

She blinked back tears. "I miss her so much."

"Me too. But she would want you to find your own happiness with your own husband."

"I know."

"Shall we proceed?"

She nodded and descended. Only her family was present and the judge and his wife—old family friends. Hugh had agreed to let the church host a gathering in honor of their marriage on Sunday.

He stood with her brothers at his side and little Evan at his right hand.

She couldn't stop smiling as her heart overflowed with love for everyone in the room and a special love for Hugh and his son. Pa took her to Hugh's side and slipped her arm from his to Hugh's.

Judge Harder cleared his throat to signal the ceremony was about to begin.

It was short and simple though the judge gave a strong admonition to honor the vows they were making this day.

"You may kiss the bride," he said. Hugh did so with enough enthusiasm to earn him a round of chuckles from her brothers.

"May I present Mr. and Mrs. Hugh Arness."

The family clapped.

Evan tugged at her arm and she bent to hear what he had to say. He took Hugh's hand on one side and hers on the other. "I love you," he said, loudly and plainly.

She laughed. She cried and she hugged him.

Hugh wrapped his arms about them both.

She turned to him. "I have found a love worth more than anything."

"God is good." If his voice seemed a little husky, no one mentioned it.

* * * * *

If you enjoyed this story, pick up the first three
BIG SKY COUNTRY *books,*

MONTANA COWBOY DADDY
MONTANA COWBOY FAMILY
MONTANA COWBOY'S BABY

and these other stories from Linda Ford:

A DADDY FOR CHRISTMAS
A BABY FOR CHRISTMAS
A HOME FOR CHRISTMAS
THE COWBOY'S READY-MADE FAMILY
THE COWBOY'S BABY BOND
THE COWBOY'S CITY GIRL

Available now from Love Inspired Historical!

Find more great reads at www.LoveInspired.com

Dear Reader,

I had such fun writing Annie and Hugh's story. I loved bringing these two reluctant, wary people together. They were a perfect match for each other even if they were the last people to discover it. Annie is such a loving, giving person. Watching her make Christmas special for her new family made me realize yet again how much I enjoy Christmas—not necessarily the gifts but the special things we do to create long-lasting memories. I hope you find joy in the season. God's gift to us is the reason for the season and the source of real joy. May His love and presence bless you.

You can learn more about my upcoming books and how to contact me at www.lindaford.org. I love to hear from my readers.

Blessings,
Linda Ford

A LAWMAN FOR CHRISTMAS
Smoky Mountain Matches • by Karen Kirst

After lawman Ben MacGregor and avowed spinster
Isabel Flores discover a four-year-old boy abandoned on her
property at Christmas, they must work together to care for
him. But can their temporary arrangement turn into a forever
family?

MAIL-ORDER CHRISTMAS BABY
Montana Courtships • by Sherri Shackelford

When a child arrives with the Wells Fargo delivery with
documents listing Heather O'Connor and Sterling Blackwell
as the baby's parents, they are forced to marry to give the
baby a home—and save their reputations.

THEIR MISTLETOE MATCHMAKERS
by Keli Gwyn

Lavinia Crowne heads to California planning to bring her late
sister's orphaned children back east. But Henry Hawthorn,
their paternal uncle, is intent on raising them in the only
home they know...and three little matchmakers hope their
mistletoe-filled schemes will bring their aunt and uncle
together.

A CHILD'S CHRISTMAS WISH
by Erica Vetsch

After her home is destroyed in a fire, pregnant widow
Kate Amaker and her in-laws take refuge with Oscar Rabb—
the widowed farmer next door whose daughter has one
holiday wish: a baby for Christmas.

———————

Get 2 Free Books,
Plus 2 Free Gifts—
just for trying the Reader Service!

Love Inspired HISTORICAL

LIHI17R2

SPECIAL EXCERPT FROM

Love Inspired HISTORICAL

*When a child arrives with the Wells Fargo delivery
with documents listing Heather O'Connor and
Sterling Blackwell as the baby's parents, they are forced
to marry to give the baby a home—and save
their reputations.*

Read on for a sneak preview of
MAIL-ORDER CHRISTMAS BABY
by **Sherri Shackelford**, *available*
November 2017 from Love Inspired Historical!

"The only way for us to clear our names is to find the real parents. If Grace's mother made the choice out of necessity," Heather said, "then she'll be missing her child terribly. Perhaps we can help."

Grace reached for her, and Heather folded her into her arms. By the looks on the gentlemen's faces, the gesture was further proof against her. But Heather was drawn to the child. The poor thing was powerless and at the mercy of strangers. Despite everything she'd been through, the baby appeared remarkably good-natured. Whatever her origins, she was a resilient child.

The reverend focused his attention on Grace with searing intensity, as though she might reveal the secret of her origins if he just looked hard enough. "Who is going to watch her for the time being?"

Sterling coughed into his fist and stared at the tips of his boots. The reverend discovered an intense fascination with the button on his sleeve.

Heather's pulse picked up speed. Surely they wouldn't leave the baby with her? "I don't think I should be seen with her. The more people connect us, the more they'll gossip."

"It's too late already," Sterling said. "There are half a dozen curious gossips milling outside the door right now."

Heather peered out the church window and immediately jerked back. Sure enough, a half dozen people were out there.

If she didn't take responsibility for the child, who would? "I'll watch her," Heather conceded.

"Thank the Lord for your kindness." The reverend clasped his hands as though in prayer. "The poor child deserves care. I'll do my best to stem the talk," he added. "But I can't make any promises."

Sterling sidled nearer. "Don't worry. I'll find the truth."

"I know you will."

A disturbing sense of intimacy left her light-headed. In the blink of an eye her painstakingly cultivated air of practicality fled. Then he turned his smile on the baby, and the moment was broken.

Heather set her lips in a grim line. His deference was practiced and meant nothing. She must always be on guard around Sterling Blackwell. She must always remember that she was no more special to him than the woman who typed out his telegrams.

He treated everyone with the same indolent consideration, and yet she'd always been susceptible to his charm.

She smoothed her hand over Grace's wild curls. They were both alone, but now they had each other.

At least for the time being.

Don't miss
MAIL-ORDER CHRISTMAS BABY by Sherri Shackelford,
available November 2017 wherever
Love Inspired® Historical books and ebooks are sold.

Inspirational Romance to Warm Your Heart and Soul

Join our social communities to connect with other readers who share your love!

Sign up for the Love Inspired newsletter at **www.LoveInspired.com** to be the first to find out about upcoming titles, special promotions and exclusive content.

CONNECT WITH US AT:

Harlequin.com/Community

 Facebook.com/LoveInspiredBooks

 Twitter.com/LoveInspiredBks

LISOCIAL2017

SPECIAL EXCERPT FROM

Love Inspired®

*When Erica Lindholm and her twin babies show up at
his family farm just before Christmas, Jason Stephanidis
can tell she's hiding something. But how can he refuse
the young mother, a friend of his sister's, a place to stay
during the holidays? He never counted on wanting Erica
and the boys to be a more permanent part of his life...*

Read on for a sneak peek of
SECRET CHRISTMAS TWINS
by *Lee Tobin McClain*,
part of the **CHRISTMAS TWINS** miniseries.

Once both twins were bundled, snug between Papa
and Erica, Jason sent the horses trotting forward.
The sun was up now, making millions of diamonds
on the snow that stretched across the hills far into
the distance. He smelled pine, a sharp, resin-laden
sweetness.

When he picked up the pace, the sleigh bells jingled.

"Real sleigh bells!" Erica said, and then, as they
approached the white covered bridge decorated with a
simple wreath for Christmas, she gasped. "This is the
most beautiful place I've ever seen."

Jason glanced back, unable to resist watching her fall
in love with his home.

Papa was smiling for the first time since he'd learned
of Kimmie's death. And as they crossed the bridge and
trotted toward the church, converging with other horse-
drawn sleighs, Jason felt a sense of rightness.

Mikey started babbling to Teddy, accompanied by gestures and much repetition of his new word. Teddy tilted his head to one side and burst forth with his own stream of nonsense syllables, seeming to ask a question, batting Mikey on the arm. Mikey waved toward the horses and jabbered some more, as if he were explaining something important.

They were such personalities, even as little as they were. Jason couldn't help smiling as he watched them interact.

Once Papa had the reins set and the horses tied up, Jason jumped out of the sleigh, and then turned to help Erica down. She handed him a twin. "Can you hold Mikey?"

He caught a whiff of baby powder and pulled the little one tight against his shoulder. Then he reached out to help Erica, and she took his hand to climb down, Teddy on her hip.

When he held her hand, something electric seemed to travel right to his heart. Involuntarily he squeezed and held on.

She drew in a sharp breath as she looked at him, some mixture of puzzlement and awareness in her eyes.

What was Erica's secret?

And wasn't it curious that, after all these years, there were twins in the farmhouse again?

Don't miss
SECRET CHRISTMAS TWINS
by Lee Tobin McClain, available November 2017
wherever Love Inspired® books and ebooks are sold.

www.LoveInspired.com